CW00326975

A beautiful piece. It is obvious that gradu
are emerging. You do not know how it gla
that when we are long gone, the light will keep snining.

*Wole Soyinka*
*Writer*


An emotional, thrilling and mind blowing novel. It is full of suspense and will definitely be a bestseller.

*Femi Anikulapo Kuti*
*Son of the Legendary*
*Fela Anikulapo Kuti*


I am impressed. The story line is perfect, and continuous, never a dull moment. He has a gift for creating scenes in such ways that you get a feeling you are there.

*Dele Momodu*
*Publisher*
*OVATION magazine*


A best seller from a young African. It only goes a long way to tell the world that Africa is a land of untapped resources.

**Bishop Desmond Tutu**


It will make a beautiful motion picture.

*Richard Mofe-Damijo*
*Actor*

# DESIGNS OF DESTINY

## AUTOBIOGRAPHY

Femi Akinwunmi

Protea Publishing

Copyright ©2003 Femi Akinwunmi. All rights reserved.

Designs Of Destiny. Autobiography.
Femi Akinwunmi

First Edition


ISBN   1-59344-028-6          softcover

ISBN   1-59344-029-4          hardcover


US Library Of Congress Control Number: 2003112658


Protea Publishing. USA.
kaolink@msn.com
www.proteapublishing.com

## *About The Author*

*F*emi Akinwunmi was born on the 19$^{th}$ of November 1975. He attended Remo Secondary school Sagamu, Ogun State, Nigeria from where he proceeded to read Pharmacy at the University of Benin, Benin City Edo State Nigeria.

A multitalented young man who has a flare for writing and acting, has featured in some stage plays with one or two local theatres and was the Publisher/Editor in Chief of Passion Intercampus Journal Inc.

A guru in the Public Relations Industry, Femi Akinwunmi is the Chairman/Chief Executive of Ekius communications, a Public Relations/Marketing company.

This is his first book, but has many of his articles published in a number of Nigerian local newspapers/magazines.

He enjoys playing lawn tennis, dancing and listening to music.

He loves adventures and is an admirer of good works of arts.

He also runs a NGO, a non-governmental organization.

He has a dream for a better Nigeria,

A place to call home.

## *Dedication*

To the meek at heart,
The poor in spirit.
The helpless widows,
The motherless child.
The victims of war and
The generation yet unborn.
To them I dedicate my piece.

## *Acknowledgement*

To some he gave five talents,
To some he gave two, and
To some he gave one.
Some turned in returns in duplicate.
One hid his under the earth.
I thank God for giving me the grace to use mine.
          This is just the beginning.

My father, my Mother, my Brothers, Sisters, Friends, loved ones.

# Prologue

*A*yo was born in East London. His Mum then was in Bradford University studying for her Masters Degree, while his Dad worked for a petroleum Company, Texaco. He grew up in Klientwood where his parents lived, and schooled there till he was in Fourth Grade when his father got transferred back to Nigeria.

As a kid, he was very shy and couldn't stand the discrimination amongst Whites and Blacks. When he wasn't in school, he was at his aunt's place, some eighty minutes drive from where they lived.

His mum however made sure he never misses his baseball lessons and his father, whenever he is around makes sure they spent as much time as possible together.

When they settled in Nigeria, he was enrolled in one of the private schools on Victoria Island, one of the highbrow areas in Lagos State. There, he met children who made it a point of duty to flaunt affluence. Children who came to school with bales of Naira notes that left him wondering where the mint came from.

He didn't retain his shy tendencies too long. He had lots of opportunities to frolic because his friends had the money and he had the personality. To them, he was a mulatto, because he was light complexioned and had an American accent.

Ayo's first experience with a girl was at a party he attended with his friends at the Mainland, which was his first outing away from the Island.

His father was abroad and his mother did not object, as long as he returned before midnight. Immediately they arrived the party scene in their usual convoy of three cars, their presence was noticed because they were accorded preferential treatment.

Ayo had just finished his drink and was contemplating on having another when from nowhere; he heard this sonorous feminine voice.

"Mind dancing with me."

He turned back and behold, a cutely dressed pretty girl stood there smiling at him.

Shy and surprised at the girl's guts, he didn't know whether to say yes or run; because that was the first time he was being asked. Ayo was used to making the first move after much pressure from his friends. He looked up and his glance met a series of nods, so he summoned enough courage and said.

"With all pleasure."

They had barely danced for five minutes when she asked if they could go outside for some fresh air. The place was a bit stuffy he admitted, but the central cooling system in the fairly large sitting room was at full blast, so he saw no reason for going outside but as things were, he obliged.

"Toyin is my name," she said as they stepped out on the platform.

"Ayo is mine," he replied, "Ayo Arigbabuwo."

"Your surname when translated, means wealth or something," she paused turned to face him before she continued.

"That means you must be very rich."

He looked at her and they both laughed. That was what he needed, because immediately, he felt relaxed and was himself again. They talked for about thirty minutes, within which she told him close to everything about herself.

A girl of sixteen, daughter of the Chief Justice of Lagos State and a Lagos based businesswoman. Her parents were out of the State and she was alone at home because her brother had gone to a nite-club, and would not be back till the early hours of the next day.

When she finished, she asked if he could take her home to pick something. As innocent as he was, he smiled and said,

"Why not."
He got the keys to one of the cars they brought, a Honda Prelude sports automatic and drove her home.

She seemed to have enjoyed the short ride home because she was alive and in a light mood, when he parked in front of her house.

Her house, a big White House could be described as a mini mansion with a standard size swimming pool, separated from the sitting room by a platform and a set of sliding doors covered by thick velvet curtains which length seemed endless.

"How about a quick swim before we leave?" she asked as

9

they entered the living room.

"I'm sticky all over."

Luckily, Ayo had his swimming trunks on.

"That wouldn't be a bad idea," he said, "I have my trunks on."

Obviously elated, she turned and disappeared into the interior of the well-decorated house.

Ayo was admiring the works of art in the sitting room and was particularly engrossed in a painting on the wall, a portrait of Cleopatra when she spoke, making him jump with fright.

As he turned, he felt rooted to the spot, shocked at the scene that beheld him. For the first time that evening he really saw how beautiful she was. Why he had not noticed all night, he didn't know or probably the bikini added a touch of sensuality to her beauty.

The mistake he made however was telling her what he saw, which to him, was expressed with utmost sincerity.

"You look wonderful in that bikini," he said. And for the first time, he saw a black lady blush.

Things happened so fast after they dived into the pool, that by the time they started dressing up to go back, he had been initiated. Initiated into the unclean world. He had reached the heights of pleasure, he had climbed the sacred hills, and there was no turning back. He had eaten the forbidden fruit and his thirst became insatiable, even as he gained admission into the University of Benin, until one fateful day.

# Chapter 1

Strolling in leisurely, a moderately tall, fair complexioned beautiful lady, with long beaded braids, a tight fitting black pair of jeans and red short sleeved body hug top caught the attention of everybody in the Lecture theatre.

To Ayo, She could be mistaken for a perfect piece of art or better still, a Greek goddess, come to life. She slowly took the steps, one at a time, drawing along with her glances from virtually every male in the lecture theatre.

*"See better person,"* somebody said behind Ayo. Quickly, he shook off the series of nasty thoughts that was on his mind and continued to read his books because he was scheduled to have an eight O'clock paper, the next day.

What transpired within the next few minutes to Ayo was beyond man's understanding.

Was it fate, was it meant to be. Was it destined that they were meant to meet each other?

Unknown to Ayo, the boy sitting next to him had left. The clattering of chairs disturbed Ayo's concentration, so he put his head on the table to relax till the class went silent again. Almost immediately, he felt someone sit down beside him. Slowly, he raised his head but stopped, shocked at whom it was.

Mesmerized and flabbergasted, he became demoralized.
Slowly, she put her books on the table uninterestedly, as Ayo turned around to look for the guy that was sitting on that seat a few minutes before, but he was nowhere in the Lecture Theatre. Instead, his eyes met different glances virtually from all corners of the Lecture Theatre.

"Jesus Christ." Ayo said quietly to himself. "Why tonight of all nights." He continued trying to concentrate on his studies, telling himself he could ignore her. All of a sudden, he realized he had been reading for twenty minutes, and had assimilated virtually nothing.

What next, he sighed. He had to talk.

"What time is it?" he asked.

"10.30," she replied.

"That's a literature text, are you studying literature?" he

tried again.

"No, English Arts." She replied not taking her eyes off her books.

He pretended to read for about ten more minutes before he raised his head. He saw in a pamphlet beside his books, a poem and slowly whispered the title.

"My Coy Lady."

She looked up and smiled. A smile that sent shivers up his spine.

Gently, Ayo's face broadened as he returned her smile and saw she was impressed.

They talked for about ten minutes in which she told him a few things about herself. Unlike Ayo, her next paper was in three days time, so she was more relaxed. They strolled to the café for a drink and walked around as he doled out the best of his collection of jokes. Suddenly, he felt so close to this stranger, yet still far. He wanted to know her for himself alone, to share her with nobody else.

When they came back to the L.T., they read for about an hour before she turned to tell him that she was leaving.

Ayo walked her a few yards and decided to go back, but she insisted he went further. He had a girl friend in her Hall, who by that time would be in the common room, reading. He summoned enough courage and walked on, hoping to turn around at the Hall entrance.

As they approached her Hall, he couldn't interrupt what she was saying so he made up his mind to face anything. Moreover, he wouldn't risk losing this girl for any of his girl friends. Not on my life, he thought.

They entered her hall, and he quickly scanned the common room but didn't see Chichi his girl friend. He then proceeded to know her room.

"You have not even told me your name?" she asked as they approached her room.

"Oh," he exclaimed. "That was bad mannered of me." He said pretending it wasn't deliberate.

Usually, he preferred being asked. That way, he would be sure the girl is interested in him.

"If it pleases my fair lady, I would say my name at thy request." He said, trying to tease her, but to his surprise no blush came. Instead, she answered with a teasing smile playing around her lips.

"Speak oh handsome prince, I am all ears."

Usually, when he made such jokes, girls shy away, blushing but she played along. This impressed him and he immediately realized things weren't going to be easy.

"That was a nice act," he said. "Ayo is my name."

"Come on, I am an art student or have you forgotten so soon. Anyway, Amaka is mine."

"I sure will see you very soon, probably tomorrow in class." Ayo said when they got to her room.

"May be," she shrugged, before gently tapping on her door.

"Sweet dreams," he whispered as he turned to leave.

As he walked past the common room on his way out, he caught a glimpse of Chichi reading. Obviously, she had seen him, so he went to meet her.

"Hi Love." He said, giving her a peck on the cheek but she refused to answer. He tried talking to her but still she ignored him. Seeing she was in a bad mood, he left promising to be back. He was back in less than fifteen minutes with a cup of vanilla ice cream and a bag of popcorn. To his surprise, Chichi relaxed immediately. After some cock 'n' bull story about who he was walking with, things became normal and he left.

That was the beginning of his transformation.

He got back to the Lecture Theatre and read till the early hours of the next day. When he got back to his room, he couldn't sleep. He tossed and turned in his bed, waiting for dawn to come, the dawn of a new era, the Amaka era.

His flat mates were surprised that he was so anxious to go to the Lecture Theatre to read the next day. Usually, he never left his room to read in any of the Lecture Theatres, unless any of them persuaded him to go. Unfortunately for him, he didn't see her. He spent half the night checking round all the Lecture Theatres for her, thinking she might come but got tired of checking round.

He left for his room, refusing the urge to look her up in the hostel. She would come to me he consoled himself as he staggered, worn out from his fruitless search.

✧

# *Chapter 2*

*"H*ow about buying me a cup of ice-cream." Furo said, "and popcorns too," she added chuckling.

"Meet my friend, Ade. He is in Ogun State University, O.S.U.

Since we entered your room, you didn't bother to offer him anything or know his name, all that is in your head is me buying you ice cream."

It was the beginning of a new semester, Adeola Okunoren, one of Ayo's friends had come to spend some time with him since they hadn't resumed in his school. Ayo had taken him to see some of his girlfriends, intending to give him a treat, but it ended-up making him sulk for the better part of the night

"Ahhh! Ayo," she exclaimed. "Why should you talk like that? Hello," she addressed Ade, a bit embarrassed. "Furo is my name, I'm sorry I did not offer you a drink. Do you mind a bottle of soft drink?"

"Thanks," Ade replied, smiling, "We just finished eating at the main café."

"What did you eat? Eba?" she asked looking at Ayo, chuckling.

"And what's wrong with that?" Ayo asked.

"Mmh, I was only joking." She started quickly to avoid his wrath. Turning to Ade, she said. "So your name is Ade, mine is Furo."

"I know…" Ade answered.

"How did you know?" she asked, confused.

"You said it once, besides, Ayo has said so much about you that when I saw you, I knew immediately why he is always so crazy about you,"

"This one, talk about me, please spare me the details," she concluded waving it off with her hand.

"So when are you going back to your school and how are you finding ours."

"Well, your school is okay and when I'm going back,

probably in a day or two."

"Get something to wear," Ayo interrupted, addressing Furo. "We will be back in five minutes. I want us to see one of Ade's friends in the other block. We'll wait for you outside while you change," he added moving towards the door, followed closely by Ade.

"I thought we were still going to the other female block?" Ade asked when they were outside. "What is the need for her coming along, I want to see that Amaka that made you sulk for six good weeks in Lagos."

"Well," Ayo started. "We'll drop her one way or the…"

"What's dropping." Furo said as she came out of her room making Ayo swallow the rest of his sentence.

"Oh, he was just err… talking about dropping some money for my cousin in *Ago-Iwoye*."

"Where's that."

"Somewhere in Ogun State." Ayo answered, knowing she knew little or nothing about the towns in the West.

"Hi Gloria," Ayo called as they entered her room. "Were you about going out."

"Not actually," Gloria answered. "Ovie was about buying me a cup of ice-cream, but he is still contemplating."

"What's happening Ovie," Ayo said shaking his hand. "Let's all stroll down to the ice-cream shop. I know Furo definitely will be in support of that. She had wanted it all along."

"Alright," Ovie said. "Let's go add some colours to our ladies cheeks."

"One more cup." Ayo called to the lady selling the ice-cream as he took part of Furo's ice-cream before he passed it to her. Knowing she was talking to someone but not seeing the person, he turned to play one of his jokes.

"Hope you don't mind me taking part of her ice…" he stopped short, his jaw, as his mouth fell opened in surprise. He was starring into Amaka's face.

He felt his heart skip a beat, he felt his legs shake so much that he lost his voice. She was the last person he wanted or expected to see, there and then.

Quickly, he gained composure.

"Amaka I presume," he started feigning a smile.

Furo surprised, said helplessly. "So you know this one too," before moving away to join Ade.

"Ayo," she drawled. "It's been a long time, so you are still in this school." Ignoring her statement, he turned to order another cup for her. She had company, so she declined the offer. Some minutes later, she left with her escort, while Ayo left with his friends, after buying a bag of popcorn each for the girls. Since then, Ayo lost touch of every other thing that happened that night. It was as if he had left his heart at the ice-cream shop.

He couldn't sleep. He paced the room all night like a wounded Lion, grunting what seemed like incantations.

"...Why did this happen, what have I done, what did I do," he concluded when he was tired, addressing nobody in particular.

"You don't have anything with this girl, why should you keep blaming yourself?" Ade asked when he realized Ayo was getting sober.

"A bird at hand, is worth millions in the bush," Brian, one of his flat mates added.
"You better hold on to those you have and let the sleeping dog lay."

"Listen," Ayo replied. "No sleeping dog will lie until...well," he shrugged
Paused in his tracks, and looked at his friends.

"Wait a minute..." He started, "What's happening to me? Why am I so tensed?" He sat down, holding his head in between his palms.

"I am not supposed to be feeling this way," he continued. "Why am I so conscious of her? Why can't she just leave me alone?" He started again, getting angry at the way he allowed his emotions get a better part of him.

"You are in love Ayo. It is written all over you. You love this girl, heaven knows why but you do. I did stake my life in a bet."

"Then you won't live long," Ayo replied, smiling at the thought of being in love. "...'Cos you are sure to lose that bet." He sat on the bed, then laid on his back. In no time, the call of nature came as the stress he had been through took a toll on him with the forces of sleep overpowering him, sending him into the dream world and he was rendered motionless.

Ayo finished one of his courses one Tuesday afternoon and was on his way to the main café to have lunch, when he realised he forgot his keys on his table. On his way back to get them, he saw her on a bike. She gave him that same sweet smile, and his heart began to melt.

"Christ," he grumbled. "Can't this girl just stay out of my life?"

The bike was about moving so he stopped the bike man and told her to get down. He got his keys and together, they left for her hall. After the usual chitchat, he asked if she would like to go for a show coming up the next day at the main bowl of the school's cultural Center.

"I don't know yet," was the answer that came but the worse was yet to come.

"Maybe my boy friend will want to take me there." That served its purpose because Ayo suddenly went mute. He walked on, looking blankly ahead, seeing his future crumble.

"Are you still here," she said, touching his shoulder when she saw the expression on his face.

"Oh! Err... I'm sorry," he stammered. "I was trying to recollect something."

"Are you sure? I was only joking about my boyfriend, so when are you picking me." He couldn't believe his ears, but he pretending not to be moved.

"How about picking you at about eight p.m. We could have something to eat at the Main-café and then relax at the Shopping Mall before moving, 'cos its going to be a long night."

"Hey!" She exclaimed "I only said pick me, not make plans."

"Okay... okay gorgeous," he said, raising both hands. "I'll be here eight p.m. I didn't mean to push things," he continued, " I..."

"Its okay," Amaka broke in. "Lets see what happens."

"Alright," Ayo shrugged. "Cool..." he continued as she turned to face him on getting to the entrance to her room."

"Lets see what happens," he concluded taking a slight bow before turning to leave.

"I don't like late comers," she called out before she opened her door.

✧

## Chapter 3

"Come in". He called out as the knock came from the door; "BOY, I was beginning to think you had changed your mind," he continued, but was cut short seeing who stood at the entrance. It's not my love, he thought, it is not Amaka." His heart stopped beating, his jaw dropped open in surprise and shock at whom he saw.

Standing at the door was Tessy clad in a pair of faded blue jeans, a blue denim shirt and basket woven high-healed platform suede shoes that made her some inches taller.

"My... O... My," she started, as she came in dropping her bag on his table. "Look at his face," she continued, "I was sure I was going to shock the living daylight out of you, but are you not happy to see me or were you expecting someone else."

Ayo was dumb-founded. O my God he thought trying as much as possible to look plain and composed as his eyes traveled from her smashing face to the heavy traveling bag. Not when Amaka was to come, his mind kept telling him. He had to get her out, one way or the other, he thought as his mind began to run riot.

"You didn't tell me you had an aunt or relative here in Benin. Where are you coming from?"

"Don't be stupid you dumb head of course I came from school, to see you," she answered thinking he was playing some of his dirty jokes.

"And the traveling bag?" he asked as they both shifted glances to the traveling bag which looked as if it might burst any moment.

"Oh! She said, we were given a two-week holiday, so I thought I should spend some days with you before going home. Boy... am... I' tired," she concluded as she slumped on the bed.

"J-e-s-u-s," he exclaimed. "We have to talk Tessy," he continued. "You see, for the past one month, some things have been happening, and this is not the right time or place to talk about it."

"I'm in no mood to talk either, can't it wait till tomorrow," she said.

"Tomo.... what!" he exclaimed. "You are spending the night here," he said, more like a statement than a question.

"Where else will I spend it?" she asked.

"Err... em, you see... em... you'll sleep with my cousin Tosin, you know her room, don't you? I'll explain everything tomorrow, honestly this is..."

"What!" she exclaimed sitting upright. "What did I hear you just say? Okay... I came all the way from Ife just to see you and all I get in return is; sleep with my cousin," she mimicked. "In the first place, who told you I was a lesbian, ... oh. I see, you are expecting someone and I have to get dumped all of a sudden because of a one night stand with one bitch."

"Please... Tessy-, this..."

"...Is that not what you do, trip them, use them and dump them. This is the most important part eh and you can't shelve it for me."

Now, she was crying. Furiously, she ran towards him directing a series of light blows at his chest. He grabbed her, trying to control her as she struggled frantically until she became worn out before she fell limp on his chest sobbing seriously. Suddenly, he felt guilty and he pitied her. After traveling that long, she should be tired and tensed, but she should understand my position he thought. She could not possibly spend the night there, not that night, not in that room, the thought kept ringing as Amaka's last word kept floating in his subconscious.

*"Ol boy, you sure say na show you dey go so*, because the way you *dey take polish that shoe, e get as e be.* Mmh. For the past ten minutes, you have been polishing that shoe," Biodun, one of Ayo's flat mates was saying.

"Didn't you see how he ironed his shirt, and for the first time, he ironed his pair of jeans trouser," Brian added.

*"Na una know*, may be it is now a crime to try maintain the few things have got."

"Are you sure its your few things, you are taking care of or you are preparing for an assessment night. May be Amaka is giving him her final answer tonight."

"Mind your own business," Ayo answered cutting them short. He looked at wall clock, "Six p.m. If I stay with you guys, I will end up running late," he concluded before he rushed to the bathroom. The unusual ten minutes in the bath of course, went down as an observation to his friends. Not minding their talks, he enjoyed himself under the luxury of the cold needles spraying from the shower and the beautiful fragrance from the imported toilet soap with which he lathered as if there was no tomorrow.

The night was fun, as he had passed the first test. Eight p.m. on the dot, he was at her doorstep. This surprised her and she tilted her head before she told him to give her five minutes to get ready, this stretched to about thirty minutes, but it was worth the while as Ayo stared in admiration at his date.

The night was fun as the show turned out to be a success, and with Amaka it was more fun as they shared light secrets and laughed at each other's jokes. She had a beautiful kind of laugh that came from the inside, this made Ayo relax as he felt a place deep inside him, a place he never really knew existed regardless of being empty begin to dwell in her love.

It was the best night in his life, and they ended the show in his house.

Trust "the Boys", they had cleaned up the whole place, enslaving the air in the room in a beautiful, thick fragrance from a mixture of "Calvin-Klein-1 perfume", and the little "Eternity," Ayo had left in his case.

As she sat on the couch, absorbed in the beauty of the room coupled with its fragrance, Ayo pressed the power button on the remote control and to his surprise, Kenny-G's. "You are my love," floated through the room and that was the climax because, one, two and three, the game had begun.

As she lay in his arms the next day at about two p.m. because they woke up late due to the activities of the previous night, she asked him a question that shocked him.

"Ayo," she began. "I want to ask for the first and probably the last time, you wouldn't leave me for someone else, would you?" It was more like a statement than a question, as she looked so innocent and concerned.

"Of course I wouldn't do that, not on my life," he answered.

The second and most dangerous question came when she was about leaving. "Tell me," she started. "I wouldn't mind if you tell me now before things go far, at least I'll know you didn't lie to me. Do you have any other girlfriend as at now, serious or unserious."

Like a bad odour, the question filled the room and to make matters worse, she stared into his eyes as if the answer lay there.

"No, none that I know of," Ayo replied jokingly as he hugged her for the last time before he opened his door to prevent her from reading his thoughts.

Definitely, they all must go he kept telling himself. I could always deal with them he concluded as he waved the topic off his mind.

Like a fool he stood there five minutes after thinking of her last words. Like the same old fool, he stood looking into space as Tessy, leaned on him now sobbing noiselessly.

The loud thud shocked him back to reality as he looked up and saw Amaka standing by the door. He looked from her bag that fell back to her horror stricken face just in time to catch a glimpse before it disappeared.

"I am sorry, I didn't mean to interrupt," she said as she bent down to pick her bag. "I... err... didn't know you would be busy," she managed to conclude in a shaky voice trying hard to control her tears, as she turned and left.

Like the same old fool, Ayo stood there staring at the door after her until the reality of losing her dawned on him. As if on reflex, he left Tessy, it was so sudden that she nearly fell because she lost balance but he quickly caught her.

"Sorry," he said, sitting her down before he continued, "you just sit down right here and I'll be back in a minute," He dashed down the stairs with the speed of lightening but saw no one. She was gone. All of a sudden he felt his heart ache, his shoulders dropped with despair as his brows began to perspire. Slowly he walked back to his room and slumped on his bed.

"Was that her, was that why you didn't want me to stay," Tessy asked from beside the desk where she stood.

"It doesn't matter anymore."

"Oh, but before now, it mattered."

Getting angry, he sat up and growled "will you keep your mouth shut and stay if you want to stay..."

"And if I don't," she chipped in

"Then get the hell out of here..."

"Ayo," she screamed. That shocked him back to his senses 'cos his shoulder dropped for the second time in one night and he became sober.

"Ok - a - y," he drawled "I'm sorry I said that, but I have to see some people." He got up before she could reply and left after wearing his shoe. She only stood where she was and stared at him in bewilderment.

His first port of call was Amaka's room. "Of course she left for your place," one of her roommates said.

"I've not been home yet, I just wanted to be sure," he lied, taking his leave. "Take care of her," one of them, an ebony beauty called out as he left. She must not get hurt.

"God knows I wouldn't think of hurting her," he mumbled as he stumbled down the staircase to the common room. And I hope she is not yet hurt. He thought scanning the busy common room for the beautiful long beaded braids. He checked four of her friends but none had seen her that evening except for the last one who said she walked her to the shopping complex to buy some provisions before she left for his place.

As he left the room, he couldn't help but think that the bag that fell must have contained the things she had bought for him. Thought of where and what Amaka would be doing filled his mind as he struggled to a nearby bar where he drank a cold bottle of big stout, after which he ordered for more until his purse was empty. It was then he knew he was drunk as he fell back into his chair in an attempt to get up. He tried to look at the table surprised at his state, but with a blurred vision he had to count the bottles on the table over and over again without success.

He woke up the following afternoon and saw he was lying naked under his sheets. He looked round and nothing really made sense until Tessy appeared with a cup of black coffee.

"Just in time for your coffee," she said. Getting some tablets for him from his drawer before she placed the tray by the bed. He sat upright, leaning on his pillow, his head aching from events of the previous day, which floated back in succession.

"How're you now?" she asked.

"Perfectly okay but for my head, it aches," she kept quiet.

"I didn't remember undressing yesterday." He said looking

22

at her from the corner of his eyes. Then she raised her head. "But you remember vomiting. Let's get something straight..." She began, getting up. "Did you drown yourself because of me or that bitch..."

"Watch your mouth lady. She is no bitch..."

"Oh... okay," she said, raising her hands in despair. "Some girl has taken over your heart. That's even if you have a heart," she chipped in before she continued. "While I come all the way from *Ife* just to be the one to mop your room which you messed-up with vomit."

"Gaw-d," he drawled, "not again why am I sitting here listening to you ranting," he said, making to get up but fell back. This made him groan as his head ached.

"Okay, I am sorry," she apologized as she handed out the coffee which he downed almost immediately not minding the taste. It served its purpose, 'cos his head became less cloudy and he lay to sleep.

"Wake me up by six," he said before dozing off. "I have a test tomorrow."

# Chapter 4

*A*s he walked into the west wing of the schools central cafe, he heard someone call him by the name only his close friends use. He turned back, and saw it was Ugo.

"Ever Fresh Prince," Ugoh repeated. "Where have you been, we don't get to see you again. You have since become an essential commodity; everybody has been looking for you."

"Everybody," he murmured, as he prayed Amaka was included.

"Yeah... Kachi, Iyke, Tola as a matter of fact, Kay just left for Amaka's room to check for you, because Abbey said you'd be there."

"I wish I were." Ayo replied as he dropped his books on the table.

"...And why can't you?" Ugoh asked surprised at his answer.

"Men, it's a long story. I don't know where to start from."

"Well, let's see," Ugoh said, looking at Ayo with concern. "Start from the beginning. I'm not in a hurry," In a bid to lift off part of the burden on him, he started talking.

"You see, there is this girl I was seeing when I was in secondary school..."

"You mean you had only one girl there..." Ugoh interrupted.

"C'mon, don't be dumb, I meant the serious one. Why I stayed so long with her beats me, possibly because she was or still is. I probably don't know, 'cos its been quite sometime, a good lover or because she was out-spoken. The funny thing about it was she never complained about my other girlfriends. She always believed I would come back to her and her arms were ever open when I went back. It got to a stage that I had to do all my other girls underground.

"When I left high school, she left for the University of Ife, and God knows what happens to her there never bugged me for one minute."

24

"Or, you're bored already with my story?" he asked, "I told you it's a long one."

"No, not at all," Ugoh answered. "I was just wondering why that should bother you now."

"Yeah... yeah... I was about entering that phase," he replied as he leaned back on the rest.

"Yesterday evening, she appeared at my doorstep. You can imagine after eleven months, she just appeared out of the blues."

"H-e-y!" Ugoh started. "Stop acting the hurt one, why not enjoy yourself while she is here and may be the next time you'll see her again will be on her wedding day. What's your stress."

Sighing heavily, Ayo stared into space. "May be before I met Amaka, that might have been exactly what I would have done, but you see," he continued, "Amaka was supposed to be in my room by six yesterday, so when this girl came, I became confused."

Now Ugoh sat upright on hearing Amaka's name come up. He sensed real trouble. "So..." he said not wanting to wait any longer for the joker.

"Amaka came in without my knowledge and saw her in my arms."

"Oh L-o-r-d". Ugoh drawled. "How could you have been so careless?"

"Mmh, I wish I could blame myself for being careless but I wasn't. Tessy started crying when I said she couldn't stay, charging at me like a wounded Tigress. I held her and calmed her down as she sobbed away on my chest, that was when Amaka came and she left almost immediately."

"I went after her, but was too late. She disappeared before I got outside."

"Men, that's real bullshit you are in," Ugoh said as he relaxed on his chair, shaking his head. He pitied Ayo, knowing what the name meant to him.

"Yeah big shit," Ayo agreed. "You should have seen the expression on her face as her bag fell when she saw me."

"Have you checked her since then."

"Immediately, I went to her room after calming Tessy to settle down."

"Settle down?" Ugoh asked in surprise.

"Well, I couldn't have told her to leave that time of the day. After all, Amaka wouldn't come back, so there was no use thinking at how to get rid of her."

"Men, I was destabilized," continued Ayo, "I was confused damn. I have never been so disorganised."

"And did you see her?"

"No. Even all her friends I checked didn't see her either."

"A-a-rgh that's tough you know. Hope she hasn't done anything drastic", Ugoh said.

"She's not that kind of a girl," Ayo said, as a smile crossed his face. "She's not that fragile," he continued but paused as the smile disappeared as if it never was there "or is she," he murmured. May be that was a part he had never noticed. I hope not, he prayed silently.

Ugoh stood up to see one of his friends, who were at the entrance with two girls. One of them he recognized as his girlfriend, while Ayo settled down to read his books, as his test was due in two hours.

"How was the test?" Onafue, one of Ayo's coursemates was asking him as he stepped out of the hall.

"It wasn't bad," he replied. "To be honest, it wasn't too good either."

"That means you didn't go through your notes because they were key points," she said.

"I wish I had but honestly, I did not concentrate, not with an unsettled mind."

"B-O-Y - you look troubled, are you okay."

They were passing the basement lecture theatre as he answered.

"Yea… You can't be of help any way," he concluded strolling on absent-mindedly. Suddenly, something attracted his attention.

"You never can know what..." Onafue paused when he held her arm

"Err.... Onafue, please you'll excuse me, I have to see someone. May be I'll check you in the evening," he said, as he hastened his steps.

"Where could she be going," he thought as he followed Amaka and her friend.

"Okay love, I should be around," she called out after him. At least some people care, he thought as he strolled into the Medical students hostel.

"Yes who is it?" A voice came from inside as he knocked.

"It's me," he answered, dreading to mention his name. "Can I come in?" he asked silently praying.

"Come in, the door is not locked."

As he opened the door to enter, he saw the surprise on Amaka's face when she saw him. She was alone in the room with a girl who possibly was her coursemate he thought.

"Hello," he said to her friend who was sitting on the bed facing that on which Amaka sat.

"Hi," she said before getting up. "I will just get my towel before we leave," she said to Amaka as she left the room, leaving two of them in the room. This didn't surprise him, as he knew Amaka must have narrated what she thought she saw to her friend.

"Hi," he said slowly moving closer. He sat opposite her. "Where did you go last night, I searched every where for you."

"And if I may ask, why were you searching for me?"

"'C' mon you know I did search for you, not after leaving my house like that."

"Oh, it was the way I left your house."

"No, Amaka I won't start explaining anything," he continued trying to control her temper "because you wouldn't believe, but I assure you, it wasn't what you thought you saw."

"And what did I think... you know what I feel like doing," she continued now getting annoyed. "I feel like smashing that gas lamp on your head."

He looked at the beautiful gas lamp on the table top at the end of the room, and assured himself she wouldn't do anything like that, the lamp looked too heavy for her.

"Please listen to me Amaka," he tried again. "I'm sorry things happened like this, things probably went too fast for you to see the reality in it. Please relax and give me a chance to prove myself. Now he was on his knees begging her. "Yesterday till this moment seemed the longest hours in my life.

Another chance is all I ask for, and I promise I won't fail you, please don't say no, don't say no, don't..."

"Oohps! Sorry," her friend apologized as she entered

cutting him short; I'll be outside when you are through.

"No, wait Yinka, Let's go." She said getting up.

"But Amaka, can't we settle this before you leave."

"Settle what?" She nearly screamed as she was near tears. "There's nothing to settle please, just leave me alone; alright," she concluded as she turned, packed her books and left.

Ayo was still on his knees, looking at the floor when Yinka's words tore into his sub-conscious.

"I want to lock my door," she said. "Are you going to stay or leave."

He had never been humiliated in his life as he was that particular day, but he stood up and told himself he deserved it, at least a punishment for the play boy he used to be.

"And if I were you," Yinka whispered as he stepped out of the room, "I would stay away from her for sometime."

"Thanks," he replied without knowing. At least, she was on his side he thought, consoling himself as he watched Yinka walk up to her.

It was two weeks after he last saw Amaka as all attempts to see her failed. Those two weeks were the worst Ayo had ever through. He did nothing but drown himself in a bar, sleep and think. People kept complaining he was losing weight but he was unperturbed.

Even Tessy's beautiful body could not change his mood as all attempt to get to him failed. She left, depressed and annoyed at his state. He was on his bed reminiscing on his time with Amaka when he heard a bang on the door. He got up to open it and saw Ugoh's angry face.

"I've been banging this fucking door for the past five minutes, were you sleeping? But for that final year student down-stairs, I would've left. She assured me you were in, or have you suddenly gone deaf," Ugoh ranted on and on, annoyed at Ayo's attitude.

"Gawd," Ayo drawled,  "Not again. Not from you of all people, that was why I jammed my door."

"Oh, you decided to seek consolation in the solitude of your room."

"Say whatever you want to say," Ayo answered. "It's not your fault, you can talk." He sat down on his bed as he continued,

28

"Come in and sit down men, or don't tell me you are leaving now."

"Mmh, in a way, yes," Ugoh replied now relaxed as he walked in shutting the door behind him and with you."

"With me?" Ayo asked, astonished.

"Yes, with you," Ugoh replied

"Then you better leave because no Jupiter can move me from this place, not till evening anyway."

"C' mon Ayo, we're supposed to go to Brian's place together, you know he has not been okay for quite some time."

"And what makes you feel I am?" Ayo asked.

"Okay if you feel because you have a minor emotional problem that you won't care for others, well… Good luck and bear your burdens alone," Ugoh said pretending to be annoyed as he turned to leave.

"Okay… Oka-y you fool, Ayo grunted, why not ease myself while I see my friends."

And make sure you shave, your face looks untidy." Ugoh frowned making himself comfortable on the bed. I'll be waiting."

Ayo entered the bathroom attached to his room and stared into the fairly large dressing mirror that swayed loosely on a small rusty nail.

"Christ," he groaned seeing his reflection. He looked ten years older. "I look a sick old fool," he called out as he fumbled with his electric shave.

After what seemed like an endless war, he came out of the bath looking good and smelling fresh. He clad himself in a pair of black "Tommy Jeans," and a "Ralph," multicolored sweat shirt. He looked up for approval and he got more than that. For the first time Ugoh mixed a bit of his native Igbo Language with the usual pidgin which was the "Lingua Franca," on campus.

"*Nna you be my guy*, this is the Fresh Prince I use to know", he continued. "*Bobs nack ya shoe make we go.*"

"Do I need to wear something formal, why can't I wear my leather slippers?" Ayo asked reluctantly, I'm really in no mood for a shoe.

"NO-O-O we might check on someone on our way back."

"Mmh…mh, if it's a girl's place, count me out. I have enough on my mind to start smiling at any girl now."

Suddenly, he looked up into Ugohs eyes and sensed he had

29

something up his sleeve but Ugoh avoided his eyes, pretending to read the Magazine in his hand.

"Look Ugoh," he said at last. "I'm in no mood for girls now so if that's what you have in mind, let me stay in my room, I have some thinking to do."

"After two weeks, you've not finished thinking, I hope you finish one day. Well, about girls, let's see what happens. I just hope you'll forgive them one day."

"I think we better leave before you change your mind," he concluded as he got up, leading the way.

# Chapter 5

*A*yo had seen surprises, but the one that looked him in the eye that day was a heart breaker.

The moment he stepped into Brian's room he felt uncomfortable as the whole place, usually noisy was unearthingly quiet.

Ugoh opened the door, which wasn't strange since it was always opened to whoever cared to say "hi", like his too, Ayo thought.

As they entered, the room was almost dark but for one or two rays which the drapes couldn't prevent from coming in.

Ayo was about telling Ugoh he was better than some people, at least he wasn't in darkness but like a contradiction to his thought, the light came on as voices rang out in unison. Singing a beautiful birthday song for him.

Fear, shock and surprise showed on his face as he gaped, mouth open till they rounded it up with a, "Happy birthday Fresh Prince." Then, he looked back at Ugoh who gave a slight bow.

"Happy birthday my friend," he said.

It was after he heard it from Ugoh's mouth that things fell into place. It was November 29, my birthday He thought. How could he have forgotten, he had planned taking Amaka to Warri to spend his birthday at the Hotel Presidential, the best in Warri from where they were supposed to go to a party which was to end in the early hours of the following day.

Applause followed a speech made by some one in the crowd. He woke up from his daydream looking round helplessly not knowing what to do or say.

Knowing the state he was in Ugoh led him to a table to blow out the candles on a fairly large birthday cake, which in his normal state would have looked mouth-watering. Sub-consciously, he bent down and was about blowing out the candle when a voice rang out from behind.

"Make a wish."

The voice sounded familiar but in his state he recognized

no one so he couldn't make out who really said so but he must have guessed it was one of Amaka's friends.

Silently, he said "God, How I wish Amaka was here." When he was young, he read fairy tales where fairies made wishes come true. He never thought he would ever get to make a wish and watch it come through.

Immediately he blew off the candles, which took all the strength he had, somebody clapped behind him and Brian who was supposed to be ill, walked to the wardrobe opened it exposing a mighty box wrapped beautifully and tapped with a beautifully mixture of red and blue ribbon.

Slowly he read what was written on it.

"Hurray! Fresh Prince is a year older."

For heaven sake, this was becoming too much he thought. If this was a dream he thought, he had better wake up but when he saw the content he changed his prayers to; He had better not wake up. He imagined what was in the box. A TV, a C. D. Player, a fridge, series of items raced across his mind, as he stood rooted to the spot.

Ugoh ever at his service cleared his throat breaking into his thoughts as he stepped forward.

"Err…" he began, Ayo or should I say Fresh Prince. This is a Present we feel you and only you deserve, and we all contributed to get it for you. I see you are a bit tired, so we will help you open it.

"Abbey," he called.

"Ugoh, you shouldn't have done this, I have a fridge you know."

Ayo whispered across as he walked past.

"Never mind my friend, when you see this one you will forget you ever had one."

"Please Biodun, can you give me a hand," Ugoh called but as they approached the box, a voice, which sounded like the previous one, called out.

"Please let the celebrant open it himself."

Now, his head a little clear, he saw it was Yinka, Amaka's friend. To be sure Amaka wasn't there, he looked round and sighed helplessly, confirming his fear.

He bent down loosening the ribbon with a fragile fidgety

hand while whispers kept floating from behind him. He wondered what was making them giggle as he loosened the last of the ribbons, and slowly pulled the lid.

What made them giggle he now saw. Like a mighty python, she uncurled herself from her sitting position, got up and stepped out of the box as Ayo moved back sub-consciously out of fear and shock.

"No..." he said. "This is a dream," he stood rooted to the spot not taking his eyes off her afraid she might disappear.

As if she knew what was on his mind, she stretched her left hand and moved a step closer just as the same Kenny G's "You Are My Love," which filled his room some weeks back came floating into his head.

Perplexed as he was he looked round and saw a series of movements which made gestures that he should go on. Afraid she might have disappeared, that he might wake up and realize it was all a dream, he turned back to Amaka and there she was in a sparkling white body hugging stoned evening gown that showed the beautiful outline of her body from her bare shoulders to the fish tail end, inches above her gold coloured shoe on a white round shaped platform heels.

Her hair a series of curly waves flowed down her shoulders, revealing less than half of her beautiful face adorned with a perfect set of white teeth that glowed as she smiled looking as beautiful as ever.

The gap between them reduced as they became one, swaying to the rhythm of the beautiful track that filled the room. After the second track; he began.

"Amaka... I'm sorry. You see..."

"S s sh..." she hushed. Leaning back on his shoulder, they allowed themselves get lost in a world of their own.

Ayo noticed the room was empty but for two of them so he held Amaka tightly in case she too decides to disappear like the others but a round of applause brought the music to an end and he raised his head to see everybody exactly where they had been.

"I thought they left," he whispered to Amaka.

"Gosh," she sighed.

"Is it thirty minutes already, time sure flies?"

"Thirty what?" Ayo asked nearly shouting in surprise,

33

"...so..."

"S sh..." she stopped him again. " Don't ask questions," she said looking straight into his eyes, "please."

Looking into the depth of her eyes, he nodded, lost in Love. As long as she was there he thought, as long as she never leaves him again, anybody can do anything he or she wants, as long as they don't come between them, he raised his head.

The drinks please, Brian called and almost immediately two girls, Brian's girlfriend and the other Ugoh's sister came in with trays containing cups, half filled with red wine garnished with grape fruits floating in each glass.

Ayo looked at Amaka, as one of the girls brought the tray to them, and she gave a slight nod.

Tired of the game, he shook his head helplessly as he picked two cups, handing one to Amaka. Brian continued when everybody had his or her drink.

"We are gathered here today to wish a very good friend, brother and husband to be," he paused and gestured towards Amaka who giggled at the thought "...a happy birthday as he is a year older today.

Many happy days like this to come my friend.

"Amen," the boys chorused as Brian stained the rug with a spill of his wine. Unlike Biodun, he didn't complain. Instead, he smiled and did the same.

"Hope you appreciate our birthday gift," he joked. "Though it's not much but I can assure you that it cost us a lot, but anything for you my friend," he concluded, "anything."

He downed his wine in a gulp calling for another cup, as they all halved their drinks, he continued

"Now three hearty cheers to our friend."

Hip !!! Hip !! Hip !

H u r r a y

Hip !!! Hip !! Hip !

H u r r a y

Hip !!! Hip !! Hip !

H u r r a y

Almost immediately, Abbey raised a song and others joined.

For he is a jolly good fellow

For he is a jolly good fellow

For he is a jolly good fe - I - I -a

And so say all of us

And so say all of us

H u r r a y

And so say all of us.

H u r r a y ! ! ! .

For he is a jolly good fellow

For he is a jolly good fellow

For he is a jolly good fe - I - I -a

And soo - say all of us they all drawled as the song came to an end. "Hip Hip Hip ! ! ! H u r r a y," they all chorused.

"Happy birthday Ayo." Brian concluded before they all gave him a hug one after the other. It was all so formal that Ayo thought they must have planned and rehearsed for days. It all seemed like something out of a well-edited American film, but this time in Benin.

"You have anything to say Ayo?" Ugoh asked.

"Err… men," he stammered, looking at the wicked smile on Ugoh's face. " I must say," he continued, "this came as a blow below the belt. You guys caught me unawares," he paused as they all laughed.

"But thank you anyway, I just realized the advantage of having friends, I mean real friends. You all proved I had never been alone and will never be. I hope I would prove the same to each and every one of you and Amaka," he paused. "I think we'll reserve that till evening," he concluded cuddling her as they all laughed.

"Yeah that reminds me," interrupted Brian. "Sorry birthday boy, you will continue in a minute. Hope you're all aware "POSH," Club is having their black boogie tonight in *Warri* so all the dancing would be done there. When you leave here, which I hope will be soon, you all should go home, get ready and by seven p.m., we meet at Ugohs place, so that we can all leave in the traditional convoy by eight in order to be in *Warri* by Nine at most. Please keep that in mind and as for you big boy," he continued, addressing Ayo. "Reservations have been made for you at the international de-presidential hotel. A table for two and a double room so we would understand if you wouldn't be at the party but be ready by 6.30 p.m. I will pick you and then Amaka before joining others."

Confused, he turned back to look at Amaka - "Is *Warri* still fixed?" he asked.

"Not if you don't want to," she answered. "Do you have

any other plans?" she asked

"No--- no--- its' just that I'm beginning to feel faint, the world seems to be moving faster than I can bear."

"Relax my love, it'll soon be over. Just a matter of time and it will be you and me."

At the mention of my love he regained consciousness as it kept ringing in his head "my love."

He hugged everybody as they started leaving. On getting to Yinka he said "thanks," and hugged her. "I will pay you back."

"You don't have to," she answered in a matter of fact tone. "Next time you hurt her I will have your balls chopped off."

"Never mind," he answered. "There wouldn't be need for that you have my word," on getting to Ugoh, he said, "you know something."

"What?" asked Ugoh.

"You are a fucking son of a bitch."

"My mum wouldn't like that if she hears, you know," he said smiling.

"Okay, a beautiful one," Ayo added.

"Well, I guess I could settle a beautiful bitch," Ugoh whispered. "Maybe you should know, it wasn't solely my idea, Yinka supported it all the way."

"You know Yinka?" Ayo asked astonished.

"Come on Ayo, She is now my girl."

"Girl! What!" Ayo exclaimed. "Okay... Okay..." he continued now becoming restless so it was a set up from the beginning, now what else don't I know, tell me Amaka is your sister."

"Are you ready". Brian broke their conversation. "I am leaving, I have to fill my tank - it's nearly empty"

"Yeah... I'm ready, I think I should get out of this place or I might faint the next minute.

"Relax boy." Ugoh called after him, you'll get over it don't worry you will."

## Chapter 6

"Like how?" Ayo asked, ignorant of what Amaka had been saying. "What were you saying?"

"Thank God you're back," she answered. "I was beginning to think you would be in that trance forever."

"What trance?" he asked surprised.

"It doesn't matter anymore," she said sighing heavily with relief. "I was beginning to blame myself for playing along with them, I didn't know the extent of psychological effect it would have on you." Leaning on the table, she continued, "What matters now is that you're back and I hope you don't go again. We are at the presidential hotel."

"Of course I can see that," Ayo answered. "But when did we get here."

"That was what I was complaining about, you've been quiet since we left Benin. Brian just left, he promised to call when he gets to the party to know your condition, but he assured me you would come out of the trance, he said it was excitement."

"Excitement!" Ayo thought as he looked at the table without saying a word. Afraid he was going again, Amaka leaned across the table to shake his hand. "What is the matter?" he asked looking up, surprised.

"I thought you were going again."

"C'mon, I wouldn't do that. You see," he stated leaning on the table, "I don't know where to start from but I want you to know that I'm sorry. These two weeks was hell for me. I didn't know how to get you, but you must know, it wasn't what you saw, you see…"

"It's okay," Amaka whispered, taking his hands on the table. Ugoh explained everything to me. I would have seen you myself but I couldn't bring myself to face you not after I walked out on you in Yinka's room. That was why he suggested we give you a surprise party, all expenses paid by your club. Whatever the name is, I know, it's made up of great guys."

I pray you never know the name, he thought. I'm not yet a

member, but I know I wouldn't be able to hold on for too long without joining, after tonight.

"Ugoh," he said after a moment of silence. "Ugoh has always been a devil full of surprises. He sure pulled this one on me and I'm grateful." He smiled as he held her hands across the table.

Just then, the waiter brought some fish pepper soup for them. "Do we need an appetizer?" he asked spreading his serviette on his shirt.

"Well," she shrugged. "It doesn't smell bad."

"I felt our joy was enough appetizer," he teased as they both laughed. As they were about finishing the main course, Ayo made a suggestion.

"How about taking our desert in our suite?" he asked.

"Err..." She paused raising an eyebrow, pretending to think.

"You know," he continued. "We could talk about other things apart from eating."

"Things like?" she asked playing along.

"Err... you know, em... your lips, your cute small ears, your beautiful eyes, those two mountains especially the peak..."

"Ayo," she exclaimed! "In the restaurant when will you change?"

"Well, you asked for it, didn't you?. I was only making a suggestion," he added innocently leaning back.

"You know, the agony I went through this past two weeks, thinking I had lost you."

"Not now, that's gone with the past, you're a year older, that's enough to think about," she broke in before he continued to explain himself.

They stared at each other, passing a million and one messages to one another as he reached out across the table to touch her face. Quickly, she covered his with both hands to feel the warmth from the depth of his hand. "If only you know how much I..."

Just then the waiter arrived with their dessert. The fresh Pineapple juice looked mouth-watering, but Ayo had other plans.

"Excuse me," Ayo leaned closer to the waiter, "My...err friend isn't feeling too well so she'll prefer to take her dessert in her suite, me too," he whispered.

"Okay sir," he bowed. "What is the number sir?"

"Room 10-0-6."

" At the top floor?" he asked to be sure, his stare moving from him to Amaka and back.

"Yes," Ayo replied, adding when he saw the surprise on his face. "Our company paid for it, we are on official duty."

"Oh… yes sir," he nodded before taking his leave.

"Born Liar!" Amaka said as she looked at the waiter who efficiently hurried towards the elevator.

"Well, I did it to protect your interest you know, aren't you proud of me?" He giggled before they both laughed, and they left for their suite. Like two long lost lovers, their desires rose as they went up in the elevator holding and cuddling, while two old women watched from behind giggling.

They had hardly entered their suite when they began to strip. By the time they entered the stadium, there was no going back, the pitch was set they were ready and without a referee, they played till it was full time.

As they lay spent under the sheets, which covered less than half of their bodies, the waiter knocked and entered almost immediately but stopped in his tracks as Ayo quickly pulled the sheets to their shoulders.

"I'm, err... Sorry," he started, "I saw the door was opened and thought you were expecting me."

"That's okay," Ayo smiled, we were expecting you. We were just err… planning how to do our... business, remember," he added winking.

"Yes… Yes, I can see that," he replied shaking his head as he left.

"You're impossible," Amaka said, "You really made him feel at ease, he was really embarrassed at first."

"Yeah… talking of embarrassment, the first rule is to prevent such situations as leaving the door unlocked during the match."

"Match," she teased.

"Yeah, match. In a stadium as big as this," he gesticulated towards the double bed. "Casablanca to be precise," he continued, jumping into the bed after locking the door.

Dropping a kiss on her lips he said, "let's kick off." A kiss on her neck, shoulders and clavicle and, "should we score?" he asked raising his head.

"Come on," she pulled him impatiently and the second goal slipped in. They dozed off almost immediately, waking up when a knock came from the door.

"Excuse me sir," the voice came. "There is a Mr. Brian waiting for you at the reception."

"Go... S... h!" They both exclaimed in unison as they sprang up.

"Can we make it?" Ayo asked Amaka looking for an excuse.

"Come on don't be naughty," she said getting out of bed and rushing to the bath.

"Tell him we will be with him in twenty minutes," Ayo called too tired to get out of bed.

"Okay sir," the answer came faintly before the waiter left.

"I didn't know Amaka could dance so well," Brian said on their way back to Benin. The party was a success as people came all the way from Ibadan, Ife, Lagos and the environs.

One time at the party, Ayo saw Tessy. This however did not surprise him, he silently prayed she didn't see him but almost immediately, she caught a glimpse of Ayo and their eyes locked in a stare for some minutes before she blinked when her friend asked her to dance.

She knew better than to cause him another heartbreak, Ayo thought because she never came close since she had seen Amaka around.

With Tessy around, Ayo got fed up of the party and asked to be dropped off, at the hotel. Nobody complained because they all thought he wanted time with Amaka, while Amaka on the other hand preferred their match to dancing.

"Hope you'll teach Ayo some dance steps," Biodun added so he wouldn't disgrace you when next you go to a party.

"You think I can't dance ehh?" Ayo asked.

"Not that we think," replied Biodun "we know."

"Okay, wait and see. Moreover, if Amaka can dance, what makes you feel I can't do better or have you forgotten what a woman can do a man can do better."

"Sit down there."

They laughed as they headed for Benin.

# Chapter 7

"Come---- come," Bola was calling the class rep. one Friday morning. Year II Pharmacy was supposed to go on an excursion to Delta Pharmaceutical Company in Warri, but they couldn't secure a bus.

"This can't continue like this," she continued. "This trip fucked up twice because of your absolute incompetence. Why can't you secure a bus for us, it's either we go today or never," she concluded as they got to the front of the Pharmaceutics Lab. Where others were gathered, tired of the whole situation.

"Relax honey," the class rep. Said, trying to cool her down, "Segun has gone with one of the drivers to pick up the Bedford. Is that okay?" he continued patting her on the back. "We would have preferred the beautiful civilian, but now that we have no choice we'll do with what we can get."

"This is not a matter of what we can get," Bola started again. "I mean," she continued raising her hands in despair. Everybody has something reasonable to do m-e-n, instead of wasting our time sitting around this deserted lab.

"Okay... Okay, I promise we'll go, is that alright?" he asked getting tired of her naggings.

"Well," she shrugged. "We had better leave on time if we'll go or else..." She turned, and left to join her friends leaving the sentence hanging.

"What was he telling you?" Kayode asked her as she joined them.

"They have gone to get the bus at the mechanic workshop."

"But the bus is in front of the Student Union building," Kayode countered. "I saw it there not quite ten minutes when I went for a drink or is it not the new civilian bus?"

"Nooo," he said. "That's been booked for today, so we have to do with the Bedford. Talking about a drink, I think I wouldn't mind one myself, a Chilled one," she emphasized as she got up. "Where's Prince," she continued looking around, before picking her bag.

"I wonder," Tosin answered, I 've not seen him today."

"C'mon," Yormies answered defensively as they all got up. "He should be around somewhere, we came together."

"Okay... I've seen him," Bola said moving towards Ayo, followed closely by Tosin.

"French Prince darling." Tosin called out in the usual way she teased him, "why are you sitting there like a married man with wives and kids at home."

"So you don't know he's married," Bola answered before Ayo could say anything. "Wife, yes." She continued "but Children, none to his credit. Or," she said slowly. "That's what's giving him concern, have you scored," she asked, others laughing.

"I wish it was only that, I know more than a hundred Doctors around you know,"

"A..y..o!" Exclaimed Bola, "you know it's illegal to...."

"In any case," Ayo broke in before she started preaching. "That's not the case. You can imagine I left home this morning without breakfast just in time to meet up with this thing but here I am sitting, waiting. If I had known, I would have taken something before coming."

"Well not everybody took breakfast you know," Tosin consoled "I had to join Bola this morning all in the bid to beat time."

"But... You girls were supposed to prepare something to take along. Did you?"

" Yeah, sandwich." She answered "Though not much, 'cos we were in a hurry."

"Err... It seems we have to start munching the sandwich before we leave. That's if we'll leave anyway," he added looking round for support.

"C' mon," Bola pulled him down from the pavement on which he was sitting. "Remember, man shall not live by bread alone."

"Hey... Relax... Love," he exclaimed staggering to regain balance. "I got little or no energy, or you want to go on excursion with a corpse."

"Lazy man," Tosin laughed and they all left for the buttery.

"Don't carry those stools," Professor called out as Segun and Jide carried two stools from the lab. The bus finally came and some of them were to stand since the seats were not enough.

"We'll return them when we get back." Jide called back before he climbed into the bus. Following them into the bus, he continued.

"Can't you people understand, these are school properties, and I'm to account for them if any one gets missing. It's not that I don't want you to use them but you all must understand my position," he continued as they hailed him.

"P-R-O-F-E-S-S-O-R."

The short, stern looking man earned the name "Professor," from his thick round-framed lens, which was always at the tip of his nose.

As nobody was willing to return their stool, he climbed down depressed while the students kept hailing.

"God knows you students will never change." He said before he strolled into the lab. With his back hunched. If only they knew what damage the stool would cause, if only they knew what awaited them as they prepared for their long expected excursion.

"Let us pray," the class rep said just as the driver went behind the wheels.

"Sit down Mr. Man," Someone called from the back as other boys yelled, telling him to sit down.

"Some of you don't know the power in prayers," he continued not minding their yells. "Last week, sixty-one students of the. Great Kwara State Polytechnic got burnt to ashes in a bus which collided with a petrol tanker and I said let us pray, some of you are shouting."

That did it because everybody in the bus kept quiet. The idea of an accident sent cold shivers down their spine and everybody closed their eyes.

They set off, everybody keeping quiet like a bunch of naughty children scolded by their wicked teacher, everybody dreading to make the first statement.

The excursion turned out to be an interesting one as they all got one thing or the other as souvenirs from the company ranging from T - shirts to face - caps.

That seemed to have brought life back into them as they sang and drummed on their way back.

Not long after they left Warri, the driver parked beside a

43

kiosk and got down to ease himself. Seeing this was an opportunity to relate with the students, or was it just another way God wanted to test the Students, a Christian sister stood up to preach.

"Well done my brothers and sisters in…" She started but before she could continue, Devil raised his angels. Like a triumph call they all shouted and loud, forgetting the initial warning before the journey began.

Ayo and Segun got down to get some fruits. Coincidentally, they saw the driver coming out of a small shed where some old men sat drinking what looked like locally brewed whisky popularly called *"Kainkain"*.

*"Oga,"* Ayo called. *"Hope you go see road so, this one wey you don go shack ogogoro."*

*"Haba,"* he answered. *" Na water I go drink o no be ogogoro I drink."*

"I hope so," Segun answered and they all walked back to the bus.

As they entered, the sister sat down after a long battle, talking amidst their noise. She rounded up by saying.

"I pray God forgives those that are shouting for you know not what you are doing," Like the biblical story of Jesus Christ in his last hours on the cross, some said amen, taking after the sinner on his right hand side while some remained unrepentant and kept booing, taking after the unrepentant thief on his left hand side.

If only what was to happen in the next few minutes occurred to any one of them, they would have all fallen on their knees to beg for forgiveness, and probably that would have prevented the unexpected, but as the Romans would say; "As it had written, so shall it be done," because events started unfolding as the brandy took its toll on the driver.

The sound, which kept echoing in the minds of most of them, came all of a sudden. This sent the last Tangerine Ayo was about taking, flying in the cold misty air.

The driver had failed to slow down while negotiating a bend by a steep cliff. Unknown to him, a taxi was coming on the other lane also at top speed. In an attempt to swerve a bit to the right and avoid the cliff, he brushed the side of the Car with a loud "B-A-N-G", brushing off the door on the drivers' side alongside his left leg before sending the taxi flying down the cliff. In an attempt to balance the bus, he swerved back to the road and the bus somersaulted with the force with which it balanced and spun round facing Warri where they were coming from.

All the while, amidst screaming and chaos that arose in the bus, they flew from one side of the bus to the other scrambling for balance.

In the process, Jide hit his head on the stool that he refused to return and blacked out. As the bus drew to a halt, they started rushing for the window.

Ayo who had tried as much as possible to remain conscious was one of the first few to climb out through the window, praying silently that the bus shouldn't explode forgetting it was running on automated gas oil (diesel) and not premium motor spirit (petrol).

Meanwhile, back in Benin, news had reached some people who were at the park through the passengers that were in a particular bus that was behind them when the accident happened. As the bus arrived the park, people gathered around them to see why the passengers were crying, wailing and mumbling all sorts of prayers and the rumor spread from there.

Tunde, a three hundred level economics and statistics student was in a *bar* when "Shayo," walked in to drop the bombshell.

"Men," He began. "I was coming from Warri When I passed our school bus, those that went for an excursion."

Immediately he heard excursion, Tunde dropped his drink to listen to what "Shayo," was saying. He never really liked him because of the laters rough and careless attitude towards life. He drank carelessly and took pleasure in alcohol, which earned him his name "Shayo". Tunde never thought he could say anything reasonable, but since his younger sister was supposed to be in the bus, he decided to hear him out.

"Only two survived," he heard him saying "they were moving the dead bodies from the bus, laying them on the road."

"Dead bodies," "two survived,"

"What was he saying?" Tunde asked a girl sitting close to him, "Is he making sense to you."

"Well," she shrugged. "As far as I can comprehend, he was saying those that went for an excursion had an accident and only two people survived. They were…"

45

"Impossible," Tunde said, before he stood up not listening to the rest she had to say. Immediately, he left to find his friends.

"Yormies! Yormies!! Yormies!!!" Tosin was screaming at the top of her voice as they all ran around helping those in the bus get out and treating those injured.

As people ran helter skelter making sure all was safe, Ayo stood where he had been since the accident happened staring into space.

Is this how people die, he thought and he began to murmur series of prayers of forgiveness.

"Have you seen Yormies?" Tosin asked him bringing him out of his trance.

"No," he replied, "I'm sure he should be around somewhere, he should be out of the bus by now," he concluded now getting afraid himself.

"Gawd, I've not yet seen him anywhere," she said, leaving, more depressed.

Selfish girl, he thought. How cruel this world is, she was not concerned about others apart from Yormies.

"Well," he shrugged, then moved forward to see how others were doing. I guess after saving ones head, the next person is a loved one

Ayo got to Benin in the early hours of the next day, looking forward to the solitude his room would offer but to his surprise, he saw his flat was unusually noisy.

"Oh God," He groaned as he got to the door. "Not again, what next, my room's on fire," he said helplessly as he walked into the flat.

At first, nobody spoke. They all moved back as if he was a ghost and he entered his room as the last set parted by his bed. Shock, fear and devastation over-shadowed the tiredness he felt when he saw Amaka lying motionless on his bed.

"No," he said suddenly. "It can't be." He walked towards the bed, trying as much as possible to hold himself together.

Standing by the bed, he looked down straight into her face and saw stress written all over it. What might have happened he thought and like an answer to his question, Titi spoke.

"She blacked out when she heard only two survived the

46

accident. On Hearing that he heaved a sigh of relief, at least things was under control. He then closed his eyes trying as hard as he could to hold back the tears of joy flooding his eyes.

"We were buying a book at *the Salami* Bookshop when Tunde walked up to us..." Titi continued, waking Ayo from his slumber. When he didn't raise his head, she continued. "He said he heard your group had an accident on your way back from the excursion and only two people survived."

"Two people what?" Ayo said raising his head in annoyance. "How could people be so cruel?"

"Actually, we didn't believe him anyway so he asked us to drop him at the Health Centre. There we confirmed it was the other way round that two people died."

Tunde followed a bus that was organized to carry some Union Executives to the scene while we went to the hostel, only to be told Amaka had left the room on hearing the news. At once, I knew she came here so we followed.

Surprisingly, I saw her by your table crying and as I came in, she asked if it was true and I said yes. Not knowing it was the wrong version she heard. She asked if they were two and I said yes. Before I knew what was happening, she slumped and fell hitting her head on that table. I should have thought that would bring her back but instead, she blacked out completely.

We took her to the University Benin Teaching Hospital, and as usual they were unconcerned, so we brought her back while Telma went with Biodun to get her uncle at the Specialist hospital because taking her there might be quite expensive.

He came and after a detailed check-up, said she would be okay with time and since then, she had been like this," She concluded looking at Amaka's motionless figure.

Sitting down on the bed beside his love, he sighed heavily, realizing how tired he was. Silently he held his head in between his hand digesting all Titi had said.

"Gawd," He moaned. To think that after all that stress and a sleepless night, one would face another problem. Why today, he continued, of all days. Barely eight days after his twenty-first birthday.

At the thought, a cold sensation ran down his spine, how horrible it would have been if the unexpected had happened, if I had, no. He shook off the thought, at least I am alive and Amaka is too he thought consoling himself that was all that mattered for now.

"We'll just go home and freshen up," Titi said at last bringing him back as he raised his head. The room was now empty but for Titi and three of her friends who came in the same car.

"We'll be back in about an hour. You need to do the same yourself," She pointed at his soiled sweatshirt and the stained pair of jean trousers he had on.

"I'll prepare some breakfast for you when I come back and hopefully for Amaka if she's up."

"Thanks," He managed to say, "I don't think it would be necessary, moreover, I'm not hungry. All I wanted was to close my eyes for sometime but with the situation now, I don't even know what I need anymore."

"Okay," Titi said. "Relax boy, I'll be back in an hour or two, and don't play the Romeo," She said, before closing the door behind her. Talking about old folk tales, he looked back and stared into her face. Feeling like the handsome prince, he remembered the prince that kissed the sleeping beauty awake after a hundred years and smiled sub-consciously as he bent down to steal a kiss before she woke up but got the shock of his life when he felt her hands curl around his neck. He froze with shock and gently reached out for her hands to pull them apart but she held on tight.

"Please don't go," pleaded her voice so faint that he thought he was hallucinating. Gently he raised his head and looked into her eyes they were still closed, but she blinked just as he was about confirming his hallucination.

"I won't," he answered gently, stroking her hair. "I'm not going anywhere," he continued confused. "When did you regain consciousness," he couldn't help asking. "Definitely not…"

"Ssshhh," she whispered in tears. "Kiss me Ayodele, Please don't talk, just hold me," she pleaded and he gently pulled her towards him in an embrace that lasted for what seemed like hours.

"I regained consciousness when Titi was talking, but I didn't quite make out what she was saying," She spoke at last, not letting him go. "They sounded like strange voices from a distance, so I tried opening my eyes," she continued "…then I heard your voice. That was when I knew it was all a dream. I couldn't open my eyes, for fear of realizing I was dreaming. I didn't want to wake up and hear you were dead, oh God, she groaned now crying, soaking his skirt with tears, I would rather sleep forever, as long as I keep hearing your voice, as long as I know you're close."

"Come on," he said holding her closer. "Nothing happened to me."

"Yeah, at least I now know. How would I have known, when I heard only two people survived. I didn't know where your voice came from, but I prayed you come closer, close enough for me to touch you and I'd never let you return to the world of... well... Of the dead."

"So, you waited till I kissed you and you didn't miss the opportunity."

"Gawd." She continued. "The thought of you under the bus in your own pool of blood was so scary, I..."

"That's okay," He said before he made to get up.

"Where are you going?" she asked, fear written all over her face.

"C'mon, I just need to get out of this mess. Don't worry, I won't leave, not now, not ever."

"I don't mind them," she quickly said. "Just stay with me, please," Seeing she hadn't recovered fully from the shock, he sat up in his bed allowing her lean on him.

There was a bang on the door and he woke up, startled, with Amaka still sleeping on his chest. He tried getting up but a tight grip on his hand told him she was awake.

"Relax love, someone's at the door."

"Let the person go," she said, not bothered.

"It might be Titi, she promised to check back in an hour. Gosh," he exclaimed. "Is it one hour already."

"Well," she said helplessly releasing him at last. "We fell asleep."

"Christ," Titi exclaimed pushing her way into the room "I was beginning to think you've played The Romeo, I was just praying Amaka wouldn't be stupid enough to play Juliet when she wakes up and finds you dead beside her."

"O-o-o-ka-a-a-y, so I am the one to do something stupid *eh*."

"Well," she drawled, "love can tempt you know...."

"O-k-a-y---- okay," He replied shutting the door behind Ugoh who stood by the door staring at him.

"Don't get nasty," she snapped. "I was only joking," she said then turned to her friend.

"And how are you my friend, you scared me you know," she continued. "You didn't even give me a chance to explain that only two died, not two survived,"

"My sister, mmh." Amaka started from the bed where she lay "how would I have known ehn, everybody in the hostel were shouting two survived and there you were to confirm it. Ah," she sighed. "They want to kill me, imagine, what will I tell his mother," she joked and they both laughed.

"You can now joke Amaka, after lying still all night," she concluded sitting beside her.

At the door, Ugoh stood rooted to the floor staring at him. "Will you say something for heaven sake, instead of standing there looking like a moron."

He opened his arms and embraced Ayo. "You're rugged would have been the best thing to say, but I hope you will soon be. Congrats anyway,"

"Thanks." Ayo replied embarrassed at the way Ugoh held him, shaking vigorously with fear.

"Thanks," He repeated as they joined the girls.

"Great Pharmaceutical Association Of Nigerian Students"
"Great"
"Great University Of Benin Students"
"Great"
"We mourn this day the death of two students of this great institutions we…" It was the President of the Student Union that was addressing the students at the main auditorium after a procession round the school.

"So there will be a transitional service to be held at the St Alberts Catholic Church by two p.m., and…"
Ayo left, letting the voice trail behind him. I think I need to get some sleep he thought, with his lids very heavy.

"A D I E U," he murmured at the entrance, staring at the poster carrying the pictures of the two deceased, a boy and a girl. "I pray you rest in peace," He concluded before he stepped out of the mighty auditorium into the brightness of the midday sun.

# Chapter 8

*W*hat in the heavens does that letter mean, he said to no one in particular as he paced up and down his room at the top floor of a one story building where he newly moved into.

It was a Tuesday afternoon, about four weeks into the rain semester. Ayo came back home after one of his lectures to relax before his four O'clock practical class when he noticed a letter at his doorstep. Immediately he picked it up, he saw it was not an ordinary letter. Stained at the four corners with blood and sealed with the unmistakable sticker with the fierce looking skull on a poisonous scorpion. It was the logo of the *Scorpions*, a fraternity feared and respected throughout the whole of western Nigeria.

For the first time in his life, Ayo knew real fear and his blood began to freeze, his pulse raced and at once he was alert. Quickly he looked back, went downstairs to check round then returned upstairs on realizing the coast was clear. On getting upstairs, he saw one of his flat mates.

"Hi Vivian, did you see anybody ask for me when I went for lectures."

"No, I was indoors throughout, and I didn't hear anybody knock. Hope no problem?" she concerned.

"No, not at all," he answered staring into space. "Bastard," he grumbled, they are sure smooth silent operators, they must have been very careful nobody noticed them.

"Hope you are alright?" she asked, coming back outside when she saw how troubled he was.

"Are you sure you're all right," she continued. "I mean are you sure there is no problem, I could help you know."

"No," he replied, feigning a smile "I'm okay."

"But you're sweating all over like a Christmas goat and that's unlike you."

"It's probably the sun," he said walking towards his door.

"But, it had been raining since morning and since it stopped, I've not yet seen the first ray talk less of enough sunshine to drench you like that."

Annoyed, he stopped in his tracks looked back and said

"Will you please mind your own business for Pete's sake and leave me alone."

"Who in the shit do you think you are, to talk to me like that," Vivian retorted, annoyed. "You asked me a question and I was just trying to help,"

"In that case nobody needs your help and thanks," he said banging his door after him.

"Damn, he's a bastard, he's a bastard he's a mother fucking bastard," she fumed as she entered her room.

"He is a b-a-st-a-rd," she screamed as she banged her door shut.

"Who is he, who does he think he is to talk to me like that, oh God, I have suffered. This has got to stop," she continued as she walked towards her table. Enough is enough, I have taken enough shit from that bastard."

She scattered the content of her drawer and brought out a small revolver, loaded it and released the safety latch. She looked at her reflection in the mirror above the table, and then a knock came from the door.

Quickly she dropped it back into the drawer, not bothering to put the latch back to the safety before she locked it.

"Who is it?" she asked but before she turned, he came in, his ever-imposing figure looking sober. Something immediately crossed her mind opening the drawer and blowing off his big skull.

It was her best opportunity she thought, she could claim self-defense but she shook off the thought when she saw how troubled he was. She quickly turned her back on him so he wouldn't see the concern written all over her face.

"I'm sorry," he finally said after shutting the door and sitting down. Turning, she frowned feigning annoyance.

"And who said you should sit down or come in at all."

"C'mon, don't start all that now, I'm in no mood for that."

"In no mood for what, you think you can just walk out on me and come back anytime you feel like."

"I said I was sorry," Ayo answered, "Can't you hear that."

"Alright, here he comes again. Who needs your apologies anyway? If you don't mind, I have some class work to catch up with. Will you please leave?"

He sat there looking straight into her eyes. When he saw she didn't mean it, he stood up without a word and walked towards the door.

As he opened it to leave, she laughed. "Idiot, come in and sit down," she said. "What will I ever do with you?" She continued, moving closer to hug him.

"I'm sorry he repeated," holding her waist with one hand, I was tensed you know, I came back to sleep and I saw a letter at my doorstep.

"From who?" she asked

"It doesn't matter now, it wasn't as bad as I thought, at least things are under control,"

"Was it from the big boys?" she asked.

"What do you mean by big boys?" He said.

"C'mon Ayo, I'm not a small girl, it's a pity you don't know what I can do. I don't blame you anyway," she continued, "but note something, never under-estimate the power of a woman"

"J-es-u-s, what's all this talk about what anybody can do or under-estimate a…"

"Lets forget that anyway," she chipped in before he got angry again. "You need to take something, how about boiled rice with spaghetti.

I bought some Chicken parts yesterday," she continued "and cooked a mouth watering soup that has…"

"…A nice Chicken flavor from the Curry Chicken sauce," he completed the sentence for her.

"Terrific!" she exclaimed, "You're now used to my Chicken soup that you know my secret recipe,"

"One doesn't need extra lectures to know that, at least, I've heard that almost every blessed day since you came back from your last trip to London."

"*A beg,*" she waved before leaving the room, closing the door behind her. Ayo stretched on the chair, and closed his eyes as his mind went back to the content of the mysterious letter.

Immediately he entered his room, he locked the door and walked up to his bed. He sat down, carefully handling the letter before he opened it.

*"Our dear friend,"* it read.

*News have reached us that you are eating the Lions share of the meat in our great institution. The fact that you have not grown milk teeth, talk less of the strong permanent teeth and you think yourself good enough to share in the actions.*

*Failure to desist from this act (in as much as you don't grow) might be disastrous to you, and her too as she does not know who's good for her. So brother (we call you brother 'cos we believe in the spirit of oneness), but if you do not leave what does not belong to you by right... Well, this will be your last warning.*

*The next one will be accompanied by a sting from the scorpion, and when the scorpion strikes, nobody......... Nobody lives to tell the story, so..................*

## LEAVE AMAKA ALONE

## BLACK SCOPION

The bang from Vivian's door brought him back to his senses, and he realized he had shouted her down in the bid to keep himself composed. She deserved it he thought; she asked too many questions he grumbled and he left for her room.

Vivian was the only daughter amongst three children of a wealthy Benin Chief, and a one time serving general cum business magnate.

The head office of his conglomerate was the talk of the town for two years after it was commissioned.

The twenty-four-story building, built from Aluminum glass with its floor marbled to the stairs. The expensive antiques displayed in the office and the well-cultured lemon grass, which covered the whole compound with beautiful roses at intervals, gave the building a class of its own.

The father made sure she had everything she needed and as

brilliant as she was, she never lacked anything. Her two elder brothers did not help matters as people dared to take a second look at her or bullied her in any way. An instance was at the Club Towers in Victoria Island where an ex-governor's son was humiliated for trying to bully her.

She was at the bar when he walked up to her and asked her for a dance. She refused, ignoring him while she enjoyed her drink.

Embarrassed, he grabbed her by the hand, trying to pull her along. "Who do you think you are to refuse me a dance, do you know who I am".

"Damn you whoever you may be," she said angrily as she emptied her glass into his face.

"What the hell," he exclaimed surprised, you ruined my top. This is a Tommy Hilfiger Sweat-shirt you know, do you know how much it costs?"

"To hell with your top," she replied before she got down from the bar stool, making to leave. Annoyed at the way he was ignored, he pulled her back and gave her a slap on the face.

In the twinkle of an eye, she replied with two sharp slaps on both sides of his face with the second coming from the back of her hand. People had gathered around them watching the scene they made.

Surprised and embarrassed, the boy stood there flabbergasted. He was mesmerized at what the girl did. Before he could put himself together, the bouncers, two hefty fierce looking men came round to ask what was wrong and before Akin could talk, Vivian dropped a card on the bar and left. One of the bouncers picked the card and saw the name on it.

*Cocoubarou Investment*
*Baro Esq.*

Immediately, they realized who the girl was. They bundled the ex-governors son and threw him out when they were sure Vivian had left.

Nobody has a monopoly of Violence a passer-by said as Akin threatened to make trouble, all that fell on deaf ears.

"Mmh, you're sleeping already," she said placing his food on the small bedside table.

"Sure smells good," he replied when he opened his eyes sitting upright. "You know something," he continued after taking a spoon I've always wondered how you learnt to cook so well.

What do you expect from a caterers daughter, I'm sure you should expect more from me," she replied, turned and walked to the bed, twisting her waist in a way that was typical of her when they were alone.

Surprisingly, he began to feel the urge he normally felt. "Gawd, not now," he groaned and he managed to concentrate on his food.

Vivian watched him with admiration and she wondered what or how he would feel if he knew she was an Amazon. How would he feel, if he knew I was the head of the "Falcons." She smiled at the expression on his face if he discovered? The "Falcons," was the only female sorority in the school.

"What's funny?" he asked seeing her smile.

"Nothing," she answered. It's not your fault, she thought, if I had blown off that little skull of yours you wouldn't have had the guts to order me around.

At the thought of blowing off his head, her body went cold. Men I would have blown off his head, could I have had the heart to do it? She thought and fear ran through her. "God, I hope I never have," she whispered the short prayer before she got up to walk towards him.

# Chapter 9

*A*s early as seven a. m. the next morning, Ayo knocked on Amaka's door.

"Get something to wear and meet me in the common room," he said before she could say anything.

"No good morning... and... I've not yet brushed my teeth,"

"Two minutes," he concluded, turned and left.

Surprised at the way he behaved, she grabbed her bathrobe and ran after him breathing heavily when she caught up with him at the entrance of the common room.

"I said, get something to wear," He repeated staring at her bathrobe, which hung loosely over her transparent silk nightgown that left her as good as being nude.

"I'm not naked am I?" she asked trying to control her voice now getting angry at the way she was being ordered around.

"Okay," he said, pulling her towards the far end of the large hall.

"So... What is this all about?" she asked as she fumbled with her robe trying to conceal her nakedness as much as she could.

Staring at her, he did not know where to start. I can't possibly leave this angel alone, he thought. Then there was only one solution; he had to see Ugoh.

No! Another voice told him that could be fatal.

"Has anyone been pestering you of recent? I mean... Err... Threatening or... err *toasting* you"

"J-e-e-z-z!" she exclaimed, "Couldn't this have waited till later, I thought some one died or something, for heaven's sake why..."

"Stop that crap. If things don't get straightened out, and fast, someone might die."

"Gawd!" She sighed. "What's this all about, nobody has threatened me and nobody ever will, not in this school anyway," she added.

"And nobody has been trying to ask you out?" he asked.

"For Pete's sake, No. What is the meaning of all these? I'm getting tired of your game, come out straight for heaven's sake," she said getting uncomfortable.

He thought it wrong to give her the letter, but what difference does it make he shrugged before handling it over to her, watching her reaction.

"Damn." She said almost in a whisper. "Alright, some boys have been threatening me. They said if I do not go out with their friend, they would make sure nobody does."

"And you didn't tell me," he said staring into space.

"Didn't think it necessary to bother you with it, I can take care of myself and it would take more than a couple of cowards to make me leave you, you know that don't you?" she asked, more like a plea than a question. "Don't get me wrong, I meant no harm. Honesty, I..."

"I know..." Ayo answered, softening to her tender pleading voice, "I just wanted to confirm some things. You can go and get ready for your lectures, I'll see you in the evening."

"Please err... Ayo, promise me one thing."

"What"

"Please don't join, I mean don't err... don't join them."

"And, who told you I intended joining them?" he asked.

"Come on, I read the note. If you do, I'll know and...well I hope you don't," she concluded and turned to leave.

"Thank goodness." He said, as he stepped into the school buttery, I have been looking all over for you. I was beginning to think you were not in school or something."

"What's up Me-n? What's wrong? You look worried. Why should you be looking for me? Not, in this cold weather m-e-n," Ugoh continued. "You should be with..."

"Cut it out Man. Can I see you for two minutes."

"What's making you so tense?" he asked after he excused himself from his friends.

"I'm in a small fix," he started. "Read this to start with," he continued handing over the note as they stepped out of the restaurant,

"W-O-W," He said folding the note.

"As if that wasn't enough," Ayo continued, "I got home this afternoon and saw my clothes turned to rags. Whoever it was poured acid on them, then left this hanging on my door," He concluded handing Ugoh a little slip on which was boldly written, *"Next time, it will be your face."*

Ugoh sighed heavily, then said, "I'm afraid you don't have a choice now."

"I don't know," Ayo replied. "All that matters now is saving my face, no matter the cost."

"That means you're in," Ugoh said.

"Men, I'm not sure that's what I want, not now anyway. May be later."

"See, we do not fight a war that's not ours. Unless one of us is oppressed, we do not do anything irrational. We never make an offensive move so you see, its either you're in or not."

"Okay… Okay, but it has to be fast."

"Not so fast. You'll have to follow procedures. First things first, you'll be at my place for the next two weeks, they won't be able to reach you there. Then, we will know when the tests will come up."

"Mmh," he sighed at the thought of being an "Axeman," How would Amaka take it, he thought. She wouldn't know, he consoled himself as he left for Ugoh's house.

Amaka entered Ayo's room some six months later while he was in school, to prepare some food for him. Seeing there was no matchbox in the room, she checked through the drawers for his lighter but was baffled when the last drawer was locked. This was unusual, but for quite sometime she hadn't observed so she went to his wardrobe, may be he had the lighter in one of his pockets.

Inside the wardrobe, a black beret hung on a nail. This surprised her as she had never seen or noticed it. Shakily her hands moved to take the beret and she noticed a key fall. Silently, she picked the key and saw it was for the locked drawer.

Quietly, she walked to the drawer and opened it. Shock, fear and surprise gripped her and her mouth fell open on seeing the contents of the drawer. Lying inside the drawer were a small pistol with six cartridges and a fairly new hunting knife. There was another ugly looking object made of metal, it was an axe.

Suddenly it dawned on her and she started crying. "Ayo had finally joined," she said almost in a whisper. She gently locked the drawer and replaced his key. "No," she muttered, now sweating real hard. She backed away and slumped into the armchair with a loud thud.

How about... If a fight broke out and he gets killed... She felt a cold shiver at the thought of him getting killed and she cuddled herself on the chair thinking of what to do. She had to leave Benin. She once lost her brother to those evildoers she thought, this time she wasn't ready to loose her heart. Instead, she'd rather leave now than when, "no," she said as she dismissed the thought.

"Amaka," Ayo called starring at her cuddled figure. She had dozed off, not realizing when he came in.

"You've been crying?" he asked surprised on noticing her swollen red eyes. To his surprise again, she flew up and set her hands around his neck.

"Hold me tight," She whispered, clinging to him as if her life depended on it. "Please hold me closer," She repeated.

Lost in the dark, he stood there perplexed, wondering what was wrong with her. "What's wrong?" he asked. "What happened? What..." he continued confused, not knowing what to ask.

"Ssh," she hushed then planted a kiss on his lips.

"Take me," she whispered. "Take me please," she repeated pressing herself hard against him.

"Now?" he asked. "C'mon, not when you're like this."

"Ssh," don't say anything she hushed, undoing his button but stopped halfway and looked into his eyes, before she continued.

Slowly it started and they went on and on until they lay spent. Ayo was more surprised when he suddenly realized his left shoulder was soaked.

Gently, he raised her head and saw she was crying.

"Why?" she asked in tears avoiding his eyes. "Why are you putting your life on a live wire, why Ayo, why," she continued before she broke down in tears again.

"See Amaka, you're getting some things mixed up. Why not cool down and tell me what you heard," he patted her trying as much as possible to feign ignorance.

"Get your hands off me," she screamed all of a sudden, getting annoyed.

"Do you think I'm a fool?" She continued, "Oh.........
You thought I would not see it eh? The beret? The drawer? Why is it locked? Why... Why?" she sobbed on the chair.

"Please, don't get hysterical, Amaka," he said trying to calm her down.

"Don't get what," she screamed, "for heaven's sake don't get what! Give me one reason why I shouldn't, just one."

"You see, I..."

"God why," she continued before he could say anything. "What else did you want Ayo that I did not give you, I gave you everything a woman could ever give. Everything a man could ever dream of, still you went to sign a pact with the devil."

"If you get killed, what do you expect me to do? Kill myself, or cry to death."

"Jeez," she sighed, "I will not wait for that, I'm sorry it has to end this way, but it's got to. I wouldn't forgive myself if anything happens to you."

She got up, picked her clothes and made for the closet.
Quickly, he jumped up and grabbed her. "Will you listen to me Amaka, I had to. I had to, for you, for me, I had to save my neck and I couldn't do it alone, I was left with no option."

She relaxed when she saw he didn't really mean to do it.

"You didn't have to join, we could have gotten police custody or something."

"Police custody, Police custody." he repeated sarcastically as he walked to his wardrobe from where he brought out a bag, and turned the content on the floor.

"You see that, that was done with acid and the next one was meant to be for my face. Against whom should I state a complaint, those I don't know?"

"See," he continued. "This thing goes beyond your understanding, you know... oh forget it," he said making a helpless gesture. "You'll never understand."

"I hope and pray I never have a cause to," she said picking her clothes before she stormed into the bathroom to dress up.
Tired, he stood staring at the door for some minutes before leaving without saying a word, gently locking the door behind him.

He got back to his room at a quarter to midnight and was surprised to find his spare key on the floor just a few inches from the entrance. Amaka must have slipped it under the door. He looked around for any sign of a note but she left none. She'll come back he thought, may be she needs a break, but he later realized what she needed was a total break, because two days later, he got a letter, delivered by her friend.

*Ayo Love:*

*It's a pity it had to end like this, but I was left with no other choice. By the time you get this note, I should either be in The States or airborne, on my way to The States.*

*I'm sorry I had to do this, but it was the best option I could opt for. On normal condition, schooling abroad was the last thing I'll do you know that.*

*How could I watch people fight over me, and of all people you. I'm disappointed.*

*As they say, a man's memory is all that stands between him and chaos. The memory of my dead brother keeps haunting me and I don't think I can watch you too die.*

*But, one thing however is certain, as the clouds are black and the skies are blue in the brightest days and the darkest nights. I'll always say to my self. What a wonderful man you are.*

*Till we meet to part no more.*
*Amaka.*

"No, this is a bluff. This can't be real," he said shaking the note in his hands as he walked towards her. "Please tell me where she is, please Titi," he begged but stopped when he saw it in her eyes.

She looked so worried herself and she tried as much as possible to avoid his eyes,

"It can't be," Ayo continued as he walked back to his bed holding his head between both palms. "She can't leave me, not now, where will I start from, where"

"I think I better leave," Titi said gently closing the door behind her, as he got lost in a world of his own.

✧

# Chapter 10

*M*oney is the root of all evil.

Is it money itself or the love for it?

Everybody is considered innocent of a crime until proven otherwise.

That was his motto as Ayo launched his debut into the crime world.

It was a Friday night and as usual, Ayo realized it was time to face another long boring weekend. He had no beer in his fridge and did not feel like driving out. Ayo looked at his wristwatch,

"10.30 p.m." He said to himself and then decided *City Tavern* would be his best bet. It was a stone throw from his place and their jazz band he thought might do him some good.

"Sir," one of the waiters said, placing a bottle of Guinness-Stout on his table.

"Compliments of Madam," he continued, dropping a complementary card beside the bottle.

"…Err… what…" Ayo stammered, lost in thought.

"Madam", the waiter answered, pointing to another table.
He picked up the card and read the message scribbled on the back.

"Mind if I join you."

He raised his head to look towards the direction the man pointed and gaped open mouthed at what he saw. An astonishingly beautiful woman who looked thirty but was definitely in her late forties or early fifties. Slightly, she tilted her head side ways as if asking if he wouldn't mind.

Ayo stood up and gave a slight bow, straightening up in time to see her stand with grace before she strolled effortlessly to his table.

"Mariam is my name," She said as she adjusted her dress, after taking her place opposite him.

"Ayo is mine," he replied, "Ayo Arigbabuwo."
From her well-nourished silk smooth skin, Ayo saw she was either

63

very rich or married to a stinking rich old man who had very little time for her. He wondered what a married woman should be doing in a club at that time of the night.

"Thanks Joe," she said to the waiter who ran helter skelter to please her.

"You seem to be a regular here," he said finally opening his ice-chilled bottle of Stout.

"Not really, on and off you know," she winked, smiled tilting her head to the left, eyes narrowed when she saw he quickly moved away his eyes. "You look lonely, do you have a wife?"
Suddenly, Yinka's memory began to flood back and he became pale.

"Hi love," Ayo said planting a kiss on her cheek then stood back, surprised when he noticed how tensed she was.

"H-e-y," he tried again, spreading out his arms. "Show me some love woman, don't I deserve a wifely hug after a hard day's job."

Sluggishly she leaned forward, hugged him and suddenly, tears filled her eyes.

"Oh God!" Ayo groaned, wrapping his arms around her. "What now?" he asked settling her down on the settee before he went back to shut the door.

"C'mon Yinka," he continued. "What ever could be making you sad or this downcast that you have to cry like a baby," Now he was beside her, drawing her closer to his chest. When he saw she was not ready to talk, he kept mute and went on stroking her hair till she cried herself out.

"You mind talking about it?" he asked when he felt she was relaxed.

"I'll understand if you don't want to, I guess I shouldn't have left you alone in the house. Not for too long anyway," he continued, "probably we need a house help or if you would not mind my niece, mum or preferable yours and…"

"Nooo," she answered, nearly screaming before she sniffed twice.

"That is not what I want," she said raising her head to look into his eyes. "I want a baby, I want a child to call my own, I've always wanted to give you all Amaka would have given you but…"

"No Yinka," he said pulling her to his chest to avoid her eyes. "I'm happy with you, and you alone, I..."

"Noooo..." she screamed, snatching herself from his grasp but lowering her head when she realized she was getting hysterical.

"Please Ayo," she said almost in a whisper; raising her head before she gently placed it on his left shoulder. "Please, don't spoil me. I know you're so nice and understanding that I can't help but wonder if I ever deserve having you at all, I know you probably had me because Amaka left..."

"P-l-e-a-s-e!" Ayo interrupted her, getting worried and confused at her state. "Please," he continued. "Leave Amaka out of this. That is a long forgotten issue. I married you because I love you, do you understand that," he said trying to convince her to forget his past, their past.

Ayo had taken the news of Amaka's trip abroad as a blow below the belt and had felt the loss for the better part of his stay in school till he graduated. Yinka, who was around to console him caught Ugoh cheating on her, so she broke up the relationship and as fate would have it, a year after their youth service, they got married. Things had gone well for them; Ayo being his ever loving and dedicated husband and Yinka, a devoted wife and career woman until she lost her third chance of have a child. Ayo never complained, believing in the power of God and the fact that he was happy with his wife didn't give him any cause either.

Once or twice, he had seen Yinka in a sober state but what he was handling that evening told him she had probably been pushed to the wall. But whom should they blame, he thought. The doctor had certified he was virile, likewise was she certified fertile. Why not wait for God's time, he had always told her. To further reduce her stress, he had suggested she resigned and have more time to herself.

"But don't I deserve to be happy. Don't I deserve to be called a mother, don't..."

"Relax Yinka, you might get hypertensive. You see, anybody that loves children is called a mother. It's not until you get to have a child. Many have given birth to children they do not care for, they..."

"Yes," she answered amidst sobs. "That is the irony of the

whole thing, millions of children are helpless in various motherless baby homes, while I can't have only one to call my own."

"That's okay," Ayo said sighing, confused as to what to do. There are times in one's life, when one keeps quiet because; silence is much better than the stupid thing that could come out of the mouth when the head is confused. Instead of keeping quiet, Ayo spoke.

"Talking about motherless babies, we could probably adopt one you know. We could…"

"Ado… what," she said, surprised Ayo could think of raising another woman's child. She jumped up, shock written all over her face as she stared at him - mouth agape.

"Oh G-o-d," she continued raising her hands in despair, "I have suffered," she concluded before she stumbled upstairs to her room.

Surprised, Ayo's gaze followed her before staring ahead.

"Did I say anything wrong?" he asked nobody in particular. Confused, he shrugged, got up and slowly went after her. He paused at her doorstep and tapped gently before slowly pushing the door open.

Shocked, he stood there watching her tear her clothes wildly off the plastic hangers that lined her ward rope and sending them in a series of missiles into a box that lay wide open on the bed.

He then became scared of the unexpected. Silently, he shut the door behind him and walked up to her.

"Yinka," he started, holding her by the shoulders but she struggled frantically.

"Will you stop what you are doing," he said shaking her so vigorously that her head ached.

"Let me go, Let me go… let me go-o-o…" she cried before she fell limp on his chest crying, not minding the tearstain on his shirt.

"I'm sorry," he finally said, stroking her hair "…I didn't mean it that way, I didn't really mean what I said," he corrected himself when he felt her body stiffen and like a response, she relaxed. Gently, he led her back to the sitting room, shutting the door to her room so quietly   that he wasn't sure himself it was shut. He sat her down and briskly walked to the shelf, poured her a glass of red wine, adding some ice cube, before walking back to meet her.

"Take this," he said handing her the glass. " It will help relax your nerves. C'mon," he urged, pushing the cup into her right hand, supporting it with the other.

"I'm sorry," he repeated again sitting beside her. "I guess I was…"

"It 's okay," she managed to mumble as she fumbled with her wineglass. "I know you were just trying to help. You always have been a wonderful and loving husband. I only want to try again, that's all, for the last time."

Ayo woke up one Sunday evening to attend evening mass. He got his Car keys and was about descending the stairs when he realized the lights in the sitting room were out. Everywhere was dark except rays from what seemed like a candle flickering, making shadows appear and disappear.

I didn't know the generator had problems he thought. No, a part of his mind told him. The air conditioning system in his room was on. Then why didn't the guards put on the generating set? Suddenly, a thought crossed his mind, where is Yinka? Who is in the kitchen? Slowly, he descended the stairs but paused by the standing and called

"Yinka."
She came out of the kitchen, rays from the candle penetrating her transparent nightgown, outlining the curves of her body.

"You didn't tell me some part of the house had electrical fault?" he asked strolling across the sitting room to join her.

"No my dear, there's no fault anywhere. I wanted a serene atmosphere while I break the news. Join me," she added going back into the kitchen before he could speak.

He paused, shrugged and followed her wondering what she had in store for him. Sitting himself behind the dinning table, he asked, "What anniversary are we celebrating, or I should start guessing."

Ignoring his question she served the food, Oysters and shrimps. She then uncorked the wine bottle with a loud pop, quickly pouring her cup full as the wine gushed out of the bottle and was about pouring his when she broke the news.

"Which do you want?" she asked. "Boy or girl?"

"It is a lie," Ayo said surprised, looking into her eyes for doubts, but it was all there; she looked so happy and radiant.

"You're..." he paused.

"Well..." She shrugged "...are you just going to sit there," she said looking at him in admiration.

Dumbfounded, he stood up and walked up to her. As he moved, she approached him and suddenly broke into tears before she jumped into his waiting arms.

"I don't want to loose this one Ayo," she cried. "Please help me, I'd rather die than let this one go. I have to become a mother... I... I..."

"You will my dear," Ayo consoled her gently, caressing her back.

"The Lord will be our strength, you will have this baby for us. We will be full of prayers and I trust that he will continue to be our God. A boy, a girl, it doesn't matter," he continued now stroking her hair.

She withdrew from his embrace, looked into his eyes and said; "Poor me, I couldn't help the tears. Alright," she concluded turning to take her position opposite him.

"Our date," she sniffed feigning a smile. "I'm sorry," she continued waving her hand. "I guess I've been so spoilt that I need to seek comfort on your strong shoulders whenever I'm down," Ayo who had been watching her comfort herself leaned back in his chair with his gaze still fixed on her.

"To our little baby," she made the toast lifting her glass "a girl probably," she giggled excitedly.

Ayo lifted his glass absent-mindedly. "Help her Lord," he whispered.

"...What," Ayo shouted into the receiver, sitting up in his bed as he rubbed his eyes clear of sleep. He looked at his bedside clock, five thirty in the morning.

He had left the hospital at a quarter past midnight on the advice of the doctor. Though he insisted on staying, the doctor persisted he left, after enough assurance that things were under control.

"We will give you a call if need be," he had said before opening the door to his office.

"I'm sorry," the voice came from the other end of the line. "She's going through so much pain as a result of the constriction of the muscles around the cervix. The best bet is to carry out caesarian operation."

"Does she want the operation," Ayo asked now on his feet struggling into a pair of trousers.

"Well, anything to save the baby is what she wants. Moreover, she knows there is no other way out."

"Can't I get there before you do anything, I mean, see her first."

"I can't be too sure but all the same, get here as fast as you can."

"Alright then," Ayo replied forcing his legs into a pair of leather sandals. "I will soon be there," he concluded dropping the receiver before he grabbed his car keys from the shelf and dashed out of his room, taking the flight of stairs three at a time.

"Shit!" he said, blaring his horn when he got stocked in a traffic jam on Falomo road. Seeing it was useless, he sighed and relaxed in his seat, his mind wandering back to the first time he noticed the bulge in Yinka's tommy.

He immediately applied for a six months leave since her pregnancy was due in less than six months. He stayed home most times with her, took her out for evening strolls and to the Bar Beach every weekend for some sea breeze where they ran after each other or picked empty shells till she got so heavy. He then opted to reading folktales to her while she laid her head on his leg. Every week, he made sure he took her to see her doctor for antenatal care and nightcaps were always followed by a series of massage while she watched cartoons.

He did the cooking and made sure she was on diet to keep her and the baby healthy. He suggested one evening they took a trip abroad so she might have her baby there but she refused.

"My baby must be a full-fledged Nigerian," she replied. I do not want a dual citizenship for my child"

She grew bigger and bigger till one evening, Ayo was busy cooking porridge in the kitchen while she munched popcorn with a glass of milk by her side. He was giving her the latest development a\on his house at the peninsula.

"I think the garden-fence should be high, or what do you think."

"It doesn't make a difference," she answered chuckling.

"What's that?" he asked, sticking his head out of the kitchen door into the living room but smiled when he saw she was all right.

"Nothing..." she replied. "Its Casper, he could be funny at times."

"When is Aladdin coming up, you wouldn't miss..."

"Arrgh..." she groaned making Ayo drop the spoon he held, and again stick his neck through the door to see why she groaned. This time, she was not smiling, her bag of popcorn had spilled all over and she grabbed at her protruded Tommy.

Quickly, he switched off the cooker and dashed out of the kitchen. He got his car keys and was by her side, confused at what to do but when she raised her head and he saw the bulge in her eyes, he bent down and gently helped her up. They slowly made their way to the car.

✧

# *Chapter 11*

*H*e prayed fervently as he walked into the elevator; "Oh God. I'd give anything in return if she can have this child successfully. My job, my house, my car, Oh God, please relieve her pains, why should she bear so much pain alone."

He stepped out on the fifth floor and hurried down the corridor towards the labor room.

"Err... Sister," he addressed one uniformed lady that just came out of the room.

"Is she okay?" he asked.

"Who?" she asked, confused. "Oh..." she continued before he could speak "Mrs. Arigbabuwo I suppose."

"Yes...yes," he answered looking into her eyes for all odds.

"Relax Mr.... Err...Arigbabuwo I presume."

"Yes, that's correct. I'm her..."

"Husband," she chipped in before he could finish his sentence. "She is in the theatre, I think you should stay here, they should be through in another thirty minutes, or..."

"Thirty what!" he exclaimed. "I'll die of anxiety before then, please where is the theatre?" he asked.

"Err... I won't advise you to..."

"Where is the theatre?" he asked again, staring hard into her eyes, his temper beginning to rise.

"I can't..."

"Where is it damn it," he shouted making her jump with fright.

"Next floor," she replied clutching the Spirometer she held to her chest.

"Thank you," he said before he turned and hurried towards the elevator.

Ayo paced up and down the corridor murmuring different prayers at intervals. At a point, he got tired of walking, looked up and saw a single chair few meters away from the theatre entrance. He decided to sit down but felt uncomfortable after some minutes. He then thought walking around was much ·better. At least, it reduces the flow of adrenalin.

As he was about to get up, the doors opened and the Doctor came out, removing his surgical gloves and mask, breathing a sigh of relief.

Ayo leaped forward from the chair and asked a question after the other staring into his eyes.

"Is she alright? The baby? Was it successful? What's wrong? Why are you so…?"

"Relax Ayo," the Doctor who is an old friend addressed him as they walked towards his office.

"She's okay for now," he continued, opening the door to his office. "Sit down," he said taking his seat at the other side of the table. "She lost a lot of blood and the way things are, her chances of surviving are slim. You've not asked after the child. Why?"

"Oh, how is… Err…"

"He," the Doctor finished, smiling.

"Yeah," he said. "How is he?" Ayo asked, not raising his head.

"I think you better go see for yourself. They should be in the ward now. Look her up before the sleeping pills take effect on her."

"Doctor," Ayo started, "I feel guilty, I don't, know why, but I do. You see, I warned her. I told her it might come to this, we could have adopted a…"

"Ayo," the Doctor called him. "Go check your wife and stop blaming yourself."

"I thought she might be too weak now," Ayo said.

"Not too weak to see you my friend," the Doctor answered him getting up to help him open the door.

"You have a bouncing baby boy. Cheer up man, you should be happy, you have a child, even if she gives up, you should be proud she sacrificed her life for your boy," He concluded patting Ayo's back before he closed the door behind him.

"Sacrifice," he murmured walking along the corridor. "I hope she does not. Why should she give her life for a child she won't live to raise?"

When he entered the ward, two nurses excused themselves and the third stood at the door till Ayo went round the bed to the

72

other side before she spoke.

"I'll be outside in case you need me," she said and shut the door when he did not answer.

Yinka blinked and opened her eyes when he placed a hand on her forehead. She smiled, held his hand and looked towards the baby sleeping peacefully in the oxygen gas chamber by her bed.

"Isn't he so handsome," she asked tightening her grip.

"Yes…yes he is," he replied admiring the boy.

"Takes your nose, don't you think," she continued.

"And your brown eyes," he added looking at her.

"You will take care of him, wouldn't you?" she asked smiling.

"Promise… Pro..."

"Don't forget two of us made this boy," Ayo stopped her before she could continue, "...so why are you asking if I would…"

"Get serious Ayo," Yinka said, her smile turning into a grin. "The Doctor must have told you that the chances of my surviving is very slim but I will rest in peace, knowing I gave you what you always wanted."

"Please Yinka," he said, his voice shaking as hot tears filled his eyes. If only she knew he never really wanted a child, if only she had known how happy he was with her around.

` "The Doctor said you need to rest, you need to gain some blood and that will be when you sleep. Rest my love, and gain some strength because you are not going anywhere. We are bringing up this boy together. I will just rush home to pick a few things," Ayo concluded getting up.

"Please don't go," she pleaded, holding on to his arm.

"You need to rest Yinka," he said again bending over her to avoid her eyes. He gave her a kiss and turned his back at her before the hot stream of tears that clouded his eyes flowed; staining his face before it dripped, drop by drop on his shirt.

"I love you Ayo," he heard her call after him. He longed to answer, but he wasn't sure of himself. Quickly, he opened the door and hurried out.

"How are you," he asked when she turned on her side.

"Mmmhh," she groaned opening her eyes, her face broadening into a smile on seeing Ayo. "When did you come?" she asked, looking around her new ward. "Where is this?" she continued, realizing she was in a bigger room filled with flowers.

"Your new ward. You'd be more comfortable in here."

"And the flowers?" she asked, her eyes resting on an ornament vase on a stool by her bedside filled with a mixture of red, white and pink rose flowers.

"Can you please pass me the vase," she said, not taking her eyes from the Vase.

Silently, he passed on the vase and held it while she removed a single stem and inhaled the scent from the white rose that crowned the stem.

"I don't know why, I of every woman on earth should be the luckiest to have the best of men. What bothers me is why it has to be for too short a time, I mean, why should life be so cruel, why do I have to leave so soon? W…"

"You've started again." Ayo stopped her, placing his palm on her mouth. He was now in control of himself after a cold bath and some cups of black coffee.

"See," he continued, sitting on the bed. "That was what the Doctor said, but not what God wants."

"You'll see…" he paused, wiping her face with his palm.

"You have slept and woken up, a bit stronger. All you need do is to eat well and in less than a week, you will be back with me in the house with the child."

"Do you think so?" she asked, looking into his eyes for assurance.

"Yeah, I know, not think so," he answered. You just relax your nerves and remember Ayo and the baby needs you at home. At the mention of the baby, Yinka looked at the glass chamber and saw that the baby was still sleeping.

"How long is he going to be in that thing?" she asked, looking a bit worried.

"Not to worry," Ayo answered. "In two days, he will be out. You know," he continued. "When you get strong enough, we can plan a trip to Paris to see the Eiffel tower or… Okay, you've seen the statue of liberty already, but we can still go to New York from there all the same, so that junior might have a chance to see it."

"Ayo…" she called but he hushed her down and continued.

"We could go to Kenya to get a view of some wild life or…

74

Yes, the pyramids of Egypt…"

"Ayo," she called again and this time, he paused.

"Hold me," she continued. "Please hold me, give me a kiss. Kiss me." Afraid death was about snatching her, he stiffened but relaxed when she smiled.

"Ayo, kiss me now before I get cold, kiss me and save the memory for when I'm gone, gone into the distant world that you can remember and be happy rather than look back and be sad." He bent over and planted her a kiss on her lips. It was so brief that he wondered if the lips touched hers at all.

"Go home Ayo," she said, breaking into Ayo's thoughts. "I want to sleep."

"Never mind," he answered. "Sleep, I'll be here when you wake up."

"I know," she answered. "Go home and rest, I will be okay. You can check me in the evening."

"Alright," Ayo said after staring at her for some minutes. He planted a kiss on her forehead, then he left.

"I'm sorry Ayo," the Doctor said when Ayo entered his office, looking straight into his eyes.

"We tried our best," he continued "but as I had told you earlier, her chances of surviving was very slim…"

"So she is…" Ayo paused not wanting to believe it.

"Yes," the Doctor answered watching him.

"When did it happen?" he asked, stunned, still looking at the Doctor.

"At a quarter past one, just some twenty minutes after you left". His head dropped on hearing it was not long after he left.

"Why didn't you call me?" he asked. Not raising his head.

"At her request," the Doctor simply answered. This shocked Ayo and he raised his head starring at the Doctor.

"At her request Doctor?" he asked surprised. "At her request," he continued, "And you really felt I shouldn't have been contacted?"

"Not really," the Doctor answered. "…But she insisted you shouldn't be disturbed till you called again."

"Disturbed?" Ayo said, still shaking his head. "So all the soothing words were meant to console me when she is gone, gone forever. Why did she have to leave Doc… she gave me everything, she taught me how to accept a loss, to be a man. She picked up the pieces Amaka tore my heart into and made it whole. She gave me a reason to live. All I wanted was for her to be happy, that was the least I could do in return. I told her not to bother herself that God would give us a child in His own time but she refused. She thought a child would make me fulfilled doctor, she thought I would be happier if she gave me a child but what now? She is no more. Why is death so cruel, doctor, why is…" He couldn't hold the tears any longer. It flowed freely.

"Err…" the doctor started, getting up to pour him a glass of scotch. "Take this my friend, to cool down. Be a man, accept your fate. Was that not what she taught you?

Yinka would be unhappy in her grave if you remain like this. She would have expected you to be proud of her, be proud she gave you a son at the expense of her life. Not every woman would do this. Now you have a son, that is what you should be concerned with, the legacy she left behind."

Ayo thought of what his friend said, poured the scotch down his throat before he rose.

"I think I should to leave, the only thing I care for is gone," he continued. "I guess I should look forward to facing the loneliness that is to come."

"How about the child?" the doctor asked, "you don't seem to be interested, or won't you…"

"A son without a mother, who will nurse him. Who…" he paused, shrugged then continued "Send him down all the same, I guess I will be saddled with the responsibilities now that I'm alone," he continued walking towards the door.

"When can I pick the corpse?" He paused at the door.

"Not to worry, the body will be in the hospital mortuary till you want to move it," the Doctor answered. I'll get all necessary papers ready for you to sign, I mean for Yinka and the boy."

"And the boy," Ayo repeated after him before he shut the door.

"Yeah… she died."

"Oh sorry! I didn't mean to…"

"It's okay, that was some years back."

"And you're not thinking of marrying again."

"Marrying," he repeated.

"I can see you're not keen on marrying again," She said, sipping her drink.

"Well… I never really gave it a thought."

"And girlfriends?" she asked.

"One or two," he lied. "Now enough about me," he said before she continued. "Let's hear about you."

"Yeah, married. His name, forget. You'll know him if I mention it. He is out of the country most times, so I spend my evenings relaxing here or a few other selected clubs around Lagos."

As she talked, his eyes traveled from her well-manicured fingernails to her diamond necklace with a small bob that lay in between the V-shape her sparkling white silk satin lace made, revealing the swell of her bust. Which glowed most? He thought, her skin or the pearl.

"…So I'll like you to meet my partner, you'll like him he is a nice guy,"

"Err... yeah… yeah."

"You've not been following, have you?" she asked, narrowing her eyes.

"Actually, no," he confessed. "I seem to be developing a kind of nasty head ache. I think I should leave," he said as he making to get up. "Thanks for the drink."

"Don't mention, it's a pleasure. You really need some rest," she observed, watching he stand up. "Should I drop you off, I sure wouldn't mind."

"No thanks Madam, I stay quite close, just a stone throw."

"Okay then, check me or give me a ring tomorrow. My number is on that card," She said pointing to the card on the table.

"Okay," he said, picking the card.

"Take good care of yourself," she called after him.

"So you got home after all," her voice filtered through the earpiece when Ayo called her the next morning.

"Yeah I did, thanks. You were talking about a business proposal yesterday, what was it all about."

"All business, that's why your head aches. Meet me at my place in Ikeja this evening, we could talk lots of other things apart from making money."

"I'm sorry Ma'am, I don't mix business with pleasure.

Let's talk business,"

"In that case," she said giggling at the other end of the line, "Forget I ever mentioned business. Let's talk pleasure."
After some minutes, he answered almost to himself but the machine did its job.

"Okay Ma'am, I'll come, but we'll talk business too. Will six be okay?"

"Okay business man, that will be fine."
At a quarter to seven, he knocked on her door and the door slid open almost immediately. "I can see you don't keep to time," she said as she stepped aside for him to enter. "A bad manner for a business man, you know."

"I have good reasons. With the traffic jam at Maryland, I couldn't have done better,"

"What would you drink, cognac or wine?" she asked as she walked to her mini bar.

"A cold beer would do," he answered picking up a magazine on the couch to read.

"You don't have a maid or something?" he asked picking up the glass she dropped on a small glass stool beside his chair.

"Not here," she answered. "This is my own house, not my marital home. I come here when I feel like being alone. And of course, that is when he is not around," She added taking her seat on the chair opposite his.

Suddenly, he realized she was putting on a transparent gown that revealed her flimsy lacy brief, which covered little or nothing.

He then realized how beautiful she was, her shoulder length silky hair making her look twenty years younger. He moved uncomfortably in his chair feeling the familiar stirrings in his loins.

She seemed to notice it, he realized because she crossed her legs revealing their beautiful long shape.

"You see," she broke the silence. "I like you," she continued, "especially because you're disciplined and I have a feeling we'll get along real fine."

When he didn't answer, she continued. "I can see you like nice art works. Mind seeing those in my room, they are quite a collection." She added getting up.

Not waiting for an answer, she strolled towards the stairs

but paused at the foot when she noticed he was not following.

"Well," she said raising her shoulders. Quietly, he stood up without a word. What ever her game was he thought, he had to play for their business. No… another voice told him, it's for her beauty.

Her bedroom, a fairly large one which looked more to him like an art exhibition room with a collection of very expensive oil paintings on the walls, sculptured pieces displayed round the room, and a beautifully carved King size bed, which had various electronic gadgets fixed to it.

He looked round and round but none of the pieces caught his interest. The only piece of art that had all his attention was her beautifully figure. She turned to face him on getting to the bed, sat down then stretched her right hand towards him and like a drugged Alsatian he pounced on her.

"He…y, relax," She struggled under him giggling. "Let's take it nice and slow honey, it's better that way"

Ashamed of himself, he relaxed realizing what he had done.

Seeing how he felt, she took charge. It was some years back since he had contact with the opposite sex, so he relaxed and enjoyed every moment of it.

The screeching noise of the crickets, and the frogs croaking didn't disturb them as they lived up their passion.

# Chapter 12

"*That's* Ayo," Mariam introduced, "Ekius pharmaceuticals remember," she added addressing the bald pot bellied man who sat next to her.

"Yes of course, I remember." The husky baritone voice answered, making Ayo sit on the edge of his chair.

"He is just not what I expected, he is such a dashing young man."

"People call me Eddy." He continued, not waiting for Mariam to finish the introduction. "It's a pleasure meeting you," He concluded stretching his hand across the table.

"Same here," Ayo answered, stretching his hands, too weak to stand. He had left Mariam's house that morning, worn out from a sleepless night and promising he would be at the Hilton hotel that same evening to see her business partner.

"Smoke?" Eddy asked displaying a collection of cigarettes and cigars neatly arranged in a portable gold case.

"Thanks, but I don't feel like it now," he answered.

"That must be pretty expensive," he continued watching Eddy sniff at the long brown cigar.

"Yeah, good stuff. You know, I love Irish cigars. They are well blended, unlike American cigars."

"No, I meant the case," Ayo corrected. "Is it gold?"

"Oh… that," Eddy said. " A gift from my boss. That was fifteen years ago, before he died."

"Sorry," Ayo said seeing the expression on his face. "You must have been very close to your boss, I mean he must have loved you so much to give you that."

"Loyalty, that's the word. Loyalty. I was loyal and honest to him," he added as he fumbled for his lighter in his expensive tuxedo suite.

Quickly, Mariam flashed hers and he took a long drag.

"She is always there for me," he said finally after letting out the smoke in a series of circles which Ayo later realized was typical of him.

Mariam chatted away from the economy to fashion, then music before she asked Eddy, "Let's dance, love."

"Thanks honey, I'm a bit light headed, I might trip and fall while dancing. You wouldn't like that, would you," he added laughing, a deep husky laugh before emptying his cup.

"That's okay, how about you Ayo?"

"I'm sorry, I'm quite a bad dancer."

"Alright… alright, it's allowed. Nobody wants to dance, then lets…"

"I wouldn't mind," somebody said from behind them and they all turned.

Averagely tall, he stood behind them, a slim handsome young man, smartly dressed in an Armani evening jacket.

Almost immediately, Ayo felt a pang of jealousy. He felt like sending a blow in between his eyes but quickly dismissed the thought and shifted uncomfortably in his chair, turning his attention to Eddy.

"If none of them will, why not?" she said then made to get up.

Swiftly, the young man helped her with the chair pulling it with one hand and holding her hand with the other before he led her to the dance floor.

"Beautiful, isn't she?" Eddy asked following Ayo's gaze.

"You like her?" Eddy continued when he didn't answer.

"Err… sir," he stammered caught off guard by the question "…err she was talking about some business we could do…"

"Yeah… Yeah," Eddy replied, taking another drag at his cigar.

"Yeah business," he continued as he puffed out the smoke.

"I like you, you know. I have a feeling we'll get along real fine. I mean, real well."

Silently, Ayo gulped his drink, listening to what he said without actually comprehending.

"…So we'll discuss in detail," He concluded just as Mariam strolled back to their table.

"Gosh…" Mariam gasped slumping into her sit. "He's not a bad dancer at all," she said gulping her glass of soda.

"I think I better leave," Ayo said almost to himself. "I have an important appointment tomorrow and I have some work to catch up with."

"Okay boy." Eddy said smiling. "I will expect you on Monday evening… okay?"

"Do you have to leave so soon?" Mariam asked surprised.

"I'm afraid so," he replied not daring to look into her eyes.

"Okay then, I'll drop you. I…"

"Don't bother," he cut her short before she could get up. "I'll call a cab." He added controlling his voice with all his strength as he turned and left.

"He likes you," Eddy grunted watching the square shouldered six-foot youngman stroll out of the restaurant. "Do you like him?" he asked avoiding her eyes.

"E-d-d-y!" She screamed.

"Relax girl, I only asked."

"Okay, he's not bad, is that what you want to hear? Or, do you mind?"

"Mind…?" Eddy asked surprised, before they both laughed.

Ayo got a bottle of Guinness, after a cold shower and sat in his living room. He then switched on his cable T.V. to M. NET Channels.

As he poured his drink, his mind went back to the Hilton. First, he thought of Mariam's soft body against the dashing young man, he then shook off the thought as his mind shifted to Eddy's proposal.

"You see, it works like this," Eddy explained, when Ayo asked what he meant by money laundering.

"I have a friend who has a big pharmaceutical company in the United States. Its products get here in little quantity, that's if it gets here at all," He added before he continued.

"This drugs are very expensive when they get to the market."

"Where…?" Ayo started getting bored with his story.

"Yeah, where do you come in?" Eddy said before Ayo finished his statement.

"Well," he shrugged.

"That will come in good time," Eddy continued after he sipped his drink and took a long drag at his cigar.

"We do some business, exporting some goods and marketing them abroad. This money is usually in a very large sum, so it is difficult getting it in without people raising a brow. You, as an established pharmacist and one of high repute will help us bring in these money."

Ayo had a sore spot for complications and Eddy was making the proposal too complex.

"You will sign a pact with him," he continued "That is you will enter a partnership deal with him. That way, it would be easier to bring the products in and we will get our money by disposing it at a cheaper price. Though we'll sell at a loss but it will be negligible to us"

Ayo sat still, ruminating over what Eddy had said watching him chew the head of his cigar, tasting the tobacco. Smuggling, he thought economic sabotage that's what all this is all about.

"This money," he started. "How large is it?"

"Very large my friend, very large and what we export, you'll get to know in good time, all in good time."

"You see," he continued. "In this game, you don't ask too many questions. That way, you will make more money with a settled mind."

"And this guy I'm to work with, or feign working with, are his drugs genuine?"

"Ah… ah… ah…" Eddy laughed, "…you're not feigning working with anybody. You will be working with him. If he sees you're good enough, you could both go into producing the drugs. He might establish here in Nigeria, where you would be in charge while he manages his over there or two of you could merge your companies or something."

"Two heads are better than one, remember," he added.

"And the genuinety of his products, they are first class. Certified by the United States Health Management board"

"So, if he is that established, why is he finding it difficult to bring in his products?"

"Capital…" Eddy mumbled, as he blew out curved circles with the smoke from his cigar.

"With the amount of money we bring in, he could produce twice as much as he does without any stress or fear of loss of any kind. We'll bear all the loss which to us as I had said earlier is negligible considering the profit we make."

"So my friend, what do you say?" he asked when he saw his attention was on the dance floor.

"You don't have to give me an answer right away, you can see me on Monday and we'll set the ball rolling."

"You speak as if you're sure I'll be interested."

"Well I don't see what better offer anybody could give you and besides, left to me I wouldn't have considered letting you in but for Mariam," he smiled before he continued.

"Her recommending you, leaves me with no choice."

"Oh… I see," Ayo said draining his glass.

"Want more?" Eddy asked as he made to refill his glass

"No thanks. Too much brandy go straight to my head." That was when Mariam came back laughing heartily. Mariam, he thought getting up to take another bottle. How could he be jealous of another man's wife, he thought gulping the whole of his beer with all the energy he had. When he sat down on the sofa, he realized he was drunk. He leaned back and in no time, he was gone.

# Chapter 13

"*N*ow guys, there is no turning back. The deed is done and we are all in this together." Dapo was saying as he released the safety latch, cocking the automatic double barrel rifle he held. Taking a deep breath, he continued.

"Make sure you cover up for each other, don't shoot unless when absolutely necessary and Sleek." He addressed the man behind the wheel. "Immediately there is any sign of trouble, honk your horn twice and off you go."

It was exactly quarter past noon, that Tuesday afternoon. A sleek black B.M.W. pulled up in front of the popular merchant bank on Adeniyi Jones, Ikeja. Not quite two minutes later, four hefty men alighted from the car; one standing guard outside while three others strolled into the bank.

The driver steered cleared of any car, sat leisurely in the car with his leg an inch away from the accelerator.

Inside, everybody was on the floor. Tee-boy searched the policemen on guard, disarming them to make sure they would be totally harmless.

"Yes, ladies and gentlemen," Smart began strolling on the counter where he could see every movement in the hall.

"Nobody gets hurt," he continued, "as long as everybody stays put. We come not to kill, steal or destroy but we come in peace to earn a living."

"Hey you there," he said cocking his gun before he pointed it to a lady behind the counter. "Any attempt to move closer to that button and I will feed your brain to the chickens."

All the while, Dapo was loading the car with sacks of money. As he lifted the last sack, he heard the sound of sirens from a distance and immediately he cocked his gun and yelled back "Let's play boys."

"I'll miss you guys," Smart said as he jumped down from the counter. "I hope we meet again," he added at the entrance.
Outside, Dapo was standing straight, legs wide apart with his gun pointing towards the direction where the sound came from. As the

police van negotiated the bend into the street, he sent a series of shots and the car went ablaze.

"Bingo! I should have done that," Tee said shutting the door just as the car zoomed off. Out of Allen Avenue, Sleek swerved towards Opebi slightly missing an oncoming Cherokee jeep. Just then he sighted two Anti Crime Patrol 504 station Wagon. Quickly, he entered Toyin Street and on he went as the game reached its peak.

Sleek had been driving for fourteen years, since he was nine. A second son of an Ex-governor and a top Military Officer, he grew up in Ikeja and was used to all the nooks and Crannies that existed in the locality.

Swiftly, he swerved off Toyin Street into a narrow street and another before he linked the main road.

On Bank Anthony Way, he headed straight towards Maryland, but slammed on his brakes when he heard gunshots ahead.

Slowly, he engaged the gear to reverse and slammed on the accelerator.

Surprisingly, every car steered clear when they saw the wild beast approaching at full speed.

At the Country Club junction, he applied his brakes, engaged the gear and with a speed he had never imagined shot into G.R.A. out on Agege Expressway and that was it, they had lost them.

"Boys, we all have to go underground. God knows for how long," he continued "but the most important thing is everyone gets his share and what happens to it is nobody's business.

Go for a vacation in the Caribbean, invest or whatever. Each of us has enough to spend for ten good years at least without investing."

It was exactly two weeks after the robbery and hell had since been raised from all parts of the country. Shareholders and customers phoned the managers of the bank one after the other, demanding for explanations.

The whole country was in chaos and calls also came from the Presidency. The police Commissioner in order to save face promised to bring the evil perpetrators to book. The media did not help matters. All television and radio stations did not fail to emphasize the insecure state of the nation despite the existence of various law enforcement agencies.

The daily papers were not left out as they all had a chance to sell out fast, since people wanted to hear more about the team that robbed one of the busiest banks successfully.

Their headlines boldly printed on their front pages ranged from, *"Nigerian Police, a shadow of our time,"* to *"Five strikes, Police incapable,"* and *"Corrupt crime fighters scared of armed bandits."*

In reaction to these, the Police started making promises in cash and kind to whomever has information that could lead to their arrest.

One of such announcements was on air when Dapo was briefing his friends on how they would varnish. *"The President, General Sanni Danjuma has offered a sum of half a million naira and a beautiful duplex at the Victoria Garden City for who ever has information...."*

"Put that damn thing off," Ekius said, getting up to switch it off when nobody made a move to turn it off.

"As you can see, a simple mistake and we all will go for it. This is the biggest hit we've ever made and by God, it was clean, so lets keep it that way."

"Why in the heavens are they so particular about us?" Ekius grunted as he walked to the bar to pour himself a shot of brandy.

"You can't blame them," Dapo answered, "Heads will roll if nothing is done, that's the more reason why we should leave."

"I think that's the best," Smart answered behind Ekius, making to pick a glass on the bar. "How will we get the money," he continued after downing his drink. "And how fast can our documents be ready?"

"Alright Smart, that's a nice question. The proceeds sum up to 2.5 Billion Naira, raw cash of about 900 Million naira, other hard currencies worth over one billion naira and jewelries worth six hundred million naira at most. To start with, we will open an account for the electrician that helped us disconnect the alarm. The account will be in his wife's name and a sum of one million naira would be deposited for him."

"As for you, my brothers," he continued, "We are all

business men. Three of you will leave for The States in two days for a meeting with our business partners, which will last for two weeks. Anyhow, you would get missing from there. Get yourself a work permit and then nobody can pick you. Or, do anything that suits you. For your money, my contact will meet you at a hotel, which of course would be booked for you, to help you complete the documents which by then should be ready for your signatures."

"You my Friends are all proud owners of four fifty million naira, all in four different Swiss accounts Congratulations again for a job well done," he concluded before he gulped the drink he had held all the while.

Ekius silently poured himself another shot.

"That's a good plan," he said without turning back. "The U.S. and the meeting stuff, but your contact. They could be tricky," he continued turning back to face Dapo. "They might screw up."

A grin crossed Dapo's face but varnished almost immediately as if it never was there.

"You're always on guard my friend," Dapo said slowly lifting himself off his seat before he walked towards the shelf.

"My contact has the other half to this five hundred naira note," he continued unfolding a small piece from his wallet. "He'll meet you at the Peak Grand Hotel in New York. Never mind," he added, "he will know your room number and of course you all know how we knock. When you hear the signal, open up and trust him. So you see," he concluded, shrugged then strolled back to his seat. "Things are not as you see them,"

Ekius silently emptied his cup and said, "Its okay by me, if they have no objections. I can always take care of myself."

Smiling, Dapo said, "You sure will. One of you have to wait for a week at least before going," he continued lighting a stick of cigarette; this is to avoid suspicions and to help clear up things here in Lagos. Who will that be?"

Everybody stared at each other for a minute before Sleek spoke.

"I'm out, I need to get out of this country for some fresh air," Tee-boy joined in while Smart stared at Ekius.

"I'll wait," he said, "I need to settle some things myself, and I'm not really in a hurry."

"That leaves me with no choice," Ekius said, "I would have

loved to stay but I can always come back when the dust has settled."

"I hope so," Dapo said, "I hope so."

"Lastly, those to leave are to meet me at the Lagos International airport lounge 9:00 p.m. on Thursday. That will be the day after tomorrow I presume, to collect your documents. That reminds," he paused to pull out his drawer, "you might need some money to do some shopping before you leave," he continued, dropping four bundles of five hundred naira notes on the table. "You take one each. Remember, no extravagant spending, you never know who is on the watch. Your *trips* will have to wait till you get to The States. Good luck brothers, we'll meet on Thursday by God's grace," he concluded stretching out his hand to take theirs one after the other in a strong handshake, before they all took their leave.

"Mhhhh," Ekius moaned as he turned on his side. There was a sharp pain in his side and his head ached making him keep still, unable to bear the pain.

"Finally, you're back, I was about calling the mortuary to send down an ambulance. I thought a week in the morgue would have revived you."

"Who... who... are you," he mumbled. "I do not know you?" he continued trying to sit up but groaned before he fell back on the bed

"Don't get up love, it will take some time before you can. And as for who I am, Rex will tell you. You just try go to sleep while I call Rex on the phone but make sure you don't go into a coma again, you're one hell of a hero."

Hero he thought, love... Rex. Who is she and who is Rex, he thought drifting away into a deep slumber.

# Chapter 14

*"G*oing to the States for the first time?" the bulky man asked when they were midway in the air.

Cautiously, he examined the man who was sitting beside him in the First class cabin. Scrutinizing him from the head to his paunch, which moved gently to the rhythm of his heavy breaths. He looked at his snow-white shirt and the black tie carefully knotted in the British fashion.

I could pretend to be a businessman, he thought and decided it was safe talking to him. After all in no time, he would be.

"No. Why do you ask?" he answered at last.

"I was beginning to think you wouldn't answer, you must be a very cautious man. Well," he shrugged "...at least, when dealing with strangers."

"Isn't it necessary?" he asked. "With the rate at which people get duped these days, one needs to be careful in dealing with strangers."

"I... see. You must be very rich I guess and conservative too," he continued "for you to take your time in scrutinizing strangers."

"If I am not," Ekius answered sarcastically "I wouldn't be flying first class. Would I? And, being cautious would have been more appropriate."

"Okay... I'm Derexo Fernerdo but people call me Rex for short. I deal in business, any form of business that has real money in it. Actually," he continued, "I'm a Pharmacist, an established one. I operate in The United States and have a business partner in Nigeria. Probably you must have heard of EKIUS PHARMACEUTICALS."

At the mention of Ekius pharmaceuticals, Ekius laughed, this surprised Rex because he did not understand what was funny in what he had said.

"Apologies for my out burst," Ekius started when he saw Rex was confused.

"Ekius is my name, Ekius Temidire. I know Ekius pharmaceuticals. At least, I have seen and heard of it but personally I have not yet met the owner, my name sake I suppose."

Rex smiled and relaxed on hearing this. "No, not at all. His name is Ayo, not Ekius. He was just fond of the name."

"It's funny you know," Ekius said still smiling, seeing my name up on the bill boards, on T. V., hearing them sing with it on radio and not having anything to do with it. I always wondered who was behind the curtain.

"And an iron curtain at that," Rex added. "An iron curtain. So, what do you do?" he asked.

"Actually," Ekius started, "I'm traveling abroad to see if I can invest in some good business. My dad left me a huge sum of money and I don't really fancy doing business in Nigeria."

"I see," Rex said after some time. "Have anything in mind, I mean any business prospect."

"Not really. I intend buying companies with financial problems, build them and sell them off bit by bit. I should be okay with that, in the interim."

"I don't think that's a good venture but we could talk more about that later in The States."

They chatted away more like old friends, than acquaintance till the plane touched the tarmac in New York.

On his arrival, his driver and two of his men met Rex.

My driver will take you to your hotel," Rex said after having a word with his men. "I'll go with the other car. They will come to pick you later in the evening, Eight probably, if that's okay."

"Its okay," Ekius replied, taking his outstretched hand.

"I'll be right back," Ekius addressed the driver, who wondered where he was going.

Boom... Boom, the sound of the explosion kept ringing in the head making it ache as he struggled to sit up. He had slept for another twelve hours before the sleeping pills wore out of his system.

Dapo is a bastard he thought. I knew it all along, it was all too neat to be true, I knew he would screw up but by God, how could he be so cruel, fucking cruel. Imagine, a bomb.

Ekius was beginning to get hysterical, and he started talking to himself.

"Hey, not again," The lady called, from the entrance. "I'll be forced to sedate you again if you continue like this."

"Sedate what," Ekius exclaimed. "How long have I been here and how am I sure they are not aware."

"No, they won't dare come here, this is Rex's base. Whoever they are, they wouldn't think of coming here.

Whoever they were," she continued, "they did a neat job, a fast one at that."

Just then, Rex entered followed by two cruel looking men.

"Leave us alone Susan," He said moving towards the window while the two men took positions behind the door and by the bed. Suddenly, he stopped, turned and stood legs apart with his arms akimbo, before he spoke.

"Who did this to you and why?" he asked. It was then Ekius really saw how tall he was. He was now different from the smiling businessman he met on the plane. He looked so mighty and mean, he looked like a Don.

"It's a long story," he said as last,

"I'm all ears," Rex said pulling a chair while the others stood still.

Ekius slowly briefed him of the small game he was into, starting with a confession.

"I'm not as rich as you think, at least not yet and the way things are going, I doubt if I would ever be."

"No... no....no," Rex said annoyed. "Then what were you doing flying first class."

"All in good time," Ekius answered, clearing his throat before he continued.

"Some guys and myself pulled up a deal that fetched us 2.5 billion naira,"

A long whistle interrupted him and for the first time he noticed the other two men move.

"How many of you?" he asked adjusting his tall frame on the chair.

"Five," he answered.

"How in the shit did you do that?" Rex asked surprisingly.

"It doesn't matter." He said frankly annoyed at himself for

trusting this stranger. For all he knew, he might be a big shot in the CIA or State Security Services but he shrugged then continued. But for him, I would not be alive. He thought.

"Two of them stayed back while three of us left for The States. It must have been a planned work between the two of them to eliminate us. I had suspected something of that nature but I never expected it so soon, and in such a cruel manner. We were supposed to meet our contact at the hotel to collect our pass books as our share was supposed to have been transferred into accounts here and in two other Swiss banks. It was risky but we had no better option. We had to leave. Actually, I decided to take another room when I got to the Plaza. I preferred those rooms overlooking the peninsula, so I booked one on my account and promised to meet them by eight. The bomb unfortunately was set to explode then or thereabout. I left for their room some minutes before eight but stopped to talk to a blonde who checked in at the same time we did. Christ," he groaned as a sudden chill ran through him at the thought of having been in the room when the bomb went off.

"You see," he continued, "I never mix business with pleasure but I guess things change with the environment, or was it intuition or instinct. I met her on the corridor and just decided to be mischievous. I guess I suddenly became time conscious because I quickly excused myself and walked on briskly.

The last thing I remember was that I was about knocking on the door when it happened, with a deafening boom and that was it, the world went dark till I saw that girl," he concluded, pointing towards the door.

"Mmmhh," Rex sighed before he adjusted himself in his chair. "So you are in the big league and you were talking like an innocent business man. I almost took you for a young graduate of Harvard Business School, about putting to practice what he paid heavily for."

"How did I get here?" Ekius asked after a moment of silence... or..."

"You forget things so quickly." Rex answered "...or may be it's the shock from the... Err... what ever. My boys were supposed to pick you by eight p.m., remember. They got there about the time the bomb exploded and immediately, they called for back up. They found you unconscious on the corridor, that was how you ended up there". He concluded pointing towards the bed.

"Gawd," Ekius said still shocked at the experience. "For the first time in my life, I give kudos to God for creating women. I wonder where I would have been now without the blonde. Burnt to ashes probably," he whispered. "Thanks," he continued. "That means I owe you a favor."

"More than a favor," Rex said standing up. "You owe me for lying, you owe me for putting my boys through extra trouble and the bill. It was quite expensive controlling your pulse when they brought you. It took the combination of two cardiologists to do that. Moving their equipments down here was no Childs play either. Anyway make your recovery very quick, I could make use of you. I think you'll do real fine with my contact in Nigeria."

At the mention of Nigeria, Ekius smiled to himself. This was the best opportunity fate was giving him to get even with Dapo. "Wait for me clever boy," he whispered as he leaned back on the pillow and closed his eyes when he heard the faint click of the door.

"Sorry guys, I think I have to leave," Ekius told four angry looking men after one of Rex's men whispered some things into his ear. "We'll play some other time, probably tomorrow. I hope I didn't inconvenience anyone of you," he smiled then winked

He had been beating them as usual in their game of cards. His experience in the game, one or two tricks and the fact that he was quite good with numbers gave him an edge whenever he played at the club.

"You can't leave like that," Franco fussed because he had lost everything including his 22-Karat gold Rolex wristwatch. "The game is about getting to the peak, so we all have to finish it."

"Come on Franky. You know you have absolutely nothing on board except," he added. "You want to lose your shorts."

Realizing what Ekius said was true, he flushed crimson with embarrassment.

Ekius stood up, dipped his hand in his pocket and brought out a bunch of keys. He dropped it in front of Frank and leaned forward. "Next time, I won't think of returning it," he growled then straightened up, adjusting his shirt before he turned to leave.

"Not a bad guy," one of them said when he left. "And a nasty player too," the fourth man added.

"What was that you dropped on the table?" his escort asked when they got to the elevator.

"What does it look like?" Ekius asked annoyed at the stupid question. "A bunch of flowers," he continued raising his hands to be searched by the guards at the reception.

Realizing he'd asked a dumb question, he rephrased his question;

"I meant those were keys to what?"

"You're now talking. That was what you should have asked. They were his car keys. He had nothing left after losing his wristwatch. That reminds me," he paused dipping his hand into his breast pocket.

"I wouldn't need this," he said dropping the Rolex in the other mans pocket. "Franky should be able to get a better one."

"Thanks." The other man flushed, bringing out the wristwatch to admire, happiness written all over his face.

"You're a nice guy you know," he continued, "...only that you could be nasty at times."

"Ah... ah... ah," Ekius laughed, "...only when it's necessary," he assured tapping gently on the door before he pushed it open.

"You're very bad at keeping appointments," Rex growled from his seat at the far end of the room. He had a long Irish cigar hanging loosely in his mouth.

"We were supposed to meet eight p.m. remember, and this is a quarter past still I had to send for you."

"Sorry Rex, I was draining some guys in a game of cards and they wouldn't let me go. Moreover, I need to make some bucks you know," he added, shrugged before he strolled to the small but well stocked bar at the other end of the room. He downed a shot and shook his head. When he was about taking another shot, he realized they were not alone in the room

Smartly dressed in an expensive marine blue suit, Ayo watched the guy enter and watched him move to the shelf. He studied him with interest as he downed the first shot. He realized his presence in the room meant nothing to the guy because he did not take a second look at him until Rex did the introduction.

"Sit down," Rex said in a sharp manner, making it look more like an order.

"That's my business partner," he continued. "You will be working with him. He knows more about business in Nigeria."

As Rex talked, Ayo watched him. He wondered Rex's life with a wife and one or two kids. He didn't look an inch like a family man.

Life behind the curtains is some times nothing but a mystery, he smiled shaking off the thought. One could not tell if he was always sober at home or could he still be the strong willed man whose only concern was money.

"Making money is the main aim in life," he was fond of saying.

Ayo thought of the first day they met. Rex had entered Eddy's suite at the Sheraton Hotels and Towers with his presence immediately filling the room. He had a domineering power over every other thing in the room.

Eddy, though a bit taller with a few more extra pounds, didn't exude as much charisma as Rex.

The first time he spoke, it was like a rhythm of the old rock samba played by the Red Indians that settled in Kenya.

Comparing the man to this newcomer, he wondered if Ekius was really the man to work with. He did not fit one bit into the picture Rex had painted Ayo thought. "He looks a reckless, careless egoistic bastard," he whispered to himself observing Ekius with interest.

"You will be in charge of the Casino." Ayo heard Rex tell Ekius as he shook off the series of thoughts that ran riot in his mind.

"It would be fifty-fifty for now," he continued. "After a year and I see you can cope alone, I'll give you a free hand to run the place. Is that okay?"

"Yeah, that's cool," Ekius answered getting up to refill his glass.

"Is that how you drink?" Ayo asked, surprised that Ekius refilled his cup for the third consecutive time.

"Why... No," Ekius replied after a few minutes of intent gaze at the other man.

"It was a habit I developed those days," he continued. "A bad one of course," He made a helpless gesture before he walked back to his seat.

"With my head filled, I could forget my worries or the task ahead."

"Worries... Task?" Ayo asked more surprised. Does this fool think working with me is that much stress.

"I'm sorry I did not tell you much about him, but if he feels it is necessary, he will do that himself," Rex broke their conversation, which to him might be heading for the rocks.

"He got himself roped in a racket which involved an international organization and it took him all the luck in this world to survive an assassination attempt."

"Racket?" Ayo asked getting more perplexed.

"I'm sorry, if I have to work with anyone, I have to know what he is into so that I would not eventually get what I do not bargain for."

Suddenly, the buzzer rang and Rex picked the receiver, dropped it. He bit his lips, tapped his large fingers on the table before he pushed his chair backward excusing himself.

"If you gentlemen will excuse me, I have to be out of here for five minutes. You two can in the mean time, get to know each other well. I'll be back as soon as possible and no quarreling," he added before he shut the door.

"Are you telling me?" Ayo asked when Rex had left.

"Well, it's nothing big actually," Ekius answered. "I was involved in some bad business with some bad boys back in Lagos and they tried to eliminate me when the time came to reap the fruits of our labour," Briefly, he gave him a summary of his ordeal, emphasizing on the bomb attempt.

"So you intend getting even with him or they are still after you?" Ayo asked when he finished his story.

"Getting even, yes. But being after me, I doubt. He should think I'm dead by now so going to Port Harcourt would be the best. I'll settle down, build an empire of my own and buy his wealth bit by bit. I want to see him crumble and fall like a pack of cards."

"I'll crush him," he continued squeezing his hand till his knuckles turned white.

"I'll make sure he ends up in the streets where he came from. Then he will die the way he killed the others."

"I'll turn him into a lunatic, he will be in a state where no

Psychiatric home would take him."

He continued ranting for what seemed like hours till he suddenly stopped to pour himself a drink. Then, Ayo realized he was worn out.

"And how do you intend doing all this?" Ayo asked after a moment of silence. "With all the money this guy has, you need a life time to earn more or enough to buy him out especially if he invests wisely.

"That's exactly what he wouldn't do," Ekius answered enthusiastically as life seemed to flow back into him.

"And how I'll do it? Wait and see."

# Chapter 15

"*H*ello," the voice filtered through the receiver as Ekius was beginning to wonder what went wrong. "Ekius please," the voice continued. "Ayo on the line."

"I was beginning to think plans had changed," Ekius answered, "...you've never been this late men, not a minute, not to think of being two hours late. What happened?"

"Nothing worth troubling your soul about," Ayo answered not moved by his concern. "There was a reshuffle in the cabinet and it affected us. Plans at the customs have changed, but things are now in control. A few phone call, you know," Ayo laughed before he continued.

"We now have our scribe back in place and clearing the drums wouldn't be any problem. Can I know, when are the drums arriving? So that arrangements could be made."

"Definitely not as scheduled," Ekius answered annoyed at the careless way Ayo expressed things, "but definitely not later that the two hours delay you caused. Though not really your fault." He quickly added

"By midnight they should be airborne if there is no... Err... err... reshufflement of cabinet."

"Cut if out Ekius," Ayo snapped into the mouthpiece.

"H-e-y relax men," Ekius teased. "You nearly bit my ear off," he continued staring at the receiver.

"Men. I was only joking, you didn't have to go wild."

"You will never change," Ayo said. "I feel like kicking your ass real hard men, real hard."

"I wish you could too, but over nine hundred square kilometers, men, you need some super natural powers to do that."

"Never mind," Ayo said. "I'll wait till you get here."

"Yeah Ayo, talking about seeing, are we to meet at Rex's place or at the club because there is a girl I want you to meet and..."

"Don't cover up my friend," Ayo cut him short before he could finish his sentence. "You think I like women that much."

"Don't worry you'll like this one. Moreover, it's my girl I want you to meet, not a blind date,"

"Never mind, I'll kick both your Asses."

"Alright strongman, I just got a signal. They are on their way now, why not tie-up any loose end. The earlier, the better you know. I'll be on my way, first thing tomorrow after I receive the code-green call. I should be there, say midnight at most. How about you?"

"Early enough to be able to kick your ass," Ayo replied. "Bye for now."

"How come he has a flare for my ass?" Ekius asked nobody in particular after he dropped the phone. "Is it that big?" He said again, then got up to check his behind in the reflection on the glass wall. "Not quite, but okay," He said tapping his flat ass.

"Tea or coffee, Sir?" the airhostess asked the fair complexioned handsome young man, clad in a hand made Ralph Lauren tuxedo. He must be quite rich she said to herself, for him to fly First class. At least, most times she noticed him. No she thought, it's all the time. I don't think I have ever seen him in the Second class or. No... no not him, a dashing young man like him should be very rich, she concluded as if convincing herself.

"I don't think I want any of those," he answered. "Thanks," he added when he saw her flush.

"These rich people," she thought. "They never smile at you if you are from the middle class. Pomposity," she grinned then asked again, "How about brandy or whisky, we have a variety of...?"

"I don't want any of those either," he cut her short, looking straight into her eyes.

"Bastard," She nearly uttered, "...I was only trying to be nice, that's my job anyway," she told herself. Don't get your feelings involved with your work, her mind told her and she made to leave. He is only a familiar stranger.

"Okay Sir. If by any chance you're ready, you can call on any of the hostesses," she concluded turning to leave. But stopped when he spoke.

"Don't you serve anything else?" he asked.

"It has a particular time we serve some things Sir," She

answered, now trying to control her voice.

"Nooo... Nooo, I mean," he stopped then gesticulated for her to come closer. "I mean," he continued. "Can't you serve your company, on special request I mean," he quickly added. "I feel lonely right now."

She looked at him, shocked to the core, dismay written all over her face. So this idiot had liked her all along but had feigned indifference. Suddenly, she started laughing.

"Not now sir," she said. "I have to attend to other passengers on board like you too. May be when we land in The States, we should have two days off. Then I will think of serving my company."

"With all pleasure," he smiled, dipped his hand into his breast pocket and handed her a complimentary card on which his hotel suite number had been scribbled.

"With all pleasure," he repeated, leaning back into his chair "I think I will enjoy it better then," he grinned. That should be an addition to my collection, he thought as the hostess left. I don't even know her name, he said to himself. It doesn't really matter. He consoled himself, it was the idea that was important and it had been passed across. We'll later talk about names when next we see. That is if we get to see, he told himself pushing the thought away from his mind, his attention shifting to the purpose of his journey.

He arrived Nigeria Seven years ago and opened a nightclub at the Government Residential Area in Port Harcourt. It has a restaurant and a Casino just like Rex's in The States. It has the same structure and setting but with an African touch.

With his experience, it was not difficult to get able-bodied men to help him maintain peace in the club. It served also as his base and warehouse where he stores most of the exhibits they import.

He supplied rebels in neighboring countries, arms that were smuggled in alongside the pharmaceutical company.

Without Rex's knowledge, he had done this for seven years alongside the drugs he exported for Rex. All these had fetched him a lot, plenty enough to buy Dapo out, who by then had gone bankrupt.

This was his last shipment with Rex, and after this he intends facing Dapo to settle his score with him. Yes... Yes, he thought. The score had to be settled or else he could not settle down. Not with Dapo alive, not with the shadows of the past haunting him every time he was alone.

Ekius smiled as he remembered his first shipment. It was a clean business. They were mere businessmen, who export palm oil to The States for sale. Drums of supposed palm oil are filled with raw Cocaine, sealed and splashed with oil. The oil at the top and around the drums makes it look authentic. Nobody opens the drums or tries sampling them. The customs clear them and in no time, they are in a cargo plane, which in less than eighteen hours would be in The States.

Nobody thought it was odd, to fly ordinary palm oil to The States when we could ship it at a cheaper cost, he laughed.

All they want was to be settled.

The shipment was made twice a year because it took some time to dispose the powder. It was done mostly on the streets, because that was where the real money was. Though they also had customers, mostly Mexicans and Italians who bought in bulk for export.

That is when Ayo comes in. He brings in the proceeds via his company in collaboration with Rex's pharmaceutical company. Alongside the pharmaceuticals they import, Ekius took the advantage to bring in his own goods. A good businessman he thought he was.

Money from his arms deal was brought to his house in raw cash, usually in the evenings. A truck drives to his heavily guarded Villa, normally with police escort. The truck parks with the rear facing a heavy metal door, which is always locked. The door leads to an underground warehouse. The truck is always screened at the gate by mean looking hefty men, to make sure there is no form of sabotage. All these money was saved to ruin Dapo who Ekius had kept a tab on. He had watched every move he made. Sooner than he expected, Dapo went bankrupt.

Ekius wondered how he went bankrupt so soon but it didn't matter to him, all that mattered was Dapo made things easier for him.

Dapo had started living big when he was informed that the

102

others had been eliminated. He furnished his garage with fleet of cars, which ranged from series of Jeeps, Sleek Sport cars and other choice cars.

He bought three pathfinders; a red, black and blue, a Toyota Fore Runner and a Cherokee Jeep, all in less than a week. Not long after, he added a Honda Prelude Coupe, a Toyota Celica and a Mazda Sports. He never once liked Mercedes Benz but when the new SLK Model was launched, he added three different models to his collection.

The C-class, E-class was not left out. He didn't stop there, he moved from his Surulere duplex to a 500 million Naira estate in Victoria Island, near the peninsula. He held parties every fortnight where popular Fuji Musicians played. He and his friends doled out money on stage to the musicians and women who cared to dance while the musicians sang their praises.

Though he invested in some companies and established a few himself, his standard of living was so high that he went bankrupt in less than five years. He applied for loans and many of the banks fell over themselves to grant loans to him because of his personality and his collaterals. Not long after, one of his companies, a mortgage bank was shut down when it liquidated.

The cost of maintaining his massive estate became so high and unbearable that he had to mortgage some of his properties.

To protect his name, he lobbied for a chieftaincy title, which was due to somebody else. To secure it he bought cars for the Oba, Chiefs and donated money to charities and local governments, all to win favour but the favour was not to last for long as his wealth disappeared to an unknown group. The organization was always around to buy or take his mortgage anytime he needed money and to him it was God sent.

To save his face, he kept his house and his cars till his name came out in the dailies amongst those owing one of the distressed banks.

He then got used to drinking, to forget his plight and in no time, he lost touch with reality till he got his estate sold. That made headlines because many newspapers flashed different stories on why he sold his estate. He feigned illness and never appeared at public functions because heads turned everywhere he went.

"How are the mighty falling;," one of the headlines read.

Another had the caption; "Dapo Tavern bankrupt, How come?" and it read.

"Dapo Tavern, the *Otun Babalaje* of Lagos, well renowned industrialist and multi millionaire was said to have sold his 500 million Naira estate in Victoria Island which according to sources close to him was his last asset but for his underground night club which will be put forward for sale soon if care is not taken. The Chiefs whereabouts for the past few days has remained a mystery and the Federal Bank which of recent was defrauded has been after their debtors amongst which is Chief Oloruntobiloba Adedipupo Tavern…"

On an on it read, covering a whole page of the Guardian newspaper. The paper littered everywhere as people longed to see what the end of the rich maggot as he was popularly called would be. One was on its way to The United States on the tray beside Ekius.

A smile crossed his face when he remembered his plan. After this deal was sealed, he would buy the club, to make Dapo homeless because he now lived in the club's guestroom. He would love to see him homeless, with no real asset. He wanted him to die penniless, when he would no longer be feared and respected. Then, he would be helpless. As the wicked smile played around his lips, he dozed off forgetting the stress of this world. He drifted into another world, a world of peace.

# Chapter 16.

As Ekius dozed in peace, another mind flowed in pieces. Dapo Tavern thought of the misfortune that had befallen him. Could it be their ghost haunting me he thought? At that, he felt his whole body go cold. He had never really thought of them once since his contact assured him none survived but the sudden thought sent a shiver down his spine.

"No…" he said to himself shaking off the thought, there is nothing like ghosts, they are just a figment of the imagination he consoled himself .He tried as much as possible to make himself comfortable in the second class cabin on board the KLM 360 Air Bus in which Ekius was. He was used to flying First class but now he could not afford any extravagancy, so he made do with the second-class cabin.

This was his last hope, he thought. "If I can get somebody to buy the club at the real price it's worth, I could leave Lagos for The States or anywhere far away, enough to get out of the mess I caused myself. "Damn," he said, hitting his hand on the seat, I should be flying first class for Gods sake, not sitting down in this uncomfortable Second class cabin."

"Hope no problem, Sir." Somebody said from above, bringing him back to reality.

He looked up, and saw this beautiful piece in a smart skirt suit smiling down at him. "No Ma'am, I'm okay. Why did you ask?" He said curiously.

"You were muttering something's and you seemed to be increasing your voice, probably the deeper you got engrossed in your thoughts."

"Sorry, I never knew my voice was that audible."

"That was why I asked if anything was wrong." She asked again, "Can I join you?" She continued pointing towards the empty seat beside him.

"Err… The lady there just left for the Ladies or something I'm not sure she'll be long."

"Yeah! I saw her leave, she probably left because of you

105

were disturbing her, to get one of the hostesses," Like a confirmation to her last statement, the fairly old lady came down the cabin, followed closely by an airhostess.

"Oh… you wouldn't mind changing seats would you?" The lady asked the young woman who seemed to have calmed the man down.

"If he doesn't mind," The young lady answered looking down at Dapo.

"Does he have a choice," The old woman said, "I'm not his wife, neither am I old enough to be his mother so, if you wouldn't mind showing me where your seat is."

"Four seats away," the young lady answered making to go get her things. "I'll just get my things," She said, but stopped when the airhostess, who had stood all the while, watching the scene, gently held her hand.

"Never mind," she smiled, "I'll help you get them."

"Oohps," she gasped as she adjusted herself in the black leather seat. "These old folks could be nasty at times."

"It's not her fault," Dapo said. "If I had been making the strange noise you claimed I was making, she had every reason to be annoyed,"

"Then you agree there is a problem?" she asked, sounding as harmless as possible.

"Not that you can help anyway," he answered.

"Amaka is my name. Amaka Nwazuegbo. I shuttle Lagos and The States, on business. I own a number of boutiques and a fashion house on Allen Avenue in Ikeja, may be you might have heard of Stop 'n' Shop in Ikeja or The-Plaza in Ikoyi. Those are some of my shops. Thanks," She addressed the hostess who handed over her things with a smashing smile before she turned to leave. "She's beautiful, isn't she?" She scattered the contents of her bag for her business card.

"Well, I didn't quite notice," he answered. That is probably the last thing I would want to notice now"

"Okay," she said suddenly, making him turn in surprise as she brought out a small gold printed business card and her passport.

"I modeled alongside Yemi Fawaz in The States before she left for Kenya while I came back to Nigeria on my uncles request.

106

As a matter of fact, I'm on my way to The States to see my uncle's wife who put to bed not long ago. I should stay a week or two but definitely not more because my business does not allow me to stay away for too long.

"How about you, how long are you staying?"

He sat listening to this pretty doll talk freely with him, he suddenly decided he could trust her. What have I got to loose anyway he thought, I've lost almost everything except what I started with, my precious club.

When she saw him relax, she knew he would talk so she kept her cool till he spoke.

"You must have heard of me," he started as he fumbled with her business card. "I'm Dapo tavern, Chief Oladipupo Tavern for full," He was surprised when she did not flinch on hearing his name. People always hissed or shook their heads in pity or in disgust on hearing his name ever since he went bankrupt.

"I once controlled a business empire, an estate, fleet of cars," Briefly, he gave her the story of how he fell from grace to grass.

"There was this particular company that bought any of my companies I wanted to sell or offered to take my mortgages any time I was broke. One thing I did not understand was why and how they always knew I had financial problems. Probably, they had a hand in it," At the thought he paused. "I never thought of it that way you know.

Anyway, I lost everything," he continued "...at the last Stock Exchange market in Lagos. I thought I could make some profit to put me back in business but like a log of wood, I fell.

Some bastard bought most of the shares and dumped it at a ridiculously low price, which left me stocked with those I bought. I had no choice; I had to sell at a loss. I wonder how much the idiot would gain from those shares, but he ruined me and that was it, I lost everything I invested on.

From somebody, I became a nobody. No one wants to assist me financially, everybody sees me as bad investment. You happen to hear the same thing from all of them."

"D.T." as they are fond of calling me, "business is bad you know, or... the economy is bad. When I helped them, before things went bad, I wonder if the economy then, was good.

That's the irony of life anyway," he paused shrugged, then turned to her.

"Are you with me?" he asked, realizing he had been talking for too long, "Hope you understand my story."

"Yeah...Yeah!" Amaka answered. "I was just wondering what happened to your club."

"Oh... the Club... That was where I was about getting to. I have an underground club in Surulere, Off Adeniran Ogunsanya, the..."

"The Spectacles," She said excitedly, before he could finish his statement.

"Yeah, so you know it," Dapo answered unmoved by her enthusiasm.

"Who doesn't know The Spectacles? Only many people do not know it belongs to the magnanimous Dapo Tavern."

He chuckled at the way she called him "Magnanimous".

"How I wish I am," he smiled watching her before he continued "I would have loved to take you to dinner," he said more like a wish.

"That means you're off your worries now, at least to see me worth taking to dinner."

"Even a man in his last hours would make taking you to dinner his last wish, how much more a young man that has a long way to go, forty years probably." He added and they both laughed before he continued.

"But I'd just ask for a favour, if by any chance you see any one that can run the club and has enough money to buy it, I could sell it off and finally get out of Nigeria to another place entirely where I am not known. Probably somewhere around East Africa you know, where I can hunt down wild life, rear cattle or do anything just to make me forget the past."

"Why do you want to sell it? Why don't you want to keep your last asset? It might bring back all you've lost. Life at times is a game you..."

"And a deadly one," Dapo interrupted before she could finish. "You see," He continued, "you don't seem to understand, somebody is after my neck. What beats me is why the person whoever he is should want me ruined at all cost. Christ, it was one hell of an amount the person blew away at the Stock Exchange,

108

just in a bid to get my ass kicked"

"After that great loss, I have decided to leave the country for him."

"And you feel this mysterious enemy of yours that sacrificed that much on you wouldn't keep a tab on you," Amaka turned now looking more concerned. "I feel its best to keep your club because you might be running away from nothing or probably you were not the main target, may be it just had to rub off on you one way or the other."

"Ah... Ah... Ah," Dapo laughed for the first time. "You are a very nice girl. I mean, lady. I appreciate your concern but as our elders would say, a rabbit does not run around in the afternoon except there is something pursuing it from its hole."

"Likewise, an eagle does not fly at night except it is troubled. When you hear the eagle cry three times, you know it is looking for chicks to carry. I have heard the cry, and I know I am the chick. So..." He paused, shrugged then continued "I have to run, the best thing is to leave the country fast and quietly too.

So if you can help me," he continued when he saw she did not utter a word, "...to get a reliable person, and rich enough of course, I would be very grateful," When he saw she did not answer, he turned and saw a frown on her face.

"I'm sorry if I upset you," he started again, leaning back slowly. "It's only that you don't know how long I have thought of this and how painful it is. Moreover, the club is now in ruins because I no longer have time for it. I drank so much alcohol of late that till now, it beats me how I got myself to make this trip."

"It took lots of guts to put myself together, and here you are trying to destabilize me instead of encouraging me. I don't blame you anyway," He continued, "...life is not as easy as you think, you are a beautiful young lady, anybody would give you financial assistance, not an old drunk fool like me"

"Don't talk like that," she said suddenly realizing the stranger's plight.

"You don't look old, and you're definitely not a drunkard. I have an uncle that can buy it, though I would have bought it myself but I know nothing about the running of a club.

If I can have your contact address, I'll let you know if my uncle in interested. I'm sure he will anyway," She concluded.

After some minutes of silence, Dapo spoke.

"Thanks for considering helping, I really appreciate your concern but if it will take you out of your way to get someone, I'll advice you not to bother."

"If only you know," he continued "how I feel seeing somebody that cares if I survive or not. Someone that could ever think that, after all my misfortune, I could still be good investment. I really appreciate your trying to help and I hope you would not end up changing your mind."

"Of course not, what are friends for. Moreover, I might someday need your help and I'd do what I'll expect from you."

"We are about landing at the magnificent New York International Airport," the voice came from the loud speakers breaking their conversation.

"Fasten your seat belts and be relaxed for in less than five minutes, we shall touch the land of honey, Gods own city. Happy landing," it concluded.

Passengers giggled at the way the lady joked. Most regulars enjoy K.L.Ms hospitality and customer service, because theirs usually is with a difference.

Back in the First class cabin, Ekius sat up adjusting his seat before he hooked his seat belt. He looked out of the window watching the thickness of the cloud fadeout till he finally saw the outline of the tarmac.

As he descended the steps from the plane, he stopped suddenly, making the lady behind him bump into him. He saw two figures that caught his attention but one made his blood run cold. Strolling towards the arrival hall was the unmistakable Dapo Tavern with shoulders a bit sagged. At the sight of his sagged shoulders, Ekius smiled and descended the stairs now more slowly.

"The end is really here," he said to himself seeing how stressed up he was. "I'll kill him bit-by-bit," he thought controlling the urge to blow out his head there and then. I'll make sure he dies twice. But the lady, he thought, searching his memory. She couldn't be with Dapo Tavern, he murmured and like a confirmation to his thought, they shook hands in the lounge and exchange a few words before they parted.

Ekius hastened his steps in the bid to catch up with the lady. Seeing she was clearing her luggage, he reduced his pace till she finished then he spoke.

"Mind if we change bags," he asked, startling the lady.

"I beg your pardon," she answered after she gasped, surprised but stopped short when she saw the dashing young man who look somewhat familiar.

"I mean, you have a big bag and I have a small one. You could help me with mine while I put your burden on my shoulder, you would feel more comfortable with mine."

"How am I sure I can trust you?" she asked, frowning. "You might have an exhibit in your small bag, trying to beat the security using me as a smoke screen."

All of a sudden, he remembered where they met. Only one beautiful girl, smart and defensive had he met. Amaka Nwazeugbo.

"I'll forgive you because you're beautiful and pretend you did not slight my personality. You can never change, Amaka Nwazeugbo," He said shaking his head. "The girl that scared me away with her beauty," he continued.

"That was then anyway, not now. Whatever you say does not matter, I'm helping you," He concluded then bent down to pick her box. When he straightened up to hand her his bag, he saw she was smiling.

"Oh... so you were pulling my legs," He grinned and they both laughed as they turned to leave.

When they stamped their passports, Ekius asked if anybody was to meet her. "Actually, I didn't tell my uncle, because it was meant to be a surprise,"
He heaved a sigh of relief realizing she was not related to Dapo. "In that case," he said at last. "My driver will drop you. He should be around somewhere," he continued looking through the crowd.

"Looking for something, Sir?" Someone startled them from behind.

"You! Today again, you won. When will I ever win?" Ekius laughed allowing the uniform chauffeur relieve him of the box he carried.

"Next time messier," the dark Italian answered in his ascent leadingd them to the white limousine parked at the entrance."

He opened the door to the rear and watched Ekius step aside for her to enter, then gave a slight bow. When he saw the surprise on her face he shook his head.

"Its not what you think baby," he said getting in beside her before the chauffeur gently closed the door and turned round to take his position at the driver's seat.

"It is for one of my business partners," he continued lighting one of his long brown cigars. "Smoke?"

"No thanks. You sure got on well," She said as they hit the highway leading into the city.

"You're not doing badly yourself. Tell me," he continued. "What's been happening to you?"

"You mean after you disappeared into thin air."

"Did I?" Ekius asked, surprised at the way she answered.

"It was a pity you didn't know," She smiled.

"I was young and beautiful, but inexperienced. You were the first guy that really had the confidence to tell me you loved me or maybe you were joking but unfortunately, I fell for you. You broke my heart almost before anything started. You did not call, you did not check me. You left me thinking everybody that knocked was you. I waited for your call till I finally gained admission."

"Then...?" Ekius asked, inhaling his tobacco, obviously enjoying the story.

Ignoring his careless attitude, she continued. "Thank God you left then because I wonder what I would have done if you had used me and dumped me just like that," she waved her hand in a gesture. It was good enough you left then, breaking my innocent heart, than playing with my body which I cherished so much as a kid. I hated you so much then, because you treated me for a kid."

"Don't tell me you're still... Err," he paused not knowing how to continue.

"Of course not," She paused to clear her throat. I gained admission into the University of Benin and then its another sad long story..."

"So, who broke the remaining part?" Ekius asked teasingly.

Laughing, she replied, "You will never change, so careless. Actually, the Prince Charming who saved my heart from the turmoil got into a feud with some boys over me so I left to save his neck"

"Couldn't he take care of himself?" he asked, looking at her, surprised.

"Well, I did what I thought was right. How about you," She switched the topic, "...don't tell me you just went round making girls fall in love with you and leaving them all of a sudden, just like that," she concluded with a snap of the finger.

"Ah... Ah..." He laughed. "It's not the way you..."

"Buzz," the buzzer rang, making him swallow the rest of his sentence.

"Yes?" he asked as he pressed the speaker on.

"We are at the hotel sir," The driver said.

"Thanks Stephen," he said not minding the click of the intercom. "How about lunch tomorrow?" he continued now facing Amaka, "or preferably dinner."

"I'll like you to meet my business partners, two of them," he quickly added. "They are pretty nice guys, you'll like them."

"Alright, I'll call you tomorrow morning to let you know if I'll make it."

"That's okay, my room is at the topmost floor 1007, knock anytime and I'm all yours," he said laughing, as he alighted.

"He'll drop you at home, I would have loved to meet your uncle but I have to receive a phone call in the next twenty minutes. You see," he made a helpless gesture, "I work with time. Probably some other time," He concluded before he blew her a kiss and allowed the driver close the door.

Silently, she leaned back and smiled as the car noiselessly cruised away.

## Chapter 17.

"*W*ho is it? A feminine voice came from inside, shocking Amaka into her senses. Afraid she was in a wrong room, she looked at the number on the door and it read 1007. As she stood there confused, the door opened revealing to her yet another surprise.

Standing in front of her, clad in a snow-white wool bathrobe was the beautiful airhostess she had seen aboard the KLM airbus the previous day. Now, her hair hung loosely, flowing over her shoulders in a series of curls.

Immediately, she recognized Amaka. "Afternoon ma'am, can I help you," she asked smiling.

The smile eased Amaka who slowly returned the smile and decided it would be best she left.

"Hi," she answered. "I thought one Mr. Philips stays here, I was supposed to drop a letter for him," she lied fumbling with the content of her bag as if to get it.

"Sorry Ma'am," she answered politely. "No Mr. Philips here."

"Is this not room 1007?" Amaka asked again, pretending to be confused.

"Who is it?" A voice came from an inner room. The voice, Amaka quickly recognized.

"Asking for one Mr. Philips", the airhostess called back. "Have any idea who that might be."

"That's okay," Amaka said dreading to see Ekius come out in towels. "Maybe he moved out or something, I'll just keep the letter or call to confirm the room number," She concluded giving the other lady a smashing smile before she turned to leave.

"Sorry, we could not help," the waitress called out before she shut the door. Almost immediately, Ekius stepped out of the bath.

"Who was that?" he asked drying his hair with a towel

"Nobody of importance," she replied. "Just a lady that missed her way or probably got duped by a guy called Philips," she giggled at the thought of being duped.

"Poor thing," she continued. "Probably it was the guy she was sitting next to on the plane."

"Which plane?" Ekius asked suddenly, almost dropping the wineglass that he held.

Seeing the shock on his face, she became surprised.

"You're not Mr. Philips, I hope?"

"Come on! I was just surprised someone on the plane we were could be knocking on my door. They might have been tailing me, or well... Hope she didn't come in, she probably came to bug the room."

"No, she didn't," She answered and quietly gave it a thought. "No," She said again, "she didn't look like a spy to me or... are you a secret service agent?" she asked, eyes narrowed as she got up to meet him. "Why else should they be after you," she continued, tilting her head sideways to make her hair flow to one side. Slowly, she wrapped her hands around his neck, raised her head and kissed him gently on the lips.

"Are you tired?" she asked rubbing her body against his, her eyes questioning.

"Now...?" Ekius asked, imagining how Amaka felt. Yes, it was her all right he thought. She would be smart enough not to disturb him.

"Why not," he said, as life began to flow into him. "Why not?" he repeated pulling her closer. "May be this time in the bath," he continued picking her up.

She laughed and cuddled herself in his arms.


As he walked into the club, one of Rex's men walked up to him "Mr. Ekius, I presume," Swiftly he turned and scanned the man from the head down then back, his hand already on his berretta, which hung loosely in its holster below his left shoulder.

"Sorry if I startled you," the man continued ignoring Ekius move to get his gun

"Rex said plans have changed. He said you are now to meet him at the Las Vegas Hilton, he is hosting his niece to a light reception and does not want to use the club."

"You seem to be new around," Ekius said after he adjusted his Evening jacket. "Learn the code, and fast before approaching anyone or else you might get your ass kicked soon," he concluded, then turned to leave.

"Hello," he called to one of the waiters who was already going past him with an alarming speed. "Is Rex around?"

"Oh… you must be Monsieur Ekius or Mon…"

"Yes, I am Ekius, where is Rex?"

"He is waiting for you sir, I'll just take you there." The stout French man said with a slight bow before he turned and moved with the same speed he was used to. Ekius had to increase his strides to keep up with him. To his surprise, the man went towards the escalator.

"They are upstairs," he said without looking back "Our VIPs eat upstairs."

Quietly, he stepped on the next step behind him, shrugged and marveled at the speed with which the waiter worked.

Upstairs, unlike the restaurant below had very few people, so he wondered how he did not recognize the lady sitting with Rex from a distance

As they approached Rex, he realized he had company, but he did not realize the niece Rex was hosting was the one he had met at the airport.

"Welcome my friend," Rex said pointing towards a seat bedside Amaka

"I hope the change in venue did not upset your program. It's unlike me you know."

"Not at all. Every disappointment they say turns out to be a blessing. I was supposed to host her tonight," he continued looking straight at Amaka "...and here she is."

"That's true," Rex began, "She told me you met at the airport,"

"A long time ago," Ekius corrected.

"Well… She didn't tell me that," Rex said a bit confused. "Small world isn't it," he continued turning to Amaka.

"In any case," he continued. "She has a business proposal I like you to handle."

"Is that so," Ekius said, still looking at her. But to his surprise she did not flinch. She looked straight at him, a wicked smile playing around her lips.

"Yes, it's quite a good one..." She started before Rex cut her short.

"But... I'll want Ayo around before we discuss anything. So, for now, let's drink to our latest success."

As they talked, Amaka gasped all of a sudden as if the restaurant had run out of oxygen, spilling her drink over her beautiful cream-colored evening gown. She went so white that Rex thought she had seen a ghost. Quickly, he looked towards the stairs where her gaze was fixed.

Ayo was in a hurry, because he knew how Rex hated being kept waiting, but stopped after stepping off the escalator.

Unlike Ekius, he had seen their outline from afar and had immediately recognized the beautiful smile that has lingered for fourteen years in his mind. Slowly, he approached their table. Not taking his eyes off her, afraid she might disappear or change to the real niece. Rex had told him about.

Perplexed, Rex looked from the strange looking Ayo to the white-faced lady who sat opposite him, and back to Ayo who by then was at the table.

"Hi Rex, sorry I'm late." He said as he pulled out a chair next to Rex and sat down, with his gaze still fixed on Amaka.

"Amaka...Amaka," Rex called for the second time before Amaka woke up from her trance.

"What's wrong with you," he asked, "you are white all over."

"I'm sorry Rex," she answered stammering. "I feel sick, I think I should go home."

"Nonsense!" Rex said, surprised at her weird behavior. We have had nothing yet and besides, the night is still very young. Look at you, you stained your dress," he continued pointing to her soiled gown.

"...And, you've not yet met Ayo: We were waiting for..."

"We've met," Ayo said. "Let her go, she looks like she needs some rest," Ekius who had been watching the scene quietly, spoke at last.

"I think I'll take her home," he said getting up, to help her to her feet.

"I should be back in half an hour," He addressed Rex.

"Tell Wendy I'll he here, just in case and..." Rex paused

before he continued. "Tell her to take care of Amaka, probably call a doctor or something."

"Alright," Ekius answered before he hurried to meet up with Amaka who by then was on the escalator.

"What in the heavens was all that about," Rex said unable to reason out the whole scene.

"Nothing much," Ayo answered. "I guess she was surprised to see me.

"And you?" Rex asked.

"Well to say I was shocked and surprised is an understatement but I guess because she was excited... well, excitement and shock is just like a mixture of tobacco and brandy. I don't blame her," he continued. "Fourteen years, fourteen good years is no joke."

"Wait...wait...wait," Rex said, "tell me everything, from the beginning," he added.

Slowly, Ayo gave him a brief history of their relationship starting from how they started, to when they broke up and then a summary of his marriage to her friend.

By the time Ayo finished his story, they had eaten virtually nothing but emptied four bottles of vintage brandy.

"Gosh!" Rex exclaimed when he looked at his wristwatch.

"Your story was quite a long one, you can imagine what the time says."

Ayo checked his wristwatch and saw it was quarter to midnight.

"How," he drawled. "So I talked for roughly four hours. Where in the heavens did I get the energy to talk for that long?"

"There," Rex said pointing to the four empty bottles on the table and they both laughed. "We'll meet tomorrow, for the final arrangements and for the business proposal my niece has," Rex said, but remembered he was hosting a party.

"No," he corrected himself. "Let's makes it the day after tomorrow but, you should be at tomorrow's buffet. Wendy wouldn't hear of your absence and there are some important government officials I'll like you to meet."

"But," Ayo started then paused before he continued, "I don't think I want to see Amaka now, I think..."

"Rubbish," Rex groaned. "Nonsense. Now, you don't be a

118

coward, that's the more reason why you should be there. You two might have a chance to talk and the way she looked when she saw you this evening shows she still has something of what she felt for you before she left. Probably, that was why she never got married after her first marriage failed. She might have had the hope of still seeing you someday and fortunately, that happened today."

"You mean she isn't married?" Ayo asked surprised as he longed to ask more questions but he controlled himself and downed the last shot of brandy in his cup.

"Well..." Rex paused "not to my knowledge anyway," He continued "but I think Ekius has an eye on her, so you better win her fast. Should I expect you or not? he asked bluntly, daring him to say no."

"I'll come," Ayo answered at last.

"Winning her back," Rexs statement kept ringing in his head.

"I'll drop you at your hotel before going home," Rex said not looking back as they stepped out of the restaurant.

"Thanks," Ayo replied, "but I'll rather hang around for some time before going back."

"But don't get yourself drunk, okay," Rex said after he settled himself into the backseat of his brilliant white Rolls Royce.

"No..." he said to himself, as he watched the car glide down the road "This can't be happening," he continued. "Amaka, Rexs niece," What a world, what a small place the world is he wondered. He then decided to take another shot of brandy before he finally left in a cab.

"Want to talk?" Ekius asked after driving half way in silence. "I'll understand if you don't want to," he continued turning to steal a glance and realized her face was wet.
As he shifted his glance back to the road, he slammed on his brakes almost immediately, seeing a small boy run ahead of his mother who was fixing a hook in the baby carrier she had strapped to her shoulders.

"Damn," Ekius gasped as the car screeched to a halt.

Quickly, the woman ran across the road to pick the little boy who stood there confused as horns blared behind Ekius, perplexed at the way his mother screamed and at the beautiful looking Beast that flashed into his eyes. Mesmerized as he was, he followed his mother looking back at the man who sat in the Beast.

As the car screeched to a halt, Amaka woke up from her trance and was surprised to see the car come to a halt a few inches from the boy.

Flabbergasted herself, she nearly screamed but she covered her mouth with both hands and looked at Ekius.

"You nearly hit him," She said.

Ignoring her look, he slowly stepped on the accelerator. "So you finally said something, I was beginning to think you lost your voice."

Ignoring his statement, she looked out of the window and tried cleaning up her face.

"Look Amaka. I know it's none of my business, but I feel since it involves you - one way or the other, it involves me too. I don't like to see you so upset," he continued.

"Come on don't start feeling concerned, not now, not ever. You have no business in this as you have said but if you insist, I'll tell you.

The Ayo, I said saved me from the heartbreak you caused is the same Ayo I saw in that restaurant this evening. You now see what the problem was. God!" she said, "if only somebody had told me his surname before hand, I would have known how to warn myself against all odds. Christ," She continued. "After fourteen years, what else would you expect?"

"Its okay," Ekius said when he saw she was now sobbing.

"No it's not," she continued trying to control herself. "How would I face him again after behaving like a fifteen year old school girl."

"H-e-y! Come on honey," he tried soothing her nerves. "Anybody would have done the same thing, I'm sure he understood. Probably that was why he told Rex to allow you get some rest. He might call you when he gets back to his hotel or later," At the thought of him calling, the hairs on the back of her head stood on its end. "Could he?" she asked herself.

Could he call after the way she left him. As she thought of the possibilities, her pulse increased. Ekius pulled over in front of the pavilion in Rexs compound.

"Here we are," he started, turning to face her.

Silently she turned to look at Ekius. "You know you could be a darling," she said finally. "Its just that you spoil things when its just beginning by your disappearing acts and…"
She paused looking into his eyes.

"Never mind, it's none of my business, not anymore," she concluded, smiling as she leaned over to give him a peck on the cheek.

"Thanks," She said again, before she got down and walked briskly towards the butler who had held the door open at the sound of the car.

## Chapter 18

*A*yo walked in earlier than scheduled to see if he could have a chance to talk to Amaka before the party began but did not see any trace of her. Rex was on the phone in his private chambers so he decided to hang around in the living room. He helped himself to some Irish cream; it's too early to start taking alcohol he said to himself as he settled down on a business magazine.

The party started and still, no sign of her. He quietly avoided Rex since he was the only one that could notice he was uncomfortable. He bumped into Ekius and asked him if he had seen her but Ekius said he hadn't. As Ayo made up his mind to ask Rex, Ekius pulled him to a corner of the ballroom.

"You know something," he started. "For once, I'm jealous you have something I will never have. She's all yours, but you have to get her yourself."
Seeing he was confused, Ekius explained.

"Amaka is ill, and in her room upstairs. I learnt she is not to be disturbed but of course that does not include you. Trust Me," he continued, "Her heart is still yours, and all yours and the earlier you see her, the better."
Surprised, Ayo could not utter a word. He could only nod his head.

"And," Ekius added making him turn. "After all this hints, hope you will change your mind about kicking my ass. It's so small you know," He laughed, leaving Ayo with his problems.

"There you are." Somebody called him from behind. Absent mindedly, he turned to see Wendy in a smashing evening gown. In his usual mood, he normally showered her with flattery but instead he muttered a mere hello. Immediately, Wendy knew something was wrong because she normally enjoyed the teasing session anytime Ayo was around.

"You look sick," she said finally after quietly observing him. "Rex said I should get you, he wants you to meet the new Nigerian ambassador and one or two other Senators."

"I don't think I can meet them in this state, I think I need some fresh air."

"Should I get you some aspirins?" she asked feeling concerned.

"No thanks. I'll just get myself straightened out in the garden, and then I'll join Rex and the others. Tell him I'll be with him in less than an hour."

"Alright," she answered wondering what was on his mind. "Sure you'll be okay?" she asked again bothered.

"Of course," he answered and managed a smile.

Wendy wondered what was wrong with him because he was always cool, composed and cheerful. He was an ideal husband, unlike Ekius who was very careless. She always wondered why he chooses to remain single.

"Phone call for you madam," the butler broke into her thoughts.

"Oh... Thanks Leo, I'll get it in the study," she replied before she lifted her gown and hurried on.

The moon smiled at him as he looked up to the sky. Slowly, he took in the beauty of the garden on which the moon reflected its beauty giving it a silver luster.

From the balcony, he saw three windows upstairs and wondered which of the rooms Amaka was. There was a slight movement in one of the rooms before the lights went out and he decided that it should be hers probably she was about going to bed.

Absent mindedly, he strolled into the garden and wondered round admiring the beautifully trimmed flowers and inhaling the blend of the cool night breeze and the beautiful scent that comes out of the lilies that lined the side of the path. The path curved and he traced the curve, which led to a small gate. Silently, he walked towards the gate, surprised, because he had never seen that part of the garden. Normally, he came into the garden with Rex who was fond of plucking the beautiful lilies as they discussed business. They always avoided any discussion pertaining to business when Wendy was around.

The gate opened to what looked like a field grazed by beautiful green lemon grass with one or two trees at approximate intervals, which made it look more like a park.

He paused at the gate and was about turning back, when a movement behind one of the trees caught is attention.

He felt for his 48 police automatic, which hung loosely in

its holster under his evening jacket. He brought it out and made sure it was loaded.

He looked again and saw there was really someone behind one of the breadfruit trees. Slowly he moved towards the tree but stopped two steps away from the gate. I did not open gate he thought. I can't possibly be a ghost, he asked himself confused then looked back and realized the gate was wide opened.

It suddenly dawned on him that the intruder might probably be one of their guests. Quickly, he returned his luger and moved on but stopped and brought it out, putting it in his right trouser pocket for an easy reach.

What would a guest be doing outside, he thought as he quietly strolled on - a spy probably.

Shocked out of life, he stood rooted to the spot some yards from the tree when he realized the person was no intruder, guest nor was the person a spy. It was none other than his stunning beauty. Immediately, he replaced his gun in the holster and watched her rock herself back and forth, lost in a world of her own.

How time flies, he thought. Fourteen years and she was still as beautiful as ever.

"I thought you were supposed to be ill and in bed," he said startling her.

"Oohps!" she gasped as she jumped off the swing and scrambled on the grass staggering to regain balance.

"When... how... why... are?"

"Relax Amaka," Ayo started, embarrassed that he startled her. "I did not mean to startle you," he continued stretching out his hand to help her back to her feet.

"Sit down," He said, "...and I'll explain."

"Thanks. I can help myself," she snapped pulling her hand free before she moved back. "For how long have you been there and why are you not at the party.

How did you ever get here or who told you I was here," She continued avoiding his eyes because she was shocked and embarrassed at seeing him.

She had gotten home the night before and stayed till two o'clock in the morning hoping he would call but fell asleep tired and worn out when none came.

124

She woke up in the morning with a hangover and could not leave her room for breakfast. She was still thinking of what to do when her uncle came in.

"Why didn't you come for breakfast, love?" Rex asked as he entered the room. "Mmh," He continued, "...isn't it a bit stuffy in here," he continued and he went to pull the drapes. Immediately, rays of sunlight filtered in and Amaka groaned covering her head with the sheets.

"Are you sure you are okay?" he asked again, sitting down beside her before pulling the sheet down.

"I'm alright, Rex," She blinked sitting up.

"Oh Lord!" Rex exclaimed when he saw her eyes. "You need to look into a mirror, you look terrible."

"Just a hangover, Rex. I..."

"You drank?" Rex asked surprised.

"No, of course not," she answered.

"I stayed up late to finish some paper work"

"You still love him don't you?"

"Rex - x!" she screamed, baffled at the way her uncle talked, he never hid anything.

"Now, don't start a defense. You should have seen how you looked yesterday, when you saw him. God," he sighed. "It was like you saw a ghost from your past. You went so white that I thought you had run out of blood. I thought you would collapse or something."

Amaka smiled at the thought of frightening her uncle because it usually took something extraordinary to scare him.

"There was nothing really, just the shock that's all, you know. I've gotten over it now. It's nothing really," she said trying to smile.

"Be sure you are down by eight. The guests should have arrived by then, you..."

"Sorry Rex, I have a slight headache. Can't you give me time to sleep, please?" She pleaded.

"Come, Amaka," Rex said strolling back to the bed. "For how long will you?"

"Please," Amaka said afraid what he might say might be the truth.

"Amaka," Rex said, confused at the whole thing. "Well,"

he shrugged then left without a word.

That bothered Amaka. "What did Ayo tell him," she said, everything, or the side that favoured him.

Restless as she was, she tossed and turned, falling asleep at intervals before she woke up finally by a quarter Nine in the evening. Quickly, she showered, slipped into a plain pink evening gown, tied her hair into a long ponytail before she sneaked into the garden through the Kitchen, afraid somebody might see her. Unfortunately, she bumped into the old Chef in the Kitchen but made him promise he would not tell anyone, not even Rex, where she was.

Straight into the garden she went, plucking flowers at intervals till her legs got very weak. She then went to Rex's golf pitch and rocked herself on one of the hand made swings till she lost touch of time.

"Ssh," Ayo hushed. "You don't have to talk so loud, you just take the questions one after the other and see may be I can give you reasonable answers.

C'me on... relax," he continued when he saw she was uncomfortable. He moved closer and held her hands to the rope, his body some inches from hers.

"Sit down," he pleaded and she sat. Slowly he went behind her and gently rocked her forward, slowly at first then gradually, he slightly increased her altitude.

She held the rope tight and let all her thoughts fade away into the cool night breeze; floating away forgetting she was not alone till suddenly he held the swing jerking her back to reality.

"Ayo... are you there," They heard someone call from the terrace.

"Seems Rex wants me," he whispered almost to himself.

"But is it compulsory you...oh don't mind me," Amaka cut herself short before she finished, embarrassed at her behavior.

"Don't keep him waiting," she continued not raising her head. "He usually doesn't like that."

Ignoring her, he asked. "How about tomorrow at seven?"

"Where?" not knowing.

"If you wouldn't mind my suite, I'll prefer it but if you mind, we could..."

"Its okay," She said, looking straight towards the house

avoiding his eyes.

Slowly, he turned to move towards the house but turned just in time to see her quickly turn her gaze away.
He longed to walk back to give her a kiss but on a second thought, he continued towards the house. Time, he thought. She needs time.

"Bastard," she muttered to herself. He couldn't even give her a peck. Why did he turn back, she thought. Just a peck, her heart had screamed but he turned to leave, leaving her depressed.

"For Christ's sake, where have you been?" Ekius exclaimed as Ayo approached the terrace. "The Ambassador is about leaving and you have not met him."

"The Ambassador," Ayo smiled at the word. Who was the Ambassador, when my long lost love is the proverbial Garden of Eden.

## *Chapter 19*

*"W*ho is it?" A feminine voice called from inside, I'll be right over,"

No, this can't be happening Amaka thought. Without hesitating, she turned and ran down the corridor into the open elevator before the lady inside, whoever she might be would open the door. She was in no mood to start lying about Mr. Phillips. Who could it be this time, definitely not the airhostess, or one from another airline, a beautiful one probably and at the thought, her blood ran cold.

"Why me?" She started, in tears since there was nobody else in the elevator but an old woman that did not seem important to her.

"Why does it always have to be me," she continued but paused in surprise when the old woman handed her a snow-white handkerchief.

"Thanks Ma'am," She said dabbing her eyes, trying as much as possible to control herself before she handed back the handkerchief

"You see, my child." The woman started.

"Whatever happens to you in life, be patient and see if it's worth shedding tears. There are things we feel we see but we do not so, cheer up girl for life is not worth much tears."

Surprised at the words the woman spoke, Amaka felt guilty and shy at once.

Slowly, she thanked her and got off the elevator on the next floor. She still had six more floors to go before the restaurant on the ground floor and was bound to hear more if she remained in the elevator.

"Life is not worth much tears," The words echoed in her mind as she descended the flight of stairs.

It was past eight and Amaka still had not called. Ayo had left a message with his secretary who was to wait till Amaka called, in his suite.

The Ambassador after meeting Ayo had promised to host him the next day at his place but shifted their meeting to Ayo's hotel when Ayo told him he already has a date.

"Three is no crowd," the Ambassador laughed his deep throaty laugh and told Ayo they would have dinner in his suite if Ayo preferred that.

"No... sir, that wouldn't be necessary," Ayo said, we would dine in the restaurant.

Standing up, he gave a slight bow before he excused himself from the table. At the reception, he called his room and the secretary picked the receiver.

"No sir," she echoed. "Nobody came."

"Are you sure nobody knocked?"

"Err... err actually sir"

Just then, something caught his attention on the flight of stairs that led to the lobby.

"Are you sure nobody called?" he asked again, this time with a voice as hard as steel.

"Nobody sir," the secretary replied. "Except...err probably the waiter or something. He tapped on the door while I was in the ladies and I called out that I would be right over. When I got there, he had left."

"The waiter?" He said, gently into the receiver just as Amaka took the last of the steps, and strolled into the lobby clutching tightly at her handbag. With a slight click, Ayo dropped the receiver and followed Amaka.

Immediately, the secretary knew something was wrong. Her boss never spoke like that unless he was trying to control his anger. Quickly, she picked up her jacket and raced towards the elevator. On the corridor she stopped, confused when she remembered she did not lock the door.

"Oh... God," she moaned racing back towards the elevator. Hope I don't lose my job. People like my boss are hard to find. She prayed as the electric doors slid shut on her.

"Can I be of any help to you, Madam," Ayo said, on getting to her side.

"I beg your par..." she stopped shocked on seeing Ayo. No, it can't be true, what was happening to me. She thought trying as much as possible to stay conscious. Ayo could not possibly be in the room and in the lobby at same time.

No, She thought. My mind must be playing tricks on me she concluded then turned and continued but stopped in her tracks when the unmistakable voice called her name in a very sharp tone. He usually called her that way when she was getting naughty. Afraid and confused at what to do, say or think, she stood there without turning to face him, all her legs too weak to carry her weight.

Annoyed at the way she turned without saying a word, he had called her but surprised himself, that he was getting annoyed. Gently, he called her again then walked up to her.

"Amaka," he started. "I thought we were supposed to have dinner tonight,"

"Were we?" she asked, trying to control the tears that had clouded her eyes.

"Stop playing games with me, Amaka. I know you got to my suite but why you took the stairs is the only thing that beats me," When she did not answer he continued.

"Will you say something?"

So the bastard was in his room after all, then how in the hell did he beat me to the lobby? The elevator, she thought or probably the emergency exit attached to every suite.

"If you don't mind, the Ambassador is waiting. He would not like to be left alone for too long."

The Ambassador? She thought as she allowed him lead her along. Who is he? For how long had he been with Ayo? Who answered her in his room, or was it a wrong room? As these many unanswered questions flowed through her mind, she felt him squeeze her hand and said.

"Can you please put a smile on your face. I'd prefer a smiling beauty to a stone faced one. Surprisingly, the Ambassador stood up when they got to the table.

"Sorry sir, I kept you waiting. There was a little confusion along the line," he continued pulling out a chair for Amaka.

"That's my date," he gestured towards Amaka who sat down immediately, too weak to comprehend what was happening.

"Meet his Excellency," he said to Amaka with a slight grin before he continued. "The honorable Ambassador of Nigeria to the United States."

Shakily, she stretched her right hand to the Ambassador who bent down and kissed it very gently as if it might break.

Neglecting Amaka's bad manner, Ayo apologized on her behalf.

"Sorry Mr. Ambassador, she isn't feeling too fine so she had to sit down."

"It's okay," The good-humored ambassador said, laughing. "For her beauty, I'll take anything," he continued. "As a matter of fact, I think we're now too close for you to continue calling me the Mr. Ambassador thing," he paused, wrinkled his face and looked from Ayo to Amaka and back for approval making Ayo laugh, and Amaka managing a smile. She had not yet understood what was going on, but she relaxed at the Ambassador's good humour.

"Moreover," he continued. "This is an informal dinner, so you can call me, Lawrence Aderibigbe Gold. Chief Lawrence Deinde Aderibigbe Gold," He repeated, adding the title before he sat back to let the significance of his name sink.

"To our continuous friendship," he lifted his glass to make a toast. "And to your beauty," he gesticulated towards Amaka.

Ayo poured Amaka a glass of vintage wine and they received the toast with a "Cheers," that came in unison, making the Ambassador laugh.

"You two seem to be one already," he teased laughing. Just then the secretary appeared from nowhere, breathing heavily.

"Err. Sir, I..." She stammered but stopped when she saw Amaka at the table. "Err... You've seen her sir," She continued a little more relaxed seeing he was in a light mood.

"Yeah thanks Susan, I have, you can now go home."

"You must be kidding, Ayo," The Ambassador said making the other three look at him in surprise.

"The night is still very young," he continued. "Join us young lady, let's make it two against two." He laughed heartily.

"Ayo would not enjoy me sharing his beauty's company with him, so I'll rather have mine," He concluded, got up and pulled out a chair for her.

Ayo looked at Amaka and they both laughed at the Ambassador's courtesy display.

✧

# Chapter 20

"So he wants to sell his club?" Ayo asked after Amaka told him, Rex and Ekius about the business proposal Dapo had offered.

Ekius had kept quiet while Amaka narrated her encounter with Dapo, trying as much as possible to make them see the advantage in buying the club.

"Allah be praised," Ekius had prayed silently. So it is true that you don't struggle into hell's gate. Imagine! He thought getting up to pour himself some brandy, adding a twist of lemon. "Look at the club I was planning to buy on getting back to Nigeria," He said to nobody in particular. "Now somebody is begging me to buy it."

He had requested his lawyer buy it in the chamber's name to keep him anonymous but now, it would just be buying it in Rex's name without any sense of insecurity.

All he needed to do was to be very careful. He thought as he sipped his drink and listened to what they all had to say. It was too late to turn back.

"Turn back," He laughed at the phrase, not after seven years, not after he rehearsed his last speech to Dapo over and over again till it became a part of him.

"Yes," Amaka answered. "But to someone that can manage it," she continued.

"Well," Rex said standing up, "I should have a meeting in an hour at the Hilton so, Ekius should handle that. He can do with one more club especially in the heart of Lagos."

"Or won't you," He turned to face Ekius, realizing he had not said anything all night.

Ekius took a deep breath after he downed his drink and walked to the bar. He refilled his cup and downed it without looking up.

"That will burn your throat," Amaka protested as he poured the forygolden liquor down his throat.

"Never mind," her uncle replied. "It will take more than that to burn his throat."

Ignoring her warning, he took another shot and was about taking the third when Amaka sprang up from her seat and snatched the bottle from his grasp. Ashamed at his behavior, he spoke without turning to face them.

"Remember the deal I did seven years ago, Rex?" he asked.

"Of course, who would forget what nearly killed an asset like you."

"Yes… yes, an asset," he repeated as he made a move to refill his cup but realized the bottle was with Amaka. Slowly, he raised his head to look at her and she shook her head. Seeing it was hopeless, he continued. "You remember how I nearly got killed, don't you?" he asked again still not turning back.

"Come out straight m-e-n," Rex said, getting impatient at his questions. Usually, Rex always avoided Ekius whenever he was moody.

Slowly, Ekius turned to face them and Ayo whistled with shock on seeing his face. His eyes were red and swollen with anger. Ayo had never seen him look so cruel and all of a sudden he became afraid, something might happen but he relaxed when Ekius spoke.

"That deal was planned in this same club," he continued. "And the man that set us up was…"

"Gaddemn," Rex groaned sinking back into his chair perplexed at the turn of events.

"Don't," he said waving at Ekius to forget the rest of the story but he had just started, and Ekius continued.

"Yes Chief Oladipupo Tavern. Then, he was not a chief anyway he was like any of us then. It's been a long time so I can tell you what really happened.

"I graduated from the Ogun State University as an accountant and had nothing to do - no well paying job, one good enough to compensate for the four years of stress I went through and with that dirty sun at *Ago-Iwoye*.

"The money my parents left when they died was running out fast. My dad used to be a top government official in the Second Republic and my mum, the only daughter of a First Republic minister. You can imagine what they left behind for their only Child. The mistake I ever made, was not to further my education and I nearly paid with my life.

"I visited clubs, slept in hotels and became a regular at Fela's Shrine every Friday, Saturday night and Sunday afternoons.

"Along the line, I met Dapo through one of my friends, Sleek - may his soul rest in peace," he whispered before continueing.

"I learnt Sleek was killed in Lagos, his was worse than ours... or my other two friends, no brothers," He said shaking his head, "They were more like brothers to me. With the last of my wealth, we furnished ourselves with arms as we had agreed to hit a bank," He paused but continued when none of them moved. Slowly, he walked to the window and looked up into the sky.

"It was not stealing," he continued. "It was hitting, at least that was what it meant to us then. We were all young. Dapo was the oldest and he used us. To us, it was an adventure. He got the guns, which we did not really use and bullets we got from some hungry policemen who sold it out for a token."

Amaka had dropped the bottle of brandy on the bar when she got engrossed in his story. Ekius eyed it and made sure Amaka was following his story. Slowly, he walked back towards the drink but Rex who was not carried away with the story got the bottle in two long strides.

"Okay... Okay. I am not an alcoholic," he shrugged before slumping into a chair with a loud thud.

"I can always do without the drink," he continued taking a long deep breath.

"It was fun," he continued. "I mean, everything at first. It was an adventure we all thought we would never forget. We never really knew how risky it was till it all started. All the media houses went bizarre."

Briefly, he narrated everything and laughed at the thought of the five Smooth Operators.

"It was a clean job," he added. "No insider, just the five of us, like in the movies. The only difference was, we were not caught. I mean we were the heroes.

"Now, seven years later, nobody knew those that were behind the mask. Only that God punished three from the crew and by God," he swore, "Dapo will join them. I would have gone with the others but God did not want it that way."

"He probably blessed me to avenge my friends' death, to

134

kill him the way he killed my friends. 'He that kills by the sword shall die by the sword.' As it is written, it will be done." He concluded, got up, and walked up to Rex. This time Rex gave him a shot.

"That is okay boy," he said then corked the bottle.

" I was punished by not having a share of everything, now I have worked for my own money with which I bought Dapo out. Left now is where he started, once I send him to the streets, Well," He shrugged after a pause. " Lets wait till then."

"Hell," Amaka said astonished at the whole story.

"Yeah," Ekius answered on his way to his seat. "That's where I want him to go. Poor sinners go to hell, remember,"

"Ekius!" Ayo scolded, annoyed at the way he joked with the Bible.

"Ah...ah... ah," Ekius laughed. "I'm a sinner too, I know but a rich one. I won't go to hell, that's if die soon anyway"

Troubled at the menace, which Ekius had suddenly turned into, and the way he spoke with such venom, Rex asked.

"What now do you intend doing since the ball is in your court."

"Good question," He answered, a wicked smile crossing his lips. "Good question," he repeated sitting upright.

"First, I'll buy the club and blast it up with him in it. I want to hear the bomb explode with his frame blown to pieces,"

"That will be unfair, I would have betrayed him," Amaka pleaded in a soft voice.

"See, you do not understand," Ekius said, "This is a game that must come to an end. It is either you kill or you get killed. If he hears that I am alive which I know he would, I am as good as dead."

"Well," he continued. "I'm surprised till now, he still does not know I bought all his companies. It is unlike him you know, but he was too dumb to think I would still be alive. Money makes one dumb you know especially one you did not earn. To him, I had been blown up seven feet high and thrown into the sea, but I will surprise him. I will pay him back in his own coin and it has to be soon, probably in his hotel."

"But… you don't know where he is," Amaka asked baffled.

"Never mind," Ekius laughed. "I saw both of you at the

airport and made sure I kept a tab on him, I always had."

"But, do you have to kill him? ...Please don't."

"Okay for your sake, I won't."

"Promise?" she begged.

"Cross my heart," he said squeezing his face but immediately uncrossing it and smiled at the thought of Dapo being blown to pieces.

"You can take Amaka home, Ayo," Rex said after arrangements had been made on how to buy the club. "I 'll make sure Ekius gets to his hotel."

"Ekius," Rex started when Ayo had left. "I know how important this is to you and how you have waited for this, but there is something I want to ask." When there was no reply, he continued, "Can't you settle this?" he asked knowing what the answer would be.

"No," The answer came, sharp and abrupt.

"Alright, if this has to be done, you have my support but do not involve my niece. If anything happens to her, I'll make sure you suffer for it."

The threat came so casually that Ekius did not take it serious.

"Of course not. Amaka would not be involved," He said then got up to pick his coat. "About the shipment," he said as they walked towards the door. "We will clear things up when I come back. I'll be leaving tomorrow together with and Ayo and Amaka. Probably by weekend, we should be through. We can settle that before I retire.

"I hope so," Rex replied before he called for his driver, to meet them in front of the house.

136

# Chapter 21

"*W*ho is it?" Dapo called from the inner room at his hotel suite, checking his wristwatch. It was five thirty in the afternoon, one and half hours before schedule.

What was Fawaz doing here? He thought, probably he had plans for the evening. Hope his papers are ready, he prayed as he moved towards the door. He could not possibly stay in this country a day longer, not with the media making so much noise and this bloody hotel bills, he thought opening the door.

Shocked to death at who stood there pointing a revolver with a silencer fixed to the mouth at him, he became weak and perplexed from shock and fear that he did not move.

The long expected deal had been made, the club had been sold and as expected the media and raised hell. Dapo's traveling papers were supposed to be ready that morning but he had preferred to collect it at the airport and leave immediately to avoid speculations or attracting the attention of reporters that might gather at the airport when they get a hint that he was leaving town. He had called his friend, linkman and confidant to meet him at the airport by seven and was packing the few clothes he had, his passbook, license and passport when he heard a knock on his door.

Slowly, he retreated as Ekius moved forward. When Ekius was two steps into the room, he closed the door and locked it without taking his face from Dapo.

"Sit down," Ekius ordered and Dapo slumped into the convertible sofa, too confused to talk but stared absentmindedly at the intruder.

"Nooo... it can't be," he shouted when he regained enough composure to speak. "You should be dead, you cannot be him," he continued confused.

"Ah... ah..." Ekius laughed. "Yes, to you, I should be dead but God was on my side. You know why he kept me alive," he continued without taking his face off him for a second. "To do to you, what you did to us. Only, yours would be slower and more painful. Just then, a knock came from the door, followed by three, then another two in a sequence. Immediately, he knew his boys were around.

Slowly, he backed off towards the door to let them in before he locked it again. Almost immediately, they swung into action. They dragged Dapo to a single chair and taped him to the chair with a silver electromagnetic tape. Then, they brought out a micro atomic explosive of very short range and taped it under his chair before they programmed it to go off in exactly ten minutes from then. Silently, they left without uttering a word and Ekius locked the door after them.

"Sorry for the break in transmission," he teased taking his seat opposite him. "It was what had to be done. You remember your words, Dapo," Ekius continued. "You cannot make an omelet without breaking some eggs, remember and another," He paused as if he had forgotten before he continued.

"Yeah... Yeah... and too much broken eggs could wound the hand. You broke too many eggs, Dapo and by God, your hand would wound. Unfortunately," he continued. "It would not be only your hand but your wicked soul, cruel mind and cold heart.

You b...ar...s...ta...r...d," he growled, his anger rising. "You see," he continued, "Now you cannot talk. I know you might imagine how I found you but with your little, Babalaje of Egbaland, it was easy to get you. I wanted you to die penniless, as you were before we met.

I bought all your companies and made sure you had nothing left. Oh," he laughed, "don't be surprised how I did it because God was on my side. I made it in The States and established in far away Port Harcourt from where I kept an eye on you.

You're now broke," he laughed "and you want to run away. Why Dapo? Mnh, I thought you love your country, remember what you use to say.

If you go brother," he mimicked "Who will build the country."

It was four minutes left, and he slowly pulled the trigger and sent a shell slamming into Dapo's right kneecap.

"Please," Dapo groaned, after he let out a yelp. "Forgive, Ekius, I didn't mean to do it, it was for security reasons."

Another whistle hissed and his left kneecap split open, his

blood dripping on the glittering marble floor.

"Ooooh," Ekius groaned "even your blood stinks. Look at how black your blood is, it shows how dirty your heart is. How many more did you kill and how did you kill them. It doesn't matter I guess, you will suffer for all in less than three minutes."

"Please Ekius, remember that to err is human, and to forgive is divine. Don't take revenge yourself. Leave the judgment for God to do."

"Oooooh! My Lord Bishop," Ekius teased waving his hand. "When did you give your life to christ? All right, for that. Just for that, I'll let you go," Ekius said dropping his gun on a stool close to Dapo before he loosened the tape on his right hand.

Without thinking, Dapo grabbed the gun in a swift movement and pointed the gun at Ekius.

"Stop the bomb or I'll pull the trigger," he barked.

"Please Dapo," Ekius begged moving back, not releasing Dapo's other hand. "Remember, I forgave you. Please don't shoot me."

"I said stop the bomb or I'll blow your head off."
Annoyed at his sudden change of attitude, Ekius got up and spoke.

"You will never change, Dapo," He started. "You are so cruel," he continued pulling out another revolver from his belt holster, this time, his favourite berretta.

"Remember this little thing," he smiled "You taught me how to use it. Though I had promised to end you with it but I'll let you die the way you were destined to die."

Confused at what was happening, Dapo pulled the trigger and was shocked at the hollow click that came from the machine. Silently, Ekius went back and carefully taped his hand to the arm of the chair.

"Two minutes more," he said as he unscrewed the silencer from the point-32 he had earlier used and fixed it to his little berretta, making it look horrible. He walked to the door, turned and sent two more shells, one to each shoulder before he spoke.

"Adieu. My friend," he said and he slowly shut the door behind him. Quickly, he hurried down the corridor towards the elevator. One minute left and the elevator was just leaving the ground floor. He silently walked to the staircase and descended, quickening his steps with the tick of the clock.

Wait for the lift, an instinct told him but he shook off the thought and hurried down the stairs. It wouldn't be safe standing on that floor when the bomb goes off, he told himself bracing himself to take in the sound of the explosive when it came.

The world, though a small place, is as big as it is small. If only Ekius had stayed for twenty more seconds he would have saved a soul and probably his head too.

Less than sixty more seconds to go, Amaka stepped off the elevator and walked down the corridor checking the room numbers one after the other. Ten seconds more. She got to the door and listened. When she heard no voice from inside, she gently knocked on the door. Five seconds left, she turned the handle and the door slid open.

Two seconds more, she gasped at what she saw and before she got herself together, the deed was done.

On the last flight of stairs that led into the lobby, Ekius heard the loud bang echo in his head. Almost immediately, Ayo ran into the lobby, breathing heavily.

!n a swift movement, Ekius was with him.

"What is the matter?" Ekius asked "You are not supposed to be around here, it is risky or."

"Where is Amaka?" The question came sending a cold fire into his head. "Answer me," Ayo repeated, trying to control himself.

"Did she come here?" Ekius asked, trying to rule out the only possibility of him missing her "The lift."

"Didn't you see her? She walked in here about five minutes ago."

"Gawd," he sighed, suddenly wishing he had not done what he did. "I'm sorry," he whispered and left, silently praying against all odds.

Ayo dashed towards the elevator silently praying that Amaka should by chance, still be alive.

Everywhere was in chaos as everybody hurried out of the hotel to save his or her head. The management had immediately called the fire service and the police while they tried to evacuate their customers.

"Hey Mister," The security man in the elevator called when Ayo stepped off the lift on the topmost floor and ran towards the inferno.

"People were rushing to get off the floor alive but this strange man went towards the room where something like a bomb had exploded."

These were his exact words to the hotel manager when he gave his statement.

"He was a brave man," he continued. "He entered the smoke and brought out a woman who probably someone was trying to kill. He probably took her to the hospital or something."

Unknown to them, the victim was a man and the magnanimous business magnate; Chief Oladipupo Tavern. The room was not booked in his name so nobody heard or saw his body because the bomb made sure none of his mighty frame was left as exhibit. Ayo got to the top floor and had gone towards the room down the hall from where a thick cloud of smoke on the corridor got thicker as he approached the scene. The room seemed to have caught fire and a bright flame danced at the entrance to the room. He was thinking of how to get past the flame when a movement at the entrance opposite the room on fire caught his attention.

He moved closer and nearly tripped. His leg had hit something mighty and he bent down but felt pale immediately. He could have blanked out but for the love he had for the helpless figure that lay helplessly trying to move. Slowly, he fought the nauseating feeling that was rising in him, lifted the frame and headed for the elevator.

# Chapter 22

"*W*hat?" Rex growled into the receiver.

Wendy, surprised at the way her husband shouted, rushed into the bedroom from the bath where she was brushing her teeth.

"I'll be on the next plane," he said dropping the receiver absent-mindedly.

"Amaka is dead," he said bluntly shaking visibly as he fumbled with his night robe.

Unable to comprehend what he said, she poured him some Whisky and handed it over to him.

"Who told you?" she asked, knowing better than to ask any foolish question.

"Get dressed, we have a plane to catch."

He walked towards the bath, stopped at the entrance and turned to look at his wife, he was in tears.

This was the first time Wendy had seen her husband cry. She was so stunned that she couldn't move. It took more than death to make Rex cry. He must be getting old; she thought but was shocked at the next thing she heard.

"She died in an explosion," Rex said allowing the water flow from his eyes. At this, Wendy gasped covering her mouth with her right hand, her left hand clutching at her stomach before she sank into the bed. She wanted to throw up, at the thought of Amaka being blown to pieces.

Rex realized he made a mistake telling her, so he walked up to her, pulled her up and cuddled her in his large arms. More surprise unfolded itself because Rex continued. The damage has been done already he thought. Why not give her the whole story?

"Ekius set the bomb and Amaka walked in at the wrong time."

"No... No..." She screamed. Holding Rex so close as if her life depended on it. "No-ooo," she repeated. "He would not do a thing like that, why should he."

"I warned him," Rex said anger rising in him, "I warned him not to involve my niece. Now, Amaka is gone, gone for good.

No Nwazeugbo goes like that. When a lion's head rolls, more heads must roll with it."

On hearing this, Wendy pulled back.

"No Rex, you saved his life. Don't take it with your own hands, don't."

"Wait and see," he said and turned towards the bathroom.

"With nothing we came into this world, with nothing we shall return. Life is like a journey to the market, but heaven is our eternal home. No matter how long we dwell on this earth, we shall all one day have eternal rest with our Lord Jesus Christ. Amaka, you have lived a life worthy to remember and as you go to rest, leaving us in the struggle of life..."

On and on the Reverend father preached in the graveside sermon till he called the family to bid their daughter a final farewell. "Dust for dust..."

Ayo turned before the Reverend finished his sentence, shutting everything he had said out of his mind.

"No," he said to himself. "Amaka is not dead, she is only sleeping," he consoled himself.

Just like how Juliet slept in the ancient Romeo and Juliet. He has to keep awake and wait for her to wake up. He should not lose hope like the foolish Romeo, he thought.

How could he bid good-bye to the one he loved, the only one that taught him what true love was all about? Why was she always out of his reach when things happen to be going well with them? At first, she left unceremoniously in school and now that he was trying to patch things up, she left suddenly again - this time, without saying goodbye.

Why did she come back into his life when she knew she was going to leave again, why did she not just stay out of his life, he thought trying as much as possible to hold back the hot stream of tears that clouded his eyes.

"Why... Why... Why?" he asked himself, shaking his head

He shouldn't be thinking that way he thought. Not about his love, not about the dead. Suddenly, his blood ran cold. So he had finally accepted she was dead, gone forever. He looked back and was in time to see the stream of tears that rolled down Rex's face before he wiped his face with the small white handkerchief, which Ayo realized was already soaked.

Seeing Rex cry, he left his to flow freely down his face, unto his black suit, he didn't care. How much was the suit, compared to his heart. How much can he ever lose that will be equivalent to the loss or the vacuum Amaka had left.

During the burial rites, Rex had nodded twice. It was a casual nod and nobody knew what it meant. Nobody, except the closest bodyguard and confidant to Rex. Far behind the crowd, a tall hefty man backed out of the scene to where the cars were parked unnoticed.

Gently, he fixed an explosive controlled by a small remote control on the rear wheels of a black Mercedes Benz coupe, where nobody would notice it.

Ekius had gone into a solo hide out after Amaka was killed. He knew Rex would want to get even and had avoided him like a plague but he never knew he would be so rugged as to take revenge on the burial ground.

He had appeared late for the burial and had seen Rex with others he suspected to be members of the family.

He had seen Ayo turn away and had felt sorry for him because he knew how he felt but what could he have done. If only he knew Amaka would come. He had left a message for Ayo at his hotel but unfortunately Amaka got the message before Ayo and had tried to stop him. Why did she come, or if only he had had enough patience for the elevator, he would have saved all the mess that his thirst for revenge had caused.

As the series of thoughts flowed through his mind, he kept an eye on everybody at the ground. Everybody he thought he saw, everybody but the bodyguard that dug his grave. A grave he was blind to see, a grave he would have noticed in his right frame of mind.

At a time, he and Rex held their gaze for what seemed like hours before he saw Rex nod his head twice. He had thought it was a nod of forgiveness but never knew it was a signal for his destruction.

Straight, he had gone to his Coupe after the service and waited for Rex's Rolls Royce to move, followed by Ayo's black Limousine before he followed at a great distance.

As the convoy passed the mighty gate, out of the burial

ground, and descended the *Nnewi* slope, a car went up in flames. Those behind stopped, confused, running either for cover or for help but the two long cars ahead sped on as if nothing happened.

"Buzzzz." The buzzer rang and Ayo picked the receiver.

"Yes Mark."

"You have a call Sir"

"Who?" he asked surprised.

"Rex Sir"

"Okay pass it on"

"I had to," Rex started.

"I know," Ayo replied, "...what difference does it make. The only thing that ever mattered is gone, so...."

"Thats okay Ayo. We will be on the next plane back to The U.S. I'll call you when I get there."

"Alright," was the only thing Ayo could say and the line went dead.

Slowly, he returned the receiver and picked up the order of service. He opened the first page and stared at the full sized coloured photograph of Amaka and his eye was filled with tears.

He longed to say many things as the strings of tears crawled down his face but only three words came.

"Adieu my love."

*Part II*

# Chapter 1

*"A* call for you sir," Cliff called from the platform, waving the wireless so his boss could see from the golf pitch.

"Excuse me," Ayo said leaning his Club against the bag. "I'll be back in some minutes."

"Who is it," he called out as he neared the house.

"Monsieur Scadella, sir," Cliff answered. "He wants to speak with you"

"Okay Cliff, I'll take it in the study," he said, taking the mobile phone before he hurried into the house.

"Sca'," Ayo said holding the phone to his ear as he settled down on a single chair by the table on which he normally work late into the night, anytime he had extra work to do.

"Thank goodness," Sca' replied when he heard Ayo's voice. "Where the hell have you been?"

"Sorry buddy, I've got some visitors with me on the golf pitch. So, what's happening?"

"Happiness my friend, happiness. But first, pop a bottle of Champagne man, and take a gulp before I give you the good news."

"Men, cut it out and give me the good news man," Ayo said, anxiety rising in him. He was always careful anytime Sca' came up with a surprise because oftentimes, it was always about women.

"Alright," Sca' answered. "We've sealed the deal."

"Why didn't you say that all along," Ayo said laughing. "It really calls for a bottle of Champagne. Should I pop it right away," he continued. "Or wait for you."

"Err..." Sca' paused. "I think I'll like to be there. I'll be with you in less than an hour."

"Alright boy, I should be through with my game then," he concluded before dropping the mouthpiece. He then looked towards the small bar at the end of his study.

"A shot of Cognac wouldn't be a bad idea," he said to himself then got up and moved towards the bar. After what seemed like an endless battle, the deal was finally sealed. He helped himself to a shot of the liquor, halved it before he walked back to the cushioned black leather executive chair, lowered himself into its comfort and stretched out his legs, allowing his mind drift away, getting lost in a world he had known.

Ten years after Amaka died, he traveled to New York for a memorial service organized in her memory. He had gone on Rex's request because left to him, he had preferred to let go what had already gone. After the service, he and Rex decided to stop all forms of dirty business, to commemorate the tenth year remembrance of one who meant so much to both of them. They sold off all the nightclubs in Nigeria as well as those in The States, but left the warehouses for use in storing their pharmaceutical products.

"What do you intend to invest on, now that we have stopped all forms of illegal transactions and lots of money at hand?" Rex asked.

"I don't know of anything now Rex," Ayo answered. "I should fly to Paris in a day or two, relax for sometime. No business, no meetings, no phone calls."

"That wouldn't be a bad idea," Rex said. "I would love to take a trip round the world myself but there is no hurry for that, since I am now retired. I guess I have all the time in the world, well… regardless of the fact that I am getting old."

"Come on Rex, you're still young and strong. I say ten or fifteen years in active business would not have done any harm you know."

"Hey buddy, if you don't remember, I will be sixty-one in less than a month. Is that not reasonable enough to step aside for someone young and fit to run around?"

"Ah… ah…ah," Ayo laughed. "Not when eighty years old moguls are still in business Rex."

"People like that started late in life my dear. I left Oxford at the age of twenty-four and in less than two years, I went into production. That is close to Thirty-five years in active service. That is surely a time, long enough for me to have contributed anything I'm meant to give into the business."

"I think I will take my leave now," Ayo said looking at his wristwatch.

"I'll call you when I get to Paris," he concluded, got up and picked his jacket.

"I thought you said no calls," Rex said.

"Not when it for you of course," Ayo replied turning to face Rex. "I would give you a call on my dying bed."

"Ah... ah... ah..." Rex laughed but paused as he remembered something.

"Err..." He said making Ayo pause at the doorstep. "I almost forgot.
Wendy said to ask if you could make it for dinner this evening. Though I said you did be busy but she insisted. I could tell her you..."

"I'll come," Ayo replied breaking Rex's statement. "Why not, anything for Wendy," he concluded before he stepped out, shutting the door behind him.

Ayo handed over his coat to Rex's butler who was standing by to help hang it, and was about asking if he was late when Wendy came into the living room.

"My Baby," she cooed coming towards him with arms wide open.

"Hi Mum," he said going into her arms, before dropping a peck on her cheek.

"Rex is at the table," she started, pulling him along. "We were just about getting started. He said you probably changed your mind.

"Not when you're doing the cooking, on my life. It's not everybody that has the privilege to enjoy Mama's cooking the way I do."

"Naughty boy," she said poking him at the shoulder.
At the table, Rex talked about his post retirement plans as they ate, Wendy breaking in to correct him whenever he includes what she regards as, unnecessary. When they were about taking their dessert, Glamour, Rex's twelve-year-old daughter spoke.

"Uncle Ayo," she started.

"Yes, my dear," Ayo replied, smiling at her, ignorant of what was on her mind.

"Will you marry me?" she asked the question, and Ayo choked.

"Glamour," Wendy called, embarrassed at her daughter's

forwardness.

"Its okay Wendy," Ayo said after taking some water. "What makes you feel I would want to," Ayo said turning to Glamour.

Ignoring her parents, she looked straight at Ayo before she answered.

"I know you don't have a wife like Daddy has Mummy and I know you have always called me your princess. So I thought you would... err," her glanced dropped as she stammered.

"Okay," Ayo said and was surprised at the way she raised her head and the broad smile that lit her innocent face.

"...But," he continued "...you have to study hard." He realized the condition he gave did not really bother her, all that mattered to her was his consent. What does she know about marriage he thought, surprised at what children of this age could come up with.

"Promise," she said breaking into his thoughts.

"Cross my heart," Ayo answered placing his right hand to his chest. Simultaneously his eyes met Rexs' gaze and he shrugged helplessly.

Ayo arrived Paris the next day, and checked into the ancient Monte Calos Hotel. He decided to sit by the pool a day after he checked in, wearing a Bermuda shorts, a short sleeved open neck shirt, a snake skin leather slippers and a straw hat to shield his head from the burning sun. He was busy sipping at his juice when two young ladies approached him.

"Can we join you?" one of them said while the other stood by watching, unperturbed. "All the tables seem to be occupied and an extra table might choke the poolside."

Confirming what she just said, Ayo looked around him to understand what she meant by every table was occupied. Young men that chatted away either occupied most tables, laughing or aged couples catching up on lost times.

"Why not," he said at last, just when the ladies were beginning to feel snubbed. "I don't think I remember booking all the chairs," he continued looking from one chair by the table to the other as if looking for evidence that proved they were his. The one that spoke laughed pulling out a seat while the other was indifferent, pulling the other seat all the same.

"Are you expecting someone?" the one that spoke all along asked, taking off her hat to fan her face; giving the impression she was hot.

"No, why do you ask."

"Well... I just wondered what a fine young man like you could be doing here, sitting all alone at the poolside, on a beautiful summer afternoon"

"Ah... Ah... ah," Ayo laughed. "Don't be deceived by the looks, I am not as young as you think."

"How old?" she asked leaning forward on the table suddenly interested.

"Well, try guessing."

"Late twenties, or..." she paused to think. "...Or early thirties, lets say thirty-two to be precise"

"Ah... ah... ah." He laughed again raising his hand to call one of a Waiter.

"What would you take?" Ayo turned to her as the Waiter approached their table.

"Freshly squeezed lemon, with strawberries on top, and ice cubes of course," she added.

"And she," Ayo said turning to the other lady who seemed lost in her thoughts.

"Cynthia," she called,

"Yes," Cynthia answered startled, staring angrily at the other for barging into her thoughts.

"He wants to buy us drinks and I'm taking lemon. What about you?" she concluded eyes narrowed, daring her to refuse.

"I'll, prefer Orange squash or something," she replied with a wave of the hand, not minding the look on the others face.

"Cynthia," Ayo said when the Waiter had left. "That's a beautiful name. How about you," he continued looking at the lady that had done close to all the talking.

"Sylvia," she replied "...and back to where we stopped," she continued, "How old are you?"

"Forty two," he replied and watched for her reaction, but to his surprise, Cynthia turned to look at him.

"Oh silent princess," he continued when he had seen the expression on both faces.

"My age seem to interest you."

Ignoring the compliment, she looked away before she replied.

"Not really, I was surprised, that's all," she concluded staring at the pool.

"Now," Ayo said turning his attention back to Sylvia. "If I may ask, how old are you."

"I am twenty and my sister, twenty-two."

"That's nice to hear," he replied. "I would have mistaken you for eighteen and her nineteen."

"I beg your pardon," Cynthia said swinging her head to face him with an expression full of disgust.

"I was only joking," he quickly apologized, laughing at the way Cynthia turned. "You could break your neck that way you know," he concluded but she ignored him and resumed staring at the pool.

"So what are these two ladies doing by the poolside on a beautiful summer afternoon, all by themselves? No boyfriends, no fiancés or daddy to watch over them."Ah… ah… Ah."

It was now Sylvia's turn to laugh. "Give us a break," she said in between laughter. "Boy friends, no - Fiancé, yes. At least for her… Oh here he comes," she laughed, making Cynthia look towards the platform.

"Mmh," Ayo groaned, "Fine young man," he continued watching the man stroll effortlessly towards their table.

"Hi love," the stranger said bending over to give her a peck on the cheek. "Sorry I'm late."

The fact that Cynthia was indifferent surprised Ayo but he could only watch.

"Donald," Sylvia spoke before the new comer could feel embarrassed. "Meet… err," she paused when she realized Ayo had not yet told them his name."

"Ayo," he helped her out.

"It's a pleasure," Donald said, lowering his head in a bow.

"Same here," Ayo replied as he doffed his hat.

"If you'll excuse me," the young man continued, "I'm afraid I have to take them out." He paused looking from Cynthia to Sylvia. "Or you changed your mind about going with us," he addressed Sylvia, but a look at Cynthias face told her she dare not say yes.

"Thanks for the drinks," Cynthia said, a faint smile

crossing her lips as she rose from her seat while Sylvia just looked towards Ayo, shrugged before she stood up, turning immediately to leave, visibly showing her displeasure at being used as a shield by her sister.

✧

## Chapter 2

*A*yo, back on the golf pitch, took a nice shot from the *rough,* and the ball went in a projectile; and dropped into the *hole*, making the Senator's mouth drop in surprise.

"Wizard," he groaned. "To think that my ball is in the *green* already and just a push would have dropped it," the Senator said to Ahmed, a member of the House of Representatives.

"Well," Ayo said looking towards the two men. "Don't I deserve a round of applause," he continued. "But for the fact that we are all on our feet, I would have preferred a standing ovation."

"Get o-u-t!" the Senator drawled, dropping his Club into the Bag.

"I will beat you someday," he continued walking towards Ayo.

"Ah… Ah… ah," Ayo laughed at the way his shoulder dropped in defeat.

"Hey, spirit of sportsmanship my friend," he opened his arms and they embraced each other. "Spirit of sportsmanship," he repeated and the senator pocked him in the back.

"Ouch," Ayo groaned, laughing as they disengaged and all of them strolled towards the house. Just as they drove off, Ayo turned around on the terrace when he saw the gleam from Scadellas headlights. Scadella pulled up in front of the terrace, got out from the car and slammed the door shut with a loud bang.

"H-e-y," Ayo said covering his ears with both hands. You know how much it cost to replace any Honda part.

"Relax boy," Sca' said, now by his side. "When we finish with this next contract, I should be able to buy the new Honda Harler."

"And where will you put the array of cars that adorn your garage."

"Well," Sca' paused to think. "I guess when the garage is finally filled up, we'll open a showroom," he said laughing as they entered the house.

"I thought you said it had been finalized?" Ayo asked in

surprise. He slowly poured a glass of champagne for Sca' who sat in the wide executive chair in the study.

"Yes," Sca' replied, "but for the signature of the two parties."

"And, you couldn't do that?" he asked even more surprised. "When did my signature start commanding more respect than an internationally acclaimed barrister?"

"C'mon, stop that," Sca' said when he realized Ayo was starting to tease him. Ayo only does that when he begins to sloppy in their transactions.

"My colleague insisted you see his employer on Monday,"

"What for?" Ayo asked looking at Sca' for any sign that he was pulling his legs but there it was on his face, the serious look he wore anytime they talked serious business.

"I guest you will know when we get there"

"And when is that?" Ayo asked.

"10 O'clock, Monday morning," he replied.

"Why not today?" Ayo asked, "...today is a Friday isn't it?"

"I guess they want to be sure they are doing the right thing."

"After agreeing with you," Ayo said, pouring himself another cup of champagne. "What ever could be left to think, about?"

"See," Sca' said. "We are supposed to be drinking to a success and you are asking me questions. Do you know how many people lobbied for a partnership in this contract, if only you knew you would pat me in the back for a job well done."

"Alright, alright," Ayo said walking towards Sca'. He raised his hand to pat his shoulder, but Sca' hit it off.

"B-u-z-z-o-f-f," he drawled, leaning back on the comfortable chair.

"Ah... ah... ah," Ayo laughed realizing Sca' was no more annoyed. The way he exclaimed earlier, he saw Sca' was beginning to get angry which almost made Ayo regret his impatience towards the contract they were about to execute.

"See," Ayo explained, sitting at the end of the fairly large room. "Of course I know you did a perfect job, you always have anyway," he quickly added. "...But what amazes me is the need for me to be directly involved in the business."

"Security reasons," I presume Sca' answered getting up to stretch his legs.

"Which other form of security is more assuring than a legal backing."

"Personal security," Sca' replied, "...To prevent a later scandal probably. What is the problem now?" Sca' asked. "Is it to go there, or sign, or is it just the fact that you would be involved. All that is needed is a signature for Pete's sake and the deal is sealed."

"And you're sure no other conditions need be met?" Ayo asked still perturbed.

"Well..." Sca' paused to think. "Not that I know of anyway. Hey men," Sca' said tapping the edge of the table. "This is no do or die affair. If you go, and you smell a rat, back off. Tell me to backout, and I will.

"I guess so," Ayo said dropping his glass on a stool.

Sca' walked towards the door and Ayo rose from the chair to follow but stopped when Sca' suddenly turned at the doorstep.

"Don't you think it's high time I start asking after a woman in this house? I mean I'm tired of leaving this house without asking after someone."

"Well, ask after Cliff, at least he picked up your call..."

"A woman I mean," he corrected.

"Then ask after the cook, cleaner or my secretary. They are women, aren't they?"

"Don't you ever get serious," Sca' said shutting the door before he leaned on it. "Don't you get tired of sleeping on your bed alone," he continued.

"Well," Ayo paused as if to think. "If you would move in and sleep on my bed, I really wouldn't mind sharing it with you, you know. At least, then I won't be lonely or..."

"And when did I make it known to you that I'm a fag. I mean, if you don't want to get yourself a wife, date somebody. Or..." Sca' paused as Ayo interrupted him.

"Have you ever brought one and I refused her the privilege of sharing my bed," Ayo said.

"That's more like it," Sca' said, "...you are now talking," he continued anxiety rising in him "I will definitely get you one in less than forty-eight hours. Err..." he paused. "...Come to think of it," he continued, "...a friend is having a get-together this evening at the Garden city in Victoria Island. Would you like to come?"

"C'mon Sca'," Ayo drawled. "That is closer to Ikoyi where you stay. I can't imagine myself coming back to Ikeja from the Island in the early hours of the day."

"But it's not..."

"Sca'," Ayo broke him off before he could protest. "Just find me a bed mate first, then parties later," Ayo joked laughing.

"Old fool," Sca' said opening the door.

"You will just die childless," he continued. "We shall see who will bury you when you finally die." He concluded banging the door after him.

# Chapter 3

9:45 a.m. On Monday morning, Ayo stepped into the elevator alongside Sca', on their way to the topmost floor of the magnificent Malforganza building, a nine story building situated in the heart of Ikeja.

He had to sign this deal he thought as the elevator took off. The project has to start on time. Steel was discovered in Jos, and interested bodies were invited to mine the steel at a percentage. The risk involved was let known to anybody or corporate body interested in signing in, but the net gain happens to be too much to consider the risk involved. This is where brainwork comes in, Ayo had told Sca' before they considered teaming up with Malforganza. Left to Ayo, he could take up the deal alone, but any slip, and he would find himself on the streets. Malforganza happens to be one of the best mining companies in Nigeria.

As the lift came to a halt at the topmost floor, the doors slid open and Ayo stepped out, followed closely by Sca'. They paused in what looked to Ayo like a lobby where two men dressed in well sewn black suits, sparkling white shirts, spotless black silk ties and shoes that looked so glossy he could see the reflection of the ceiling on them, ran what looked like a metal detector over them from their shoulder down to their ankle then back to their shoulder from the back. When they were satisfied, one of them spoke.

"Sorry for the inconveniences sir, it is a normal routine check."

"Mr Ayo Arigbabuwo?" the other asked in a very clean ascent that Ayo could not help but wonder if they were foreign trained security agents.

"Yes," Ayo replied "And this is Mr...."

"It does not matter," the man said before Ayo could introduce Sca'.

"But he is my lawyer," Ayo protested. "Its okay Ayo," Sca' said, waving it off. As they approached a wall, it parted as if conscious of it being an obstruction to them getting into the inner office. Realizing it constitutes no nuisance anymore, the walls slid shut after them.

"Boy," Ayo could not help but exclaim, at the sight of the marble floor that sparkled from constant polishing.

"Are these marbles or diamonds?" he asked Sca', who surprisingly was indifferent.

"What do you expect from a mining giant of their caliber. Just go in and sign the thing quickly so that we can leave. I have feeling staying here for too long might give me a feeling of nausea."

As the second set of walls parted, Sca's mouth dropped open on seeing the secretary behind the desk whom at then was the only person in the room.

"Mr…" she paused, now on her feet, going round the table to welcome them.

"Yes… yes…"Ayo said before she could finish Ayo Arigbabuwo.

Where is the office?" he asked looking around for a door, which happens not to exist.

"Sorry sir," she replied, "we follow protocols. Thank you," she addressed the two men who immediately turned and took their leave the way they came.

Ayo looked round, wondering where the one who controlled so much, operated from. The room, a spotless white, coupled with the beauty of the marble floor gave the impression of angels flying all over the room.

"Your lawyer would stay here," she continued "...but if you insist, he can go in with you."

"Of course he has to…" Ayo started but stopped halfway when Sca' spoke.

"I think I will rather stay here," he said, making himself comfortable in a single chair, which happen to be the only furniture in the room apart from the secretary's chair and table.

"Sca'," Ayo called surprised and embarrassed at the way Sca' backed off.

"You don't really need me you know," Sca' said picking up a magazine from a pile by the chair. "Never mind," he continued flipping open pages of the magazine. "If it turns out to be a battle and you need help, I'll be right here waiting for you man."

"God help you," Ayo answered, before he turned to follow

the secretary who walked towards the other end of the room. Just as Ayo was about wondering what she had in mind, the walls parted into two halves, sliding apart to reveal a door along a narrow corridor.

"I hope your boss is not as computerized as his building," Ayo said when she stepped aside for him to go in.

The main office was nothing close to what Ayo had expected. He had expected mercury lined walls, Gold plated furniture and a silver tiled floor but a thick cream-colored Persian rug adorned the floor. Its cream colour matching the well polished wood furniture which Ayo was sure were antiques. Beautiful wall paintings of various landscapes adorned the walls and statues, carved from different stones they mined were well positioned all over the room. One in particular caught his attention, a sculpture of the angel Cherub, in gold. The room looked deserted so he moved closer to a wall painting, reached out to feel the texture but stopped shocked when a beautiful feminine voice startled him from behind.

"You seem to be an admirer, of good works of art, Mr. Ayo."

"Didn't your boss ever teach you, never to sneak up on visitors like that?" Ayo said turning around to face the intruder. Obviously annoyed, but relaxed when he saw the average height beauty in a smart cream, skirt suit.

"I'm sorry," she apologized as she walked back to her seat. "I didn't mean to startle you," she continued, turning to face him when she got to the table.

"If you don't mind sitting down, Mr. Ayo, so we can go straight to business."

"Look… look… look," Ayo started, obviously enraged as he walked towards her, "I did not come all the way here to speak to a personal secretary or solicitor. He should have said he would not be around," he paused, looked up around him. "Or he talks from a speaker somewhere. I thought as much, not with the way he computerized all his walls. Is this, part of security measures too."

"Sit down Mr. Ayo, or whatever your name is. I would have taken that as an offensive, but for the fact that I startled you first. I'll take it as a one-one score line, so we'll start on a clean slate. Now, if you don't mind," she gesticulated towards an empty seat in front of him.

"Wait... wait... wait, don't tell me I went through all those routine checks just to see you," Ayo fumed, still not believing she was the one that commanded so much respect.

"Just to sign our agreement, a point of correction Mr. Arigbabuwo. You have not come to see me, you have come to talk business, and to you, it is unfortunate you have to talk with me so, if you are still interested, sit down and lets talk business."

Taken aback by her commanding tone, he obliged taking a seat opposite her, his gazed fixed on her.

"Thank you," she said with a nod of the head before she took her seat.

"My lawyer, had...err..." She paused as her glance locked with his but continued unperturbed. "...Had already done all the necessary arrangements with your lawyer, but I insisted on seeing you personally to..."

"Excuse me," Ayo interrupted.

"Have we met before?" he asked holding her gaze.

"Why do you ask?" She paused, looking straight into his eyes.

"I don't know," Ayo replied. "There is this way you raise your head when you talk or... well, I just have this feeling we've met somewhere. Its probably a figment of my imagination." He shrugged leaning back into his seat.

"Can we continue," she said, not in the least bothered by Ayo's claim of familiarity. "Of course." Ayo answered, feigning a smile. "Of course," he repeated as crossed his legs.

"We are partners as in investing an equal amount in this contract and since we are to do the mining, we automatically become an employee of the partnership. That should mean, we are entitled to more of the profit instead of the fifty-fifty our lawyers agreed upon."

"That is not fair..." Ayo started but stopped when she raised a hand.

"I have not yet finished Mr. Arigbabuwo," she broke in. "If you wouldn't mind hearing me out," she continued.

Shocked at the way she monopolized the negotiation, he relaxed, annoyed at himself for coming in the first place.

"Thank you," she said once again before she proceeded. "I am not asking for the agreement to be altered, all I am trying to do is to let you see that you owe me a favour."

"So, how do I repay this favour?" Ayo asked when she kept quiet for some minutes.

"Good," she answered getting up from her chair. She strolled towards the window, paused by the side looking outside as if the answer lay there in the open. "I am the first daughter of my dad. I have a younger sister and an elder brother who happens to be a drunkard. He returned to claim what he believes is rightly his."

"So...." Ayo said. "Let him in. Moreover, it is usually better when a man handles business matters than when a woman does. You could supp..."

"You are the most horrible male chauvinist I have ever met in my entire life. So you think a woman's place is in the kitchen, don't you...?"

"Noo..." Ayo replied confused at the venom that danced around her eyes as she talked. "I was only joking," he continued. "You didn't have to fly off the handle at that."

"I'm sorry," she apologized sobering up. "I thought you were like them. After you called me a personal secretary and then telling me to..." she paused, transformed from the strong willed confident woman she portrayed to a sober teenager.

"So...?" Ayo asked. "What is the problem? Is he threatening you, and if he is, how does that relate to our own contract. I am not a hired assassin if that is what you want."

Like a flash of lightening, she transformed back to her no nonsense state, venom and anger forming strains of lines across her face.

"Of course not," she replied, walking towards the painting Ayo had been admiring earlier on. "My grand father left me a large sum of money before he died, I was his favorite. This, I have no access to until I am thirty."

"So," Ayo shrugged. "Why the hurry?"

"My brother is making it difficult for me to have access to the family's account, and I need money for this particular contract we are to execute."

Seeing the story was becoming interesting Ayo uncrossed his legs and sat straight.

"I see," he started, lowering his glance to look at nothing in particular on the table. "And..." he paused, "when are you clocking thirty?" he asked.

"Not too soon," she answered "but there is an alternative," she continued not turning to face him. "I either clock thirty or I get married."

"So," Ayo said, impatient at the way she was beating around the bush.

"Get married and lets get this thing started," he said but got the surprise of his life when she turned around, looked straight at him and said.

"Will you marry me?"

"What..." Ayo exclaimed, shifting uneasily in his chair. "Why me? Is that how it is done in your village. And ...what makes you feel I am not married, at my age I am..."

"This is a business proposal," she said, "strictly business. We get married, no strings attached, no honeymoon, and when I get my money, we'll file a divorce."

Slowly, Ayo leaned back into his seat and crossed his legs again, this time his left on the right in order to have a good view of her. "Marry me," the words kept echoing.

"I am sure you are not married," she continued when she saw he was short of words. "How I knew is really of no importance. The most important thing is I went into a record of your past dealings and realized you would not turn around and claim authority over my company once you see I am bound to you legally by marriage. You are not one of those greedy men who would do anything to accumulate wealth only to die and leave everything for one ungrateful child to squander."

"How about if I decide to provide all the money," Ayo finally said when he could get control of his voice.

Annoyed at the fact that he did not consider her in all what she had said, she walked back to the desk, took her seat and looked him straight in the eye.

"And how about if I decide to pull out of the business deal," she said, leaning back in her seat.

Ayo kept quiet and thought of what she just said. Backing out was definitely not the solution to this problem, and looking for another mining company could be risky, as good technical know-how is required in a business like this. This brought him to the last option; marry her. Impossible he said to himself rising from the chair before adjusting his suit.

"I will think about it madam," he said and he turned to leave.

"One minute before you go..." she started, making him stop in his tracks and turned around.

"Yes," he answered.

"I am having a cocktail this evening at my place," she continued. "The secretary will give you the pass you will tender at the gate.

"Oh, so..." he paused as a smile crossed his lips. "So security measures are still very tight in your house too. Hope there are no parting walls or speaking poles?" He continued turning to leave. "They have a way of making me sick," he concluded opening the door. Just in time to catch a glismp of the adjacent wall slide open. He stepped out and shut the door behind him without looking back. Stepping into the reception, he saw Sca' on the secretary's desk, flirting openly with the lady, who giggled on her chair, forgetting she was on duty. When Sca' realized Ayo was out, he jumped down from the table, waving an invitation card in the air.

"Cocktail for the boys," he said, walking up to meet him. Ayo looked from the secretary to Sca' and to the white envelope in his hand. For the boys, he smiled. Does Sca' think he is growing younger he thought walking towards the wall adjacent, knowing it definitely would part.

"How was it?" Sca' asked Ayo on their way home. "You signed didn't you," he continued when Ayo kept mute. "Will you say something instead of staring as if you just saw a ghost?"

"Did you know who the boss was before hand Sca'," Ayo spoke at last not looking at him.

"Is that what you have been brooding over since we left. I never knew you were a chauvinist Ayo, I..."

"Did you know why she insisted we met?" Ayo asked making Sca' stop to think.

"Well... no," he answered. "That was supposed to be between the two of you, it really was not a prerequisite for the project to kick off."

"Between the two of us," Ayo repeated after him.

"No," Sca' tried again, getting a funny feeling to turn the

car around, "Are you telling me or am I to turn the car around and go back there to confirm the outcome of your meeting myself."

"She gave a condition for the project to proceed,"

"Condition," Sca' said surprised at the new development.

"Yes," Ayo said, hoping to get support from Sca'.

"What could that be?" Sca' said more of a statement than a question.

"I have to marry her before the project can proceed. She can't get access to some inheritance of hers, except she gets married."

"Ah… ah… ah," Sca' started laughing before Ayo could finish what he was saying.

"And what is funny," Ayo said turning to look at Sca'.

"Everything my friend," Sca' said in between laughter, "Everything," he repeated. "You are not married, and this is a chance to have a woman in the house, no stress of wooing and no problem of heartbreak. To think that just for this, the contract takes off and you complain like somebody who just lost his mother.

"You don't understand Sca'," Ayo tried to explain. "This is simply an informal arrangement. After she gets her inheritance, we will have to file a divorce."

"Beautiful," Sca' exclaimed. "That even makes it easier. Give her a divorce if you don't see an ideal wife in her or refuse to give her if you realize she fits in as a perfect wife, at least one you can live with."

"That would be a betrayal," Ayo said, "She feels I'll give her a divorce when she requests for it, that it why she trusts me enough to consider me fit to do business with."

"So, do it for Christ's sake," Sca' said, nearly raising his voice. "It sounds easy enough."

"For you," Ayo cut in. "I am sure we have met somewhere before, she might be using me for selfish reasons."

"Bullshit man, that's all bullshit. From all we saw today, its obvious she doesn't need your money and personality, her company can fetch her all that. If getting her inheritance is what you call selfish, bear in mind that the money is for our business."

"In that case, will you marry her in my place and give her what she wants," Ayo said, making Sca' laugh.

"If Angela hears that you are encouraging me to take a

second wife, she would definitely not waste time flying down from, U.S. to personally shoot you. And," Sca' paused, "I am not even the one she wants, or else she would have stipulated that in the agreement instead of asking to see you."

"It is still the same," Ayo replied, unsatisfied with Sca's excuse.

"So what did you say?" Sca' asked.

"I told her I would think about it," he answered.

"You will what," Sca' exclaimed slamming hard on the brakes of the Honda Civic "96," Born again series, making the alloy wheels screech to a halt.

"H-o-l-y-s-h-i-t," Ayo exclaimed. "Are you nuts? What do you think you are doing? Do you realize you are on the third Mainland Bridge," he fumed leaning over to look into the rear mirror for an on-coming vehicle but saw none. He then sighed heavily and turned to Sca' when he realized Sca' had switched the gear to reverse.

"Why did you do that?" he asked raising his head to meet Sca's glance.

"We are going back," Sca' said, anger written all over his face.

"Listen Sca', I know I'm not saying no…" he paused to let that sink into his head and on hearing that, Sca' relaxed, looking straight ahead, "but…" Ayo continued. "I only want to think about the implications. The whole thing looks strange," he paused as Sca' returned the gear back to number one and slowly stepped on the accelerator. "First, the fact that she is in charge," he continued, "…the strange familiarity and then, the proposal. I definitely will do anything in my power for the mining to commence but lets try get some facts about her background."

"That's true," Sca' agreed, finally nodding his head. "Probably I'll start my investigation this evening at the cocktail party."

"Who said he was going to a cocktail party?" Ayo asked, surprise written on his face.

"Look buddy," Sca' started. "If we are carrying out any investigation, the earlier we begin, the better. What better opportunity is there to get to the bottom of this whole thing?"

"Is the secretary going to be at the party?" Ayo asked

realizing all that Sca' had been saying was absolutely out of point.

"Well… I don't know. I guess there is only one way to find out."

"And that is," Ayo said.

"We'll go and see for ourselves of course," Sca' answered joining Ayo who tried all along to feign seriousness as they both laughed.

✧

# Chapter 4

*A*yo let out a long whistle when Sca' stepped into his room later that evening his eyes traveling from Sca's charcoal black suede evening jacket that matched the black butterfly suede bow tie which contrasted well with his snow white silk shirt, to his black mauri crocodile skin shoe.

"Good gracious," Sca' exclaimed when he saw Ayo in a dull cream coloured suit. "Have you lost your dress sense?"

"What else will I wear?" Ayo asked, looking at his reflection in the mirror. "Just because you want to impress that secretary of yours, you dressed as if you have a date with the queen."

"Don't be surprised if the President or Queen of England attends this cocktail," Sca' replied walking towards the wardrobe. "Where is your *Polo* Silk suit or your *YSL* evening jacket," he continued looking through the wardrobe. "Yes," he said, picking out a white *Georgio Armani* labeled Tuxedo. "What do you think?" he asked displaying it for Ayo to see.

"Its all the same, or is…"

"No its not," Sca' said before Ayo could make an excuse. "Didn't you see where we went today? Just imagine the caliber of people that would be at the party." His eyes traveled to the shoes on Ayo's legs. "What label is on that shoe?"

"For heavens sake," Ayo exclaimed, "will you stop all this emphasis on what to wear."

"You are not ashamed," Sca' replied picking up one of the pair of shoes Ayo had worn before he turned to watch Ayo kit himself in the Tuxedo Sca' suggested he wore. "Kenneth Cole," he continued, calling the label on the shoe, "...are you going for a board meeting or to your office. When you have close to Forty-five pairs of assorted Mauri shoes?" Sca' opened the closet and looked through before he selected a pair of glossy ox-blood Mauri shoes.

"Err…" he paused holding up the shoes. He looked from the shoes to Ayo's tuxedo then back to the shoe before he opened another closet and picked out a pure ox blood silk tie and a black silk shirt.

Dropping the tie on the bed, he picked up the phone, punched three numbers and waited for someone to pick the phone.

"Cliff," he said, looking up at Ayo, "...tell three drivers to kit up and make sure the white Rolls Royce, the six-door limousine and lets see the BMW, seven series are right in front of the porch by the time we get down," he concluded dropping the receiver.

"Are you some kind of an Italian Mafia to go in convoys?" Ayo asked surprised. "What do you need three cars for?"

"Four," Sca' corrected, "...my white 300E-class Mercedes Benz is outside with fully armed security men. Personal security matters these days you know, with the increase in crime rate in Lagos, one can't help but be careful."

The guests at the entrance turned as the first Benz pulled up in front of the porch and a man quickly came down only to wait for the white Rolls-Royce to pull up before he opened the door and stepped aside for Sca' to come down. Sca', realizing people were watching, climbed the porch as the black limousine pulled up. The bodyguard was still there to open the door and Ayo stepped out from the black limousine in his spotless white tuxedo. The contrast between their suits and the colour of their cars was so impressive and the way the bodyguards, hovered around them gave the impression of a diplomat but for the absence of flags on the cars.

"How was that," Sca' whispered across to Ayo as they entered the ballroom.

"It was all your idea," Ayo replied, "so sooth yourself."

"Ah... ah... ah," Sca laughed, picking two glasses from a waiter passing by. Handing one to Ayo, he continued. "Now, that is the first phase. In case anybody wants to know where we were coming from, it's the State house. The governor is holding a buffet."

"Say anything you like," Ayo said. "All this I suppose, is for your new secretary love."

"All for our contract," Sca' said defensively. "I mean, to show we'll make good in-laws," he joked giggling but stopped when he saw the scorn on Ayo's face.

"Err..." Sca' poked Ayo slightly by the side. "Some beauty has been staring at us. Who she wants now, I don't know. Should we toss a coin to know who will have her?" As Ayo turned to look in the direction, the lady started walking towards them.

"I think I should go and look for Kate," Sca' said quickly in an attempt to leave Ayo to cope with the girl.

"For who?" Ayo asked, surprised that Sca' could want leave him to cope with the stranger.

"The secretary," Sca' answered over his shoulder.

"Oh," Ayo said, turning around not aware that the lady had gotten to his side.

"Ohpps," she gasped, quickly stretching out her hand to avoid staining her beautiful pink Chiffon ball gown.

"I'm terribly sorry," Ayo said, bringing out an handkerchief and wiping the little stain just above the swell of her breast.

"That was most kind of you Mr..."

"Ayo, Ayo Arigbabuwo," he helped her out when she paused.

"I knew I could never mistake that face for someone else," she said smiling.

"I beg your pardon?" Ayo asked, not aware of what she was talking about.

"I wouldn't blame you anyway," she continued, "I'm twenty-six now and guess I have added more weight and changed so much.

After six years," she laughed. "What else would one expect?"

"I'm sorry madam," Ayo said innocently, "I'm in the dark, I don't really understand what you mean."

"Its okay," she said sliding her left hand under his, gently pulling him to the dance floor. "Lets dance," she whispered, dropping her glass on a tray and waited for Ayo to do the same before she wrapped her hands around his neck, pressing her softness, hard against his chest.

"Err... I... err." Ayo stammered, confused at her too familiar approach. "I think you are mistaking me for someone else," he said when he could get a hold of his voice.

"You were in Paris six years ago weren't you?" she started, watching the confused look on his face.

Six years ago, was Amakas tenth year remembrance. Yes he thought, he was in Paris after he left the U. S.

"Remember you met my sister and I at the Monte Carlos

hotel in Paris, by the pool side."

"Holy Mary," he exclaimed, pulling back to hold her at arms length. "You are now a full grown woman," he said surprised.

"I wasn't that young then," she said defensively, "or was I?" she disengaged to pick two glasses on a tray, as a uniformed waiter walked past, handing one to Ayo. "Let's get some fresh air outside, it's a beautiful site at night," she continued, pulling him along.

"You seem to know the nooks and crannies of the house," Ayo couldn't help but comment when they left the ballroom through the living room, to the dining room that opened up into a platform overlooking a well cultured maze.

"Where else would I know so well if I don't know my way round a house in which I grew up. Ayo paused all of a sudden to stare at her. Things began to fall into place. This lady was in Paris with her elder sister. She stays in this house where the no nonsense director of Malforganza definitely stays. The familiar way she raised her head in the office. Yes, he said to himself. She has to be this lady's elder sister, the one that never spoke to him except for one or two compliments in Paris.

"Anything the matter?" she asked when she realized the distant look on his face.

"No, not at all," he answered, walking on, "I was just trying to recollect if you probably mentioned anything back in Paris about being a Nigerian."

"There was no need for that," she said leaning against a railing outside on the platform. "You did not give me any reason to."

"Well," he shrugged "…just thought for the fact that you are, my name was supposed to have given me away."

"You know I never really gave it a thought," she said raising a brow on second thought. "In any case, that's in the past. Where is your date or preferably your wife?" she asked,

"Actually… I…"

"Sylvia," Cynthia's voice interrupted him, saving him from the embarrassing question. How was he to explain being single at forty-eight. They both turned and saw Cynthia at the entrance into the dinning room.

"Please try see Uncle Bernard, he has been on my throat all evening. He insists he sees you before he leaves."

"Let Uncle Bernard wait," Sylvia said carelessly. "I can always see him."

"Sylvia," Cynthia called, walking towards them.

"Alright... Alright," she said waving her hands but come and see who I am talking to." she continued. "Do you remember...?"

"Yes," Cynthia cut in before Sylvia could finish what she was saying.

"Oh... so you remember..."

"Sylvia," Cynthia said, "Uncle Ber..."

"Oh spare me the stress of going to..."

"C'mon," Cynthia cut her short but relaxed a bit when she realized she was hitting too hard on her sister. "Just say hi to him and come back. I'll keep him company till you get back," she concluded turning to look at Ayo.

Surprised at the way her sister persisted on getting rid of her, she looked at Ayo, to her sister then back at Ayo who nodded and gesticulated for her to go on. With a last glance at her sister, Sylvia turned and walked straight shouldered into the house.

"How much do you remember?" Ayo asked when Sylvia had gone. "You seem not to be in a mood to talk," he continued when all she did was, lean her back against the railing, her eyes fixed to the door, even long after Sylvia had entered the house. "Why then did you let your sister go, she was good company."

"See Mr. Ayo or whatever your name is, this can't work out if you continue to flirt with my sister."

"What," Ayo said, surprised at her outburst.

"People won't believe we are married if you continue to flirt with my sister in the open. As a matter of fact, you shouldn't even do that at all."

"Who said I was flirting with your sister?"

"Does it..."

"And who said we are or will ever be married," Ayo continued annoyed at the way she accused him wrongly and to think that she had no right.

Surprised at his answer, she turned and stared into his face, then smiled.

"You want to lose your chance of going into partnership with me, and to think that a million men would give anything for

174

my hand in marriage and…"

"I thought it used to be a million and one," Ayo chipped in before she could continue "Oh," he continued. "I take the remaining one as your fiancé who refused to marry you," he concluded smiling.

"You scornful bastard," she said, turning away to face the maze directly below the platform "he did not refuse to marry me," she continued. "I broke the engagement when I realized he was a cheat, a thief and… it doesn't matter anyway," she concluded and turned, to make for the door. Quickly, Ayo grabbed her hand and she struggled frantically.

"Let me go – o," she screamed trying to get free from his hold. "I said let me go," she screamed again, her voice cracking as she was close to tears.

"I'm sorry," Ayo began. "I didn't mean it that way, I was only…"

"Its not your fault," she cut in strings of tears now dropping from her eyes. "I just thought since we were to do business together, you wouldn't mind helping me get at my inheritance. I didn't know you would read meaning to it and back off. I…"

"I didn't say I was backing off…" Ayo said defensively.

"But you just said…"

"I only said I would think about it," he continued before she started to quote him. He reached into his breast pocket to get another white handkerchief which he handed over to her.

"Thank you," she said walking to a single cane chair at the end of the balcony. "Never mind, I will be okay," she continued. "Some breeze on my face, and I'll be okay," she paused before she looked at him. "You can go in now, I'll join you in some minutes."

"No… no," Ayo said quickly protesting. "I'm okay here." he continued walking towards her but stopped a few meters from where she was sitting and leaned on the railing, looking into the maze.

"The maze," he started again. "It's so beautiful and inviting but, I guess one would lose his way if one tries to step into it." Surprised, he turned to see her giggle.

"You want to share it?" he asked and was more surprised when she started to talk.

"Nothing interesting actually," she started, "It's just that anytime I was becoming naughty when I was young, my nanny would threaten to take me into the maze."

175

"It looks beautiful to me," Ayo started but stopped when she continued.

"That was what lured me into it that hot afternoon. I had been there a number of times though, but it was always in the company of my mother." At the thought of her mother, she paused for what looked like a minute of silence, after which a faint smile crossed her lips before she continued.

"She often times, seek condolence in the beauty of the maze. Well," she shrugged. "This particular day," she continued suddenly becoming lively again, "I was right here on the platform, taking in the beauty it radiated under the powerful stream from the golden sun. I was six years or thereabout and my parents were out for one of their numerous functions. The nanny had warned me not to wander in the maze alone and always made sure the little gate was locked." She paused to look at the little gate at the end of the balcony from where a flight of steps led down into the garden that linked the beautiful network of maze. As she talked, Ayo wondered what caused the change of expression on her face when she talked about her mother.

"I wandered around and around," he heard her say and shook his head, realizing he was not with her.

"...When I realized I was getting hungry, I decided to go back to the house."

"Ah... ah... ah," she paused laughing as she reminisced in her childhood days. "This day was nothing close to being funny at all but I guess after so many years, I can laugh over it. When I made the twelfth turn, I realized I was lost. Lost in a place that consoled my mother. What used to be a paradise I adored with my mother by my side suddenly became a house of horror. I started to think of many horrifying things that happen to disobedient children. I sat down against a wall of hedge and started to cry. Unknown to me, my nanny was up here watching everything I did. She waited till she felt I had cried enough and have learnt not to venture on such an adventure again.
Funny enough, it was when I was praying to God for forgiveness that she appeared, just like an answer to my prayer. Mum had told me God punishes disobedient children, so I had thought loosing my way was a punishment. It all sounds like one of those fairy tales doesn't it?" she asked turning to look at him.

"I bet I would lose my way in it too," Ayo said. "Even now, how much more being a six year old kid."

"C'mon," she protested, "its not as difficult as it seems. As I grew up," she continued, "I realized all I needed to do was to trace the beautiful scent of lilies, and I will be able to guess the direction towards the garden. Once out of the maze, the house is as good as being close to an ice cream shop."

"I still think to find my self lost in this beautiful network is not an impossibility," Ayo said taking in the beauty it radiated, under the moonlight, giving a metallic silver luster...

"Why not go through it," she suggested. "To come out, won't be a problem. I assure you but making up your mind to go in, especially when you cannot figure out the paths well from here is where the problem lies. Would you love to go through it?" she asked looking at him.

"If you would go with me," he replied.

"Why not," she said getting up. "I wouldn't want to hear one of my guests spent the night in the Rhodes Maze court."

"That would surely make some headlines in the dailies," he said and they both laughed. They turned to leave but stopped and turned when somebody called Ayo from the entrance.

"Your friend wants you," Sylvia continued, not bothering to come out on the platform. "He says something about a Senator wanting to see you."

"Tell him..." Ayo started but stopped when Cynthia spoke.

"Its okay Mr. Ayo," some other time probably.

At that, Ayo felt foolish. Why would I prefer staying out here with her to seeing my friend on a business deal he thought, making to walk towards the entrance.

"Mr. Ayo," Cynthia called, making him stop in his tracks and turn to face her.

"Be careful," she said lowering her gaze. "I think my sister likes you," she concluded raising her head to catch the expression on his face, but none came.

"I know," he replied nodding.

"And our..." she paused, turning towards the maze.

"I'll give you a call," Ayo said quickly before she brought up the issue he never liked to think about.

✧

# Chapter 5

"Thought you did like your tea in bed sir," Mary said, shutting the door behind her. She dropped the tray on the tea trolley by Ayo's bed and brought out a telegram from her side pocket, dropping it by the tray.

"This came in not quite long sir," she continued pushing the trolley across the bed.

"Thanks," he said sitting up in bed before he picked the telegram.

The hairs at the back of his head stood on its end when he read the content of the telegram.

"Pass me the phone," he said without raising his head. Silently, he punched some numbers before he raised his head to meet her questioning eyes.

"Hope everything is okay sir?" she asked, concerned at the way he ignored his tea to attend to the message on the telegram.

"Its okay," he replied with a faint smile. "You can go now, I'll call you if I need something else."

"Yes," he answered when somebody spoke from the other side. "Can I speak with Cynthia please," he continued. "Oh, it's you," he paused realizing the cook was still by the door watching with concern. "Hold on please," he said into the receiver before covering the mouthpiece with his palm. "It's okay," he assured the cook, who was always concerned and curious whenever she noticed he was troubled.

"Hello," he continued, when the cook had shut the door behind her.

"Yes, who is this?" Cynthia asked

"Ayo speaking," he paused and continued when she did not speak. "I called to let you know I will do as you say."

"Does that mean a yes?" Cynthia asked.

"Yes," Ayo replied. "A yes, and we should start off as soon as possible."

"Say a month or two," she said but was surprised at Ayo's answer.

"Two weeks," Ayo simply said.

"If you want it that urgently, we could make it this afternoon, in the registry."

"No," Ayo replied. "I want a church wedding."

"A church wedding!" Cynthia exclaimed, "in two weeks?" She continued. "We can't have a church wedding in two weeks, not a societal one expected of me of course. My lawyer might just as well know it's a phony. Moreover, to get enough money out of the family's account, my lawyer has to see the bank manager who in turn will seek my brother's consent. Though…"

"I'll finance everything," Ayo cut her short. "Cut a beautiful wedding gown, with a veil not less than four meters long, and pearls to adorn neck. You will get enough invitation cards by tomorrow evening for your guests. Estimate everything you need and try send it to my secretary by tomorrow. Also, I will… Hello…?" He paused; confused realizing the line had gone dead. Shocked and perplexed, he punched the numbers again, and waited for her to pick the phone. The phone rang over and over again till Ayo thought it was best to drop the phone. Just then a click came from the other end followed by a faint

"Yes, what else."

"What happened?" he asked. "What went wrong?"

"Is there any other thing you require of me?" she asked, anger straining her voice.

"…But," Ayo paused. "I thought that was what you wanted."

"No," she replied. "Not what I wanted but what I needed for my company to survive."

"Well, is it not the same thing?" Ayo asked, not seeing any reason for her out - burst.

"No its not," she replied. "Do what is required of you and I will do mine. I never begged, and will never beg any man for a *kobo*."

"I was only trying to help," he protested but stopped when she continued.

"Thank you Mr. Richie rich, I will wear my mothers wedding gown. If you don't like it or your guests do not approve of it, you could always refuse to say I do when you are required to do so. I can take care of myself."

179

"How about other arrangements?" Ayo asked

"I'll hold a light reception immediately after the church service, and after that, if you like throw a wedding party at the Lagoon or invite the President, I care less."

"How about talking this over this afternoon. Maybe lunch? Do you mind? I..."

"I'm sorry, I am quite busy. Do anything you wish," she continued "...just make sure I am updated...well at least, on issues you think I should have a say. I..."

"It's okay," Ayo broke her off, "I'll call you when you're in a better mood. I..."

"Bye..." she concluded and the line went dead.
Surprised, he stared at the mouthpiece, before shaking his head.

"This sure isn't going to be easy," he said dropping the receiver.

He picked up the telegram and once again ran through it.

"Finishing my exams in less than twelve months. Hope you remember your promise, I've waited so long."

How in the heavens could she have taken me for my word he thought getting out of bed. He walked towards the bathroom, paused, turned around and walked back to the telephone. Swiftly, he punched some numbers and before a second ring, the secretary's voice filtered through the receiver.

"Yes Ekius Conglo...oh morning sir," she cut the long receptive story short when Ayo called her name in a sharp tone that told her he called for an important issue.

"Make all necessary arrangement for my wedding..."

"Sir..." she cut him short, unconsciously, surprised. "I meant..."

"Do as you are told lady," Ayo paused almost laughing, imagining the expression on her face.
"Make all necessary arrangements for a church wedding to hold in less than a month. See Sca' for details, and..." he added "...invite as many government functionaries as possible, including the Nigerian Ambassador to France.

"But Ayo," Sca' fumed in his office latter that day. "Why spend so much money on a wedding that won't last for over a month

"More than a month," Ayo corrected, sipping his drink.

"How do you mean?" Sca' asked, baffled. "Is she not due for her inheritance immediately you guys say I do, so…what's the delay?"

"Listen Sca'…" Ayo paused "…I have to get myself a wife before Glamour leaves school."

"Even then," Sca' interrupted. "Why a society wedding."

"If a society wedding," Ayo explained "…various newspapers will cover the event and foreign magazines, particularly if the France ambassador to Nigeria and ours to France are in attendance. This way, she would get the news in Paris before she leaves. Then, well… at least she can find herself a prospectful young man."

"Don't you think it will affect her exams, and if…"

"She'll get over it," Ayo cut him short. "It's better now when she can get herself hitched in the school than come back and be heart-broken. Do you know," he continued, "what it means for a girl to say she waited for six years? Don't you think she would feel I never got married because of her."

"Well…" Sca' shrugged. "I've always told you to get yourself a wife, so why are you complaining."

"Didn't I tell you to find one for me," Ayo joked…

"What is wrong with this Glamour of a girl, that you can't marry her?"

"She is Rex's daughter."

"So…?" Sca' asked disgusted at his reply.

"She is barely eighteen or, twenty at most."

"Then?" Sca' started but stopped when Ayo continued.

"She is supposed to be Amaka's Cousin."

"Oh…" Sca' said, thinking about the last excuse he gave.

"So, that is where the problem lies. Does it really matter?" Sca' asked.

"Of course it does," Ayo replied, "First Yinka, then Amaka. Who knows, maybe the ill luck that followed me with two of them might catch up with her. Moreover," he continued "…she is far too young, enough to be my daughter. I can't do that," he concluded shaking his head.

"It doesn't really matter you know," Sca' said after a moment of silence "…Not when it involves matters of the heart."

"Mmh…" Ayo smiled, "…matters of the heart. That is a figment of our imagination. It fades away, just at beginning."

"But…" Sca' paused when the phone rang. After the

second ring, Ayo picked up the phone.

"Yes," he said into the receiver. "Ayo on the line."

"Can you meet me in my office within an hour," Cynthia's voice filtered through the earpiece.

Slowly, Ayo sat up in his chair, looking at Sca' who was surprised at the way his friend adjusted himself in his chair.

"What for?" Ayo asked still staring at his lawyer.

"We have to talk. I just saw my lawyer and I think its best I let you in on some things."

"Then we are certainly not meeting in your office," Ayo protested. "I don't think I am in a mood for parting walls or..."

"You could use..."

"I'll be in my office, if we have to talk," Ayo cut her short.

"...But... I can't make it to Lagos Island in an hour, not with the traffic jam on Third Mainland bridge. More over..."

"Okay..." he paused, "I'll meet you at the restaurant in Sheraton hotel on Bank Anthony way in... err... Let's say, forty five minutes."

"Hello..." he said when she did not say anything. "Are you still there."

"Yes, I' ll be there," she said before dropping the phone.

"She wants to break it?" Sca' asked, looking into Ayo's eyes for an answer.

"No," Ayo replied. "She wants us to talk about something her lawyer said."

"Should I come?" Sca' asked getting up.

"I don't think it will be necessary," Ayo replied. "I'll call you, as soon as possible."

Sca' pressed a buzzer on the table before speaking into it.

"Tell Ben to bring..."

"No Sca', I'll drive myself. Please help tell him to prepare the Jaguar for me." Ayo concluded, getting up from his seat.

"I'll be at the chambers or in the club later in the day in case you need me," Sca' said before starting his car. "Make sure you don't take any drastic step without my knowledge," he concluded before taking his leave.

✧

# Chapter 6

*"H*i," he said pulling out a chair for himself. Sitting himself with a smile, he glanced at her plain angry looking face.

"H. e.. y," he tried again after pulling the chair closer to the table. "That is not a way to say hi to your husband to be or better still your fiancé," he laughed out loud, making her get more furious.

"Hope, you won't be as late as this on the wedding day?" she snorted.

"Oh," Ayo exclaimed, "am I late". He continued, taking a look at his wristwatch. He realized she must have been sitting there alone, for close to one hour.

"To be left sitting alone in a table for two, is enough public humiliation but, I don't think waiting at the altar for the groom would be anything near funny," she continued ignoring his off handedness.

"Come on, you know I would not do that," Ayo explained. "I stopped by at the printers, to get you a sample of the invitation card, in case you have any criticism to make," he concluded dropping an envelope on the table.

Ignoring the envelope, she gulped the remains of her lemonade.

"I see you don't take alcohol," he started calling one of the waiters with a snap of the finger.

"So…" he continued sitting back in his chair after taking his order. "What was your lawyer saying again."

Silently, she picked up the envelope, brought out the content and silently scrutinized the well-designed invitation card. Seeing she was not in a hurry to talk, he watched her till the waiter brought his drink. He half filled his cup with burgundy, took a sip, savored the taste, took another and was taking the third when she broke news. Sharp, abrupt and concise.

"I want a baby."

"Oohps," he choked, clearing his throat "Aha …aha." "You sure have a way of surprising people. First," he continued "…it was marry me. Now, it is I want a baby. See…" he paused to catch his breath "I have tried, at least to help you get your inheritance.

Now, try look for somebody else to do that for you or…"

"I am not asking you to sleep with me Mr. Ayo, I have made arrangement with my doctor to prepare for an artificial insemination."

She concluded looking straight at the astonished face across the table.

"Why don't you just get married and settle down with a man that will father your children instead of…"

"Thank you for your advice Mr. Ayo, I think I should have a right to live my life the way I want it."

"Oh… and if your so called baby gets deformed due to a mistake on the doctors part or if in the future the child wants to know the father."

"Simple…" she paused looking down into her empty cup. "He died when she was too young to know him."

"Oh… it must be a girl, or you have that planned out too."

"Not really," she shrugged. "Anyone will do, just that…"

"What is it with you," Ayo broke her off not understanding why she decides on weird things. "Do you think yourself too beautiful or too rich for any man? Or do you…"

"Err… Mr… Ayo," she started making him pause. "Do we have a deal?" she asked point blank.

"I don't think I can have my first child via an artificial insemination."

"I beg your pardon," she said raising her head to look at him. "This is going to be my child, and not our child."

"I am sorry," Ayo started, "I don't think I am interested in this particular part of the deal I…"

"So I take it you've opted out," she concluded daring him to confirm it.

"No… of course not," he protested "… I mean, err... well… the wedding still holds but…"

"No," she said abruptly. "You won't use me except you give me what I want."

"Use you?" Ayo asked surprised. "… But… this was all your idea, I mean," he paused but continued.

"I never intended to get married, not since… not since…

well," he paused looking up at her.

"Then why did you suddenly agree and what is the need for a publicity stunt."

"I wanted your lawyer to believe the…"

"Liar," she groaned. "You have a stupid plan, and if you decide to mess up my life, I will kill you."

At that, Ayo burst out laughing raising his glass to take a sip of his drink which he hadn't touched since it nearly choked him when she dropped her bombshell.

"You know something," he started. "I am beginning to like you, you know. With what do you intend killing me, those slim beautiful hands," he laughed again. "I doubt if they would want to do any such thing."

"I am not joking, Mr. Ayo. I…"

"I think we should be comfortable calling each other by our first names. The Mr. And Miss thing gives me the creeps, especially when we will soon become Mr. And Mrs." he said laughing as he refilled his cup.

"You should learn to call your husband by his first name," he continued. "Usually, marriages lasts that way or do you want people to start wondering…" he paused reaching out to grasp her hand when she made to leave.

"Excuse me," she said looking straight at him. " I want to leave," she concluded unflinching at his gaze.

"Please," Ayo said suddenly looking plain but she rose and made to shake off his grip. Suddenly, his voice rose in anger at her stubborn behavior.

"Will you please sit down," he said in a harsh tone, which made her stop to look at him.

"And who do you think you are to give me orders." She blurted out angrily.

"Please," he said in a soft tone getting up before he adjusted his suit.

"Walls have ears you know," he continued gently. "I wouldn't wants to find myself in front of the dailies tomorrow morning," he concluded gesticulating towards her seat.

"But I…"

"Please," he repeated, now nearly in a whisper.

After what seemed like hours, she slowly lowered herself

into her chair and stared at the table. Ayo joined her and gave her some minutes to settle down before he spoke.

"I'm sorry," he began. "I did not mean it the way it sounded," he continued, "I don't know why you are ever so cautious but honestly, I admire your intelligence, beauty and the smartness your person radiates. I guess I should let you know why I accepted your proposal."

Staring into his drink, he gave a summary of Glamour's proposal as a child and the telegram.

"You now see..." he concluded, "I have to make her realize I am not her type and the earlier she realizes that, the better. Funny enough, I still don't believe she meant the content of the telegram, but if she is the Glamour I knew, then every word in the message meant what it says. Mmh," he sighed raising his shoulder only to drop it all in a second.

"I' m sorry," she said. "It's just that..."

"Its okay," Ayo said motioning her to stop.
"If you would not mind telling me why you did not marry the fiancé I saw you with in Paris."

"He was a thief," she whispered. "All they want is a connection with my fathers business and I happen to be the only link to the top."

"And what is wrong in getting into your family business, you cannot manage it yourself... well, not alone I suppose," he corrected when she raised a brow "he should help you manage the helms of affair in your absence."

"Mmh," she smiled. "What do they know, all you'll hear is daddy wants this or my lawyer would see to it. They are a bunch of spoilt pampered dummies or some stone eyed thieves, just like my dad."

"What did you say?" Ayo asked surprised at her last statement.

"My dad was supposed to be a police inspector," she started. "He helped my mum on one occasion and in appreciation, my mum accepted to go on a date with him. Gradually, my mum fell for him but was blind to see he was after her money. She was from Switzerland, so she lacked the black mentally that would have cautioned her. She did not know blacks would do anything to get at you. Even if it means changing their names the other way round.

My mother, thinking she had seen an *Apollo* did everything to make him happy. Her father, a multibillionaire made sure she never lacked and threw a glamorous wedding for her. Not too long after the wedding, all her foreign accounts were emptied into his account. By the time it dawned on her, lots of damage had been done. Everything that was hers had legally been transferred to him. She threatened to leave but he blackmailed her. He wanted to make some things public. Things till today still beat my imagination. Bastard," she growled, "...she never told me what he had on her and the fact that she was carrying Sylvia, did not make things easier for her.

He married other wives with my mothers' money, and kept so many concubines that we still don't know how many of them bore bastards like him for him.

I guess she knew I would never get married, because I swore to her that no filthy hands would touch me. She probably was afraid I would not bear her a grandchild, so she laid down conditions for me to get my hands on my inheritance, which her and my father jointly owned but was single handedly controlled by my father.

She made me promise I would find myself a man. She said not all men were like my father, though hard to believe, but she assured me few were good.

Promise, yes I did, but how betrayed I felt when I read through her will and saw the laid down conditions.

My father, I guess died of hypertension. He must have developed high blood pressure when he realized he was left with barely half a million naira. My mothers' lawyer filed a suit against him as everything they owned was to be transferred to me on my mothers' death. Mmh... I guess he forgot it was documented or probably he thought I was too young but when I appeared in court, his face broadened in dismay. He slumped and died two days later.

You might not believe, but that was my happiest moment. I mean, when I heard about his death. I guess it was my light mood that made me follow my younger sister to a party, where I met Donald. It was like revenge. If for nothing but the fact that he died in agony, equaled the pain my mother went through.

After that day, I withdrew into my shell and prepared for

the task ahead; running my mothers empire.

I allowed Donald see me though, but all he cared about was partying and clubbing. He wanted to turn me to a fool, so he could use me.

Barely a month before our supposed wedding, which of course I managed to put up with due to the conditions in my mothers will. Getting married before getting a monotony of power over the empire is annoying enough but having an access to cash on the day I put to bed is something I never could live with. Well, not till now when it really is necessary. Having some filthy pig defy my body, is something I never can stand. Sorry you are a man, but it's unfortunate you fall in that genre.

As I was saying," she continued after a few minutes of silence. "Barely a month before our wedding, I walked into his sitting room, which usually was not locked," she added before shaking her head as a disgusting expression crossed her face.

"Sweet Mary," she exclaimed, "he could not even get to his room, before... before... well," she shrugged, avoiding his stare as she continued. "And the girl, as shameless as she was, she allowed him use her, right there on the carpet." She paused, shaking her head again. "Well, different strokes for different folks," she said making a face but quickly added. "Not that it really mattered to me though, but it only confirmed what would happen after the marriage. He should thank his stars, that I did not catch him after the marriage because, I would have emptied an eight round cartridge into his skull."

At the mention of a gun, Ayo smiled and wondered if she could handle one. The orientation she has about the opposite sex is one horrible one and he hoped someday, she would learn to give her heart to a man.

Then, he realized many men would give anything to have her hand in marriage but as busy as she is, she would not be opportuned to meet them. The few she probably met, at least one, happened to be the wrong one. Once beaten, they say, twice shy he thought. She did not think it necessary to have a second chance. How about him, he had been beaten twice and...

"So you see Mr. Ayo," she spoke, breaking into his thoughts. "You see why I need a child, and marriage to get what is mine."

"But why me?" Ayo asked watching her reaction. Surprisingly, she did not flinch.

"I think we should leave," she said picking up her bag.

"I insist you tell me," Ayo said not attempting to get up.

"Alright," she said getting up.

"Well..." he said, expecting an explanation.

"Well..." she repeated after him, looking down at him.

"So..." he said again waiting for her to sit down and continue the story.

"Let's get out of here. I get tired of sitting for too long, especially if it is not in my office."

"Oh..." Ayo said getting up. "So... I'll drop you at home..."

"My driver is outside, that won't be..."

"Send him home," Ayo said joining her as they made for the lobby. "I will drop you off at home later in the day."

" And where are we going?" she asked looking into his eyes for any sign of mischief.

"Actually, I have two tickets for a performance at the National Theatre this evening," he paused to glance at his wristwatch. "I guess we're just in time to meet up with the second show."

"You did not tell me you had a date," Cynthia said surprised. "I would not have..."

"It was meant for Sca'; my lawyer." He explained. "Femi Osofisans *farewell to a carnibal rage* is one play Sca' would not enjoy missing. He is a critic and enjoys watching stage plays where he can make criticisms, especially when we are together."

"And..." she started but stopped when he spoke, gently pulling her along.

"We can't stand here all day, we would miss the beginning."

"How about Sca'," she protested in the elevator.

"He can always get himself another one. For ones at least, I would watch a play without having to analyze every scene," he concluded laughing as they stepped out of the hotel.

✧

# Chapter 7

"Akanbi my love, we should not let the hatred between our fore fathers come in - between us."

"But Olabisi," Akanbi replied turning his back at her, "Your father killed my father."

"Yes," Olabisi replied, also turning to the audience before she continued. "...And your uncle killed my father."

Suddenly Akanbi turned around.

"Then the link has been broken," he shouted.

"Noo... Akanbi," Olabisi pleaded on one knee, "...the link shall be rewoven."

As they watched the play, she gets easily startled when an actor shouts on stage. Smiling at her naiveté. Ayo stretched out his right hand to pull her closer and to his surprise, she did not object. She leaned against him, letting her left shoulder rest on his chest.

"How is it?" Ayo asked.

"Sshh," she hushed at him. "She's talking."

"...Take your ring," Olabisi shouted in between sobs. "Take and I shall henceforth be free..."

"Why is the crying?" Cynthia asked, not looking up at him. "Isn't returning his ring removing lots of unnecessary burden off her shoulders. Well..." she sighed. "I guess, probably she is lucky enough to find a responsible one."

Surprised at her change of attitude, he asked, "Why can't you desire a man the way she does?" To his dismay, she did not flare up. She only raised her head to look at him.

"You know," she smiled, "I think I might probably just start to consider doing that. Who knows, I just might find my own Akanbi walk out of the moon," she concluded laughing.

At the end of the show, he was on the way to her house to drop her when she suggested they stop off at a Jazz Club downtown for some time off with their live band.

"You see," she started, when they were seated at the far end of the club. "I always thought life was as rosy as the folktales I read when I was young. You know, the beauty and beast, the Prince that kissed the sleeping beauty awake, the Frog Prince, and the likes. It was all so expecting.

A knight in a shiny amour comes up on a glittering horse to sweep you off your feet."

"It is my dear," Ayo interrupted, "But the mistake we make is that since the urge to meet this Prince charming has been stimulated, we tend to think every available person is the right one. We do not wait to think, we allow ourselves be ruled by the emotions of the heart.

Another thing we forget is that the course of true love is not a smooth one so we really have to be careful or else, we might opt out when things go wrong, thinking we are on the wrong track."

"You talk like you know what it takes to love a woman," she paused, looked down into her glass before she continued. "How I wish my mother met someone like you, I would not have suffered so much."

"I am no better than your dad," he replied placing a hand around her right hand wrapped around her glass. "I might even been worse"

"No..." she stopped him looking up at him.

"You are wealthy and not married, surprising at this age." She continued, looking away. "Many men would have filled their houses with wives and keep lots of concubines round the globe, but you did not do that.

You seem satisfied with the way you are. Can you fill my cup please," she paused waiting for him to refill her glass.

Ayo, knowing she does not take alcohol, was beginning to get scared because she had taken three shots of brandy already.

"I think you've had enough," he protested. "It might go straight into your head," he concluded corking the bottle after refilling his own glass.

"Now, don't start talking like them. If you can take more, I see no reason why I shouldn't."

"Okay," he accepted reluctantly pouring her a shot. She talked on about her childhood, her mum and the house till Ayo decided it was time they leave.

"I think we should leave," he said getting up before moving round the table to help her out of her chair. "You look tired," he observed on their way out.

"I sure am," she replied. "It was a long night," she continued "and a lovely one too," she added smiling.

"Aren't you coming in?" she asked in surprise when he pulled up in front of her porch. "For a drink at least, before you leave."

"I... err... err," he stammered before he shrugged and said. "Why not, but... what about the car."

"Leave it there," she said with a wave of the hand. "All the drivers must be asleep by now, and..." she paused. "Anybody that comes to see me at this hour definitely must be an invited guest and to my knowledge, there is nothing like that in my diary."

"Help yourself to some champagne," she said slumping into the sofa over looking the shelf.

"Please can you mix some lemonade and soda for me please," she called out. "I wouldn't mind some cubes," she added kicking off her shoes one after the other.

"This house is really big," Ayo complemented before handing over the glass of lemonade. It must have taken years to complete." He continued, taking his seat on a single chair opposite her.

"Is it divided into wings or its just one open house. I can imagine getting lost in it."

"It is not that difficult finding my way around. Mmh..." she smiled savoring the taste of her drink "not after so many years."

"Of course," he answered. "For you, it would not be difficult. Just like the maze, you must have..."

"The maze," she said suddenly, her eyes lightening up as she looked at him. "You should see its beauty under the full moon, it's a wonderful sight," she paused getting up.

"Aren't you going to see it," she turned to face him when she realized he did not make a move to get up.

"Oh..." Ayo said, raising his brows "just didn't want to bother you."

"C' mon, it's nothing," she waved her hand walking towards the wide glass doors.

"H -o - l - y  M - a - r -y..."

"Mother of Christ," Cynthia finished Ayo's sentence

allowing him to take in the sight that over looked the balcony.

The silvery rays from the moon made the hedges sparkle like diamonds.

Carried away by the beauty the night bestowed on the once scary maze, he moved closer to the railing, bumping into it, ignorant of the fact that he was moving. Shocked back to reality, he shook his head surprised at how hypnotized the scenery made him.

Giggling behind him, she spoke.

"You want to go inside, don't you?"

"Err... em... I don't..."

"I wouldn't advise you to, its better to be lost in the warmth of the house than in the cold, harsh harmattan dews of the night.

"Yeah... yeah, its such a captivating sight," Ayo replied turning around to face her.

"But it was not like this that evening," he continued. "I mean, that night, it was..."

"Actually, this happens only when the moon is full," she explained, "...that is when you really get the hypnotic effects. Alright," she continued turning to leave. "I think I should show you round the house before you decide to jump down there, hoping to grasp a handful of diamonds."

"Hope inside isn't as breath taking as that maze?" Ayo said following her, back into the living room sliding the glass doors shut behind him.

"Ha... ha... ha," she laughed, "That's left for you to decide." She paused in the middle of the room making Ayo stop, surprised. Looking round, she raised a finger. "Err... where should we start from... Okay," she said all of a sudden turning to her left.

"Let's start from the study," she continued as Ayo, whose gaze had followed hers all along followed with his hands in his trouser pockets.

In the study, Ayo ran a left finger along a giant mahogany bookshelf.

"This must be quite old," he said, staring at the tip of his fingers for any speck of dust.

"Yeah," she replied pulling out a drawer to take a bunch of keys.

"...And spotless too," Ayo continued. "I guess you have

someone polish all these furniture regularly."

"Every morning," she corrected, "one of the maid does that. You say that is old," she said straightening up after shutting the drawer. "Wait till you see the dining room. But before then, take a look at this." She concluded, pulling open a locked part of the shelf.

"*O-l-o-r-u-n - O...* err sorry I meant, Father in heaven." He quickly corrected, realizing he just spoke in his native tongue.

"Its okay," Cynthia said. " I hear, and can speak Yoruba a little. My mother had a flair for languages."

"Those shields," Ayo said moving closer to examine the shields, plaques, trophies and various medals that furnished the shelf.

"Who won all these?" he asked.

"Family treasures," she replied. Passed down the lineage from the past three generations.

"That means..." Ayo paused when she broke him short.

"Ahn...ahn, don't make me start any explanation. Giving you a concise history on those trophies might take the whole night. All I'll say is that my mum won that trophy in college. She used to be good on tracks."

"Father Lord," Ayo nearly choked at the sight of the mighty dining table made from either Mahogany or Iroko tree. The glossy surface was evidence that the mighty frame, more often than could be imagined, was given good treatment.

"Is this a conference room or a dining room?" he asked surprised at the size of the table. About twenty meters long, chairs lined both sides with a mighty chair at the end of the long, mighty but beautifully carved mahogany dining table.

From the dinning room, they entered a corridor that lead to four well-furnished guestrooms. The linen, which the blinds were made from and satin made bed sheets made Ayo wonder how the master's bedroom would look like. They went round the house till they entered a room, which immediately reminded him of the model chamber of the queen of England.

"Did the queen once live here," he couldn't help but ask. "I mean," he corrected himself, realizing how dumb his question was but aware of the fact that an helpless gesture could not help but arise in situations like this.

"...I mean," he repeated. "Did you buy the house from those British colonialist, or you built it." He concluded, walking towards the far end of the room, to a well arranged alter where a sculpture of Cleopatra, once queen of Egypt and Pharaoh amongst others, gave the impression of a catholic confession room.

He picked a marble cross on which a miniature of Christ was nailed, thorns of grass on his head and stared at it for sometime before he spoke.

"Never knew you were catholic," he said turning to look at her but stopped stunned seeing the strings of tears that ran down her face. She was carrying close to her chest a sculpture of Cherub; one of the second highest order of angels, similar to the gold plated statue in her office. The small wings on the plump child looked so angelic, and the innocence it was meant to portray was definitely of no doubt.

"That is beautiful," he said not knowing what to say.

Raising her head, she quickly wiped the tears off her face with the back of her left hand still clutching to the sculpture with the other as she moved to join him at the table.

"What did you say," she started, forcing a smile. "I'm sorry, I... I guess it's been long I cried. I mean, it's been long I really felt like crying. I must be going soft."

"Err... em... I..."

"Its okay," she cut in when she saw her behavior surprised Ayo.

"You were saying?"

"Err... yes..." Ayo stammered trying hard to avoid looking straight at her. "Err... I was just, I mean," he paused before continuing "...are you catholic?" he asked raising a shoulder in a gesture.

"My mother was a stench catholic. As the first granddaughter of sir Richards the forth, she had no choice but to be a devoted catholic. A habit, if I may call it..." she paused looking away at the contents that made the small alter.

"...A habit she couldn't leave even when she was a million square kilometers from home,"

"And that thing you are carrying?" Ayo asked, making her stare at the small piece she held.

"It was a gift to my mum from her grandfather on her

wedding day. It represents…"

"I know", Ayo answered before she could finish "…one of the first order of angels."

"Mmh." She smiled clutching to the object. "Isn't it beautiful?" she asked, more like a statement.

"And the bed?" Ayo asked. "I guess your mother was fond of it?" he asked trying to find out what brought tears to her beautiful eyes.

"She died in it," she corrected, walking back towards the bed.

"I was by her side when she bade goodbye to this world." She stopped by the bedside rocking the piece in her arms. "I begged her not to give up," she continued but she was too weak, she was…"

"Its okay," Ayo said, holding her by the shoulders. He gently turned her around to face him. Her eyes now swollen, red and moist that he could not help but pull her into his warm embrace

"That was a long time ago," he said, squeezing her against his chest in consolement, but to his surprise, her full softness against his body began to steer a feeling he long thought was dead.

"She was the only person that really loved me," Cynthia continued sobbing away as Ayo gently caressed her back. "When she died, I wanted to go with her. Go with her to the world beyond, to eternal peace, where I forever will see my fathers nauseating face no more."

"That would have been most irrational," he said. "It would…"

"You think so?" she asked, pulling back.

"Yes," he nodded. "The first thing that comes to your mind at times like that is usually not the best option but just a reflection of the mood. That which Predominates over the others is normally the best decision to take."

"Mmh," she thought for a minute before raising her head to look at his face but quickly looked away when her gaze met a pair of brown eyes starring down at her.
He gently lifted her face and dropped a kiss on her mouth, which to his surprise opened as if on reflex. Ayo raised his head to be sure he was not imagining things and there it was, her head tilted

backwards. Her face upward, with her eyes closed and mouth open in anticipation. Slowly be lowered his head. as they became engrossed in a deep heated kiss.

"Ohhh... please," she moaned, wrapping her hands around his neck. "Please," she started. "I'm not..."

"I know," he cut her short as he allowed his emotion take a better part of him. He let out all the passion bottled in him, touching, caressing and kissing her till she lost her senses.

Gradually they turned and tossed out of their cloths on the sacred bed and by the time the crickets voice became audible, what was once the sanctity of her mother had been soiled with the product of defiled purity.

The initial groan shocked Ayo as he realized what he had just done but like a spell bound horse, he rode straight to the finish line before he stopped to catch his breath.
As he rolled off, he noticed she was crying.

"Err... Cynthia," he started reaching out to wipe her face.

"Don't touch me," she said too weak to get up.

"I didn't..."

"Oh gawd," she groaned, making Ayo pause in confusion. "You animal," she continued. "I told you to stop, why didn't you stop? You are more experienced; you could have helped me control myself.
Oh...no," she sobbed. "My mothers bed, please leave. Just leave, now." She screamed, "l - e - a - v – e."

"I'm sorr..." He went mute halfway when she shouted.

"Leave please Mr. Arigbabuwo, or I'll call the police."

Ayo knew the police was a bluff but he was ashamed of himself and could not help but consider himself a fool. Silently he got out of the bed but stopped shocked, to stare in bewilderment at the sight of the stained bedsheet.

"Okay," he tried again when he could regain his voice. "How about helping you to... I mean to," he paused, "...to clean up this mess."

"Clean up what," she scowled at him suddenly gaining enough energy to sit up in bed. "Clean what," she repeated. "You've just broken the only link, between my mother and I. You didn't even... oh no, how could you have been so heartless. I told you my mother died... oh gawd. Please go, please," she cried.

197

Quickly, Ayo slipped into his pair of trousers and then his shirt before sliding into his pair of shoes. He silently picked up his jacket and left without a word.

# Chapter 8

*"A*re you sure you should not have shifted the wedding forward, after that err... incident," Sca' explained. "I should think that, after all... well," he shrugged, avoiding the real issue, trying as much as possible to be professional.

"She should hate you so much now, that she would rather die then live you." He continued on their way out of the house to the convoy of cars that lined up in his compound.

"Yes," Ayo answered waiting for a uniformed Chauffeur to open the door of a well polished sparkling white '99 model Lincoln for him to step into his side of the back seat. After Sca' had entered through the other side, he continued. "She'll hate me so much, but not enough to put on hold the mining deal"

The beautiful Lincoln hissed, balancing on its four wheels immediately the Chauffeur release the hand brake. It slowly soared after the array of cars, ahead in the convoy, with equally glamorous cars lined up behind them.

Sca' smiled to himself in self-satisfaction at the thought of the expression that would come to peoples face when they arrive the St. Benedict Cathedral. He made sure all the cars were decorated and lined in a convoy, even if it meant going for the service without carrying anybody.

"We would need to convey some of our guests to the reception, after the service. Ikeja is quite a distance from the Island you know," he defended himself when Ayo exclaimed at the array of cars Sca' arranged to be decorated. The two Navigator jeeps that lead the convoy was practically empty but for the drivers and a bodyguard each. A black Lexus trailed behind, conveying some members of the bridal train, smartly dressed in various internationally designed outfits. Ayo's white rolls followed with only the Chauffeur a bodyguard and Ayo's aged mother. The other limousines trailed behind followed by the Lincoln, as long as two limousines joined together. Six other cars followed, four various classes of Mercedes Benzes cars, including the C-class, E-class, S-class models. Two B.M.W. jeeps trailed at the end of the convoy.

The hold up on the third Mainland Bridge, was a major headline on the Network News later that day. The Sunday papers also flashed various headlines, blotting most front pages with clips of the most glamorous wedding of the year. One in particular emphasized on the beauty of the white Millipede, referring to the custom built Lincoln.

Applause welcomed them when they stepped out of the car to see the large crowd that has gathered at the fairly large compound of the St. Benedict Cathedral church in Ikoyi, Lagos.

Bending his waist a little, Ayo gave a slight bow in acknowledgement of the cheers and applause from the crowd.

"Oh... Gawd," Sca' groaned beside him, smiling and nodding in different directions to acknowledge the cheers from the crowd. "If only Cynthia would just appear, to crown my efforts. I've done my best haven't I?" he asked looking at Ayo for any word of encouragement.

"Ah...ah," Ayo laughed, leading the way along the red carpet that ended some inches away from his car.

"Nobody asked you to show off..."

"Ohh, that is all the thanks I get *ehn*." Sca' grinned behind him, absolutely not pleased at what Ayo just said.

"Relax boy," Ayo quickly said before Sca' started a protest.

"She'll come," he continued looking back at Sca' as they moved along, "...trust me," he concluded.

Almost immediately, a thought that had never once before occurred to him, crossed his mind.

"How about if she decides not to show up," but he quickly shook off the thoughts as his mind went back to events that happened in the past two weeks.

Ayo had thought Cynthia would call him later that morning, after the way he left her house. He had avoided calling her, as what to say always eluded him each time he tried. When after a week, she still did not call him on the phone or send any message as regards their arrangement; he summoned enough courage to give her a call only to be told that she had traveled to Senegal on a business trip.

"When is she due to be back?" he had asked the secretary when he recovered from the bombshell.

"She did not really specify when sir, she only promised to

call when she gets to Senegal but she has only sent in a telegram that she is safe."

Ayo tried every now and then to get in touch with her, praying hard against all odds particularly if she decides to back out of their business agreement, all because of one unfortunate night.

"Err... Ayo," Sca' whispered across to him, tapping him before poking him in the rib when he saw Ayo's mind was far away.

"Err... err... yes," Ayo said shaking his head to clear off the series of thoughts that was building up in it.

"Look," Sca' continued, allowing his jaw drop as his mouth fell wide open.

Ayo looked up at the direction Sca's gaze was fixed and a long whistle escaped his lips.

A helicopter was about landing in the middle of two long charcoal black six door convertible limousines. Immediately the helicopter touched the ground, the secretary got down from the limousine behind the helicopter and hurried to help Cynthia climb down from the dragon fly that still hovered a few inches from the ground, making all the grass bow at the strong wind from the horizontal revolving blades.

Cynthia climbed down, holding up the tail end of her white gown, followed closely behind by her sister. As she walked away from the helicopter, the veil kept crawling after her making everyone agape, wondering if it had an end. Just as their curiosity was about to be confirmed, a ruffled end crawled out and her secretary was quick in grabbing the tail end, supported at the other side by Sylvia before they walked towards the red carpet.

Cynthia paused at the beginning of the long carpet and slipped her left hand into the void her lawyers' elbow created when he raised his right hand and slowly they made their way into the church. A few meters into the church, the secretary dropped the tail end of the veil to allow it spread across the aisle, crawling steadily behind her, as the bell chimed to the rhythm, "here comes the bride, here comes the bride."

At the steps leading to the chancel, the lawyer handed over her hand to Ayo for the last few meters to the alter, which usually is the most memorable and longest distance in ones life, a jaunt into matrimony.

Sca' and Sylvia, stood at the edge of the transept as the best man and chiefs bridesmaid, waiting to welcome the wouldbe couple. At this particular moment, the congregation was very quiet, everyone, eager to hear the wedding proceedings.

"Who giveth this woman to be married to this man?" the reverend father asked, looking at the large congregation of guests and well-wishers.

"I do," the lawyer replied, standing up.

After adjusting his suit, he walked towards the couple, took Cynthia by the hand and handed her over to the officiating minister. The reverend father received Cynthia's hand, causing Ayo's right hand before he placed Cynthia's right hand in his.

"Ayodele Arigbabuwo," he started. "Do you take Cynthia Howard Rhodes, to be your lawfully wedded wife? To have and to hold, from this day forward, for better for worse, for richer for poorer, in sickness and in health, to love and to cherish, till death do you part, according to Gods holy law?"

"I do," Ayo replied and the Reverend father repeated the same lines, now addressing Cynthia.

As the reverend father recited the lines, Ayo's mind began to reflect on what the reverend just said. "To be your lawfully wedded wife," "for better, for worse," "to love and to cherish," "till death do you part."

To think that they stood in the holy house of God to take an oath they do not intend to keep gave Ayo goose pimples. The fact that they deceive the congregation that they love each other even made things worse. The sharp "I do," from Cynthia broke into his thoughts, making him turn to look into her face. She looked blankly into the future, at her inheritance that would help save her company from collapsing, at the fact that this would only be for a short while.

She probably had arranged with another lawyer to file a divorce which if tendered in less than a month after their phony wedding will not take him by surprise.

He then turned to hand over the rings into the pastors waiting hands.

"Bless these rings O Lord, and grant they that will wear them the strength to keep true faith…"

"Oh g - a - w – d," Ayo groaned, what extent humans will

202

go to get their selfish desires. To think Cynthia stood by him as the pastor officiated without any sign of guilt suddenly gave him a nauseating feeling.

As the charge flowed back to his mind, he wondered what fate awaited him on judgement day because the minister gave him a last chance to confess before the sacred ceremony proceeded but what could he do, it was all business.

"I require and charge you both," the reverend father began. "As you will answer at the dreadful day of judgement, when the secrets of all hearts shall be disclosed." The reverend father paused and Ayo's heartbeat increased, as he could not help but think that something might go wrong but no sooner did he continue.

"That if either of you know any reason, why you may not lawfully be joined together in holy matrimony, speak it or forever hold your peace."

When none of them spoke, Ayo picked one ring from the reverends palm and slipped it into Cynthia third finger reciting his lines but did not feel as stupid as when she was reciting hers.

"Take this ring as a token of my love," she said looking into his eyes with the same expressionless look before she slipped the other ring around Ayo's third finger.

Swiftly, she turned to face the pastor who happily joined their hands to proclaim them man and wife.

"Those whom God has joined together, let no man put asunder.

For as AYODELE and CYNTHIA, consented together in holy wedlock. God being our witness, and in the presence of this congregation. I pronounce them, man and wife. You may kiss the bride."

And the moment finally came, the moment most couple look forward to. When they give each other, their first official kiss. But, instead of a joy filled fluid smeared kiss, Ayo unveiled her face to see the venom dancing in her eyes. With his right hand, he raised her chin and kissed her unparted lips, raising his head just in time to see the wrinkle across her forehead before it disappeared.

From the church, they drove straight to the Sheraton Hotel and Towers where a light reception was held to host the guests with the Juju maestro, king Sunny Ade on the bandstand.

Later in the evening, a buffet was organized in Ayo's

mansion at the peninsula. Ayo and Cynthia were at the entrance to the ballroom, welcoming guests when he noticed a frown on Cynthia's face.

"Can you please manage a smile," Ayo whispered tilting a little to her side without taking his eyes off the Governor, who at that moment was just walking in with his wife, both clad in a Navy blue lace material. Both, matching theirs with a pair of blue shoes and headgear sewed from what looked like an expensive *aso-oke*. The governor's gold plated staff of office and his wife's combination of gold necklace, clutch bag, earrings, wristwatch and bangles added the glamour required of an Excellency.

After the party commenced, with a toast to the bride and bridegroom, Ayo sipped a glass of burgundy brandy while he watched Rex dance with Cynthia.

"Funny old man," Ayo said to himself allowing a smile cross his face. Rex had left Wendy with Sca' and walked up to them not quite long after they opened the dance floor.

"Lucky boy," he started, giving Ayo a firm hug before turning to Cynthia.

"And you woman…"

'H -e -y," Ayo countered, "…that's my wife you're talking to remember," he concluded, laughing.

"Alright, my dear young lady," he corrected himself, laughing.

"You look tired," Rex commented, not bothering to give any compliments "or…" he continued "…Ayo is not taking good care of you. Alright," he said taking her hand from Ayo. "Dance with me and after the dance, you can choose who you prefer. Ayo or my humble self." he concluded taking a bow before moving to the rhythm of the saxophonist.

Ayo walked Rex and Wendy to the porch and talked with Rex for some minutes, before Rex finally entered beside Wendy allowing the Chauffeur shut the door before moving round to take his seat behind the wheels.

# Chapter 9

As they left, Ayo took a deep breath suddenly wishing other guests were still around. Rex and Wendy were the last to leave and the fact that he would be all alone with Cynthia, was one thing he never wanted to look forward to.

He finally entered the living room and saw her by the sliding doors that overlooked the pool.

"Thought you had gone upstairs," he said trying to strike a conversation.

Without turning back, she spoke.

"Just didn't want to leave without saying good bye."

"You what?" Ayo asked, not wanting to believe what she just said.

"I am flying to Kaduna in my helicopter, where I can board a plane to Switzerland without attracting the press." She then paused and turned to face him before she continued.

"I also wanted you to know that I agreed to continue with the wedding plan, not because of my inheritance… well, not after what you did in my house. I came because…" she paused "…because I wanted to give my child a father." She concluded, almost in tears as she leaned back on the sliding door, holding on to her stomach with her left hand before she covered her mouth with her right hand. Slowly she went down in a crouch before she continued.

"You animal, you violated my innocence. You…"

"No… Cynthia," Ayo started, making to go close to her.

"Don't touch me," she said, regaining her Leopards might. Suddenly, her facial expression hardened and she rose to her feet, ignoring his caring gestures. She moved towards the cabinet, stood with her back to him for some minutes before she spoke. Ayo, disorganized could only watch helplessly, too short of words. "Baby," he thought, "father," he could not believe it. It was all like a dream but Cynthia's voice brought him back to reality.

"I want to go far away, where I can see your evil f ace no more. Because of you, I sold my house; the only memory of my childhood. How would I have left it when you soiled that sacred bed, the only place I see my mother when I get lonely? I could not enter the room again, not after that night, not even till I sold it." She turned to face him and the venom in her eyes made his marrow go cold.

"Ayodele Arigbabuwo, I will never forgive you." She said abruptly before she turned and walked towards the staircase but he blocked her path, making her come to a halt some inches away from his fairly large frame.

"Will you please get out of my way," she scolded and quietly Ayo backed off but gave her no room to pass.

"Please," Ayo said in a soft voice. "Should I fall on my knees, before you can give me a chance to talk," he continued slowly lowering himself on one knee.

She did not move but quickly averted her eyes, staring at the mighty Piano at the end of the large living room.

"Cynthia," he called but continued when she did not answer. "Please, sit down and let me tell you a story, just this last time. When I finish my story, you can go to anywhere that pleases you, if you still want to, then I would not feel any sign of guilt.

Just this once," he added when she turned her gaze from the Piano, to stare at her legs.

"Please Cynthia, sit down, just for ten minutes. Please, I beg of you, ten minutes."

After what seemed like hours, Cynthia turned without uttering a word, walked straight to a single chair and lowered herself into it.

"All my life, I have always had this bad luck trailing every good thing that happened to me. Apart from my business, nothing more gave me happiness. Thirty-two years ago, I fell in love with a girl who left for The States when she realized I joined a fraternity, which I did to protect us both. I married her friend some five years. She was always around. She was the only one that made me see reasons with life. She was the pillar that prevented me from falling because never had I loved a woman that I did Amaka. Yinka, her friend on the other hand, had her own problems. We tried to have a child for years, but had one complication or the other. All in the bid to make me happy, she lost her life in the process of childbearing. Her death was a great loss to me and since then, nothing else made sense. I buried myself in the stressful task of building an empire and that empire I have today.

"Just as I was resigning myself to fate, Amaka appeared from the blues but before we could put things together, they killed her. In cold blood... well, in any case since then, I have never known a woman. I had since accepted the fact that I will never father a child.

"Then you came along, with the idea of marriage. A phony though, but I feared the ill luck that had followed me, that which infected and ate badly into anything that could make me happy, might also come to you.

"I know you have little or no knowledge about my past life or you would not have chosen me to help you get at your inheritance.

"Under normal circumstances, I would have backed out of the deal or, never even have given it a thought after our first meeting. I mean, in your office complex," he quickly added to clarify the meeting he meant.

"But, for Glamour I would not have agreed to play along. I needed a smoke screen to allow her go on with her life, and you needed your inheritance. It was all a formal arrangement, a mutual agreement and now, that you have your side of the bargain, now that you can get your hands on your inheritance you want to leave. Have you ever thought of my own side of the bargain, how will Glamour feel if she hears I got married today and in less than a week, my wife is gone?

"Don't you feel she might see it as a chance to leave school and come over to see me." Slowly, Ayo lowered himself, sitting legs outstretched on the thick Persian rug, resting his back on the long sofa.

"Mmh," he sighed, folding his legs. "Why are you doing this, why can't you just keep your own side of the bargain. I wouldn't..."

"You broke the rules, you were not supposed to touch me. So, why cry foul play. Why blame me, why..."

"Cynthia please," he drawled, not wanting to raise an argument.

"All I ask is for you to stay in your room, for as long as... well," he shrugged. "Not less than a month anyway. You can travel using my credit card or any of my cars. That way, tongues won't start wagging. I am sorry I... err..." he paused, but continued, "I... well, violated your... err innocence since that is how you choose to put it but I swear by my future, I did not mean any harm. Never have I raped a woman, but what happened, it was only human. Forgive me if I have wronged you, and, I promise that I will never touch you or intrude on your privacy. If need be, we talk, we can talk via an intercom. If it pleases you, eat in your room or the dining room. As a matter of fact, from this day henceforth, I will eat in my room. If I ever cross your path or violate any of the laid down rules, then you can leave. Even without saying goodbye."

Quietness engulfed the tension filled atmosphere for some minutes before she spoke. "Is it safe to stroll in your compound at night."

"Yes," he replied. "Though I don't have a magic maze, but I have a well cultured garden and my golf pitch overlooks the beach. Guards keep watch round the clock, so I presume its safe."

Without a word, she got up and made for the stairs but with the speed of lightening, Ayo jumped up, blocking her path again.

"So..." he said his voice almost inaudible.

"Will you get off my path, before I change my mind." She said, looking straight into his face and like a spell bound clown, he stepped aside and watched her climb the flight of stairs into his life.

Before I change my mind, her last sentence kept echoing in his head as he tossed and turned in his bed, trying to catch some sleep. The phone rang, and he thanked his stars for an excuse to get out of bed.

"Hello," he said into the receiver.

"Congratulations," the voice came from the other end of the line.

"Thank you. But who is this?" Ayo asked wondering why the caller was too anxious to wish him well without letting out her identity.

"Glamour on the line," the caller replied. "Sorry I didn't let you know earlier, I guess I couldn't just wait to congratulate you."

"Oh," he paused. "Thank you," he continued. "That was thoughtful of you."

"No... Ayo, don't get me wrong," she continued. "I probably was too young to realize the implication of you marrying me, but guess what?"

"Yes?" Ayo asked, surprised at her enthusiasm.

"I am engaged to be married in eight months. Isn't that wonderful?" she paused allowing her message sink into Ayo's head.

"Glamour," his sharp tone cut into the mouthpiece.

"You don't jump into relationships, especially marriage. It is a sacred thing and also full of..."

"And if I may ask, Mr. Professor." Glamour broke him off. "What right have you, to lecture me?"

"Err... see," he paused but she did not stop to hear what he had to say.

"I only called to invite you to my wedding and to let you know that I have a surprise for you." She paused but continued when she saw Ayo could not say anything, "Oh don't try to guess, because you won't guess right. I can bet my life on it."

"Happy honey moon uncle," she concluded, dropping the receiver before he could say anything.

Ayo only stared at the receiver, lost at what to do. After a few minutes, he started punching some numbers but stopped on second thought.

"If Rex needs my advice, he will surely call me." He said to himself, dropping the receiver before he surrendered himself to the forces of sleep.

# Chapter 10

Glamour had left on her mothers' advice, back to Paris with the intention of burying herself in her studies.

Lost in thoughts, she strolled on, in the departure lounge with a file, a handbag and an overcoat hanging loosely across her left hand.

"Oohpps," she gasped letting out the file she held as she collided with a young man hurrying to confirm his ticket.

"Err... sorry madam," the youngman said, confused whether to go on or bend down to pack the content of the file the pretty lady just dropped.

On a second thought, he quickly bent down, hurriedly packed the Papers, arranged them neatly in the file before straightening up to hand over the file.

Glamour, startled, almost collapsed on seeing who bumped into her.

"No, this can't be real." She said not wanting to believe she was not dreaming.

"Madam," the stranger said, poking her Tommy with the file.

The voice she thought, Ayo could not possibly be in Nigeria and in The States at the same time.

"Please madam, I have not yet confirmed my booking," his voice tore into her thoughts. "Can I be of help in any way," he continued smiling.

"Err... no. Thank you," she said collecting her file before she turned and hurried away. "My mind must be playing tricks on me," she said to herself resisting the urge to look back.

"Bonjour senorita," he said taking a bow. "I think I will take this seat," he continued lowering himself to the seat beside her on board an Air France plane enroute to France.

Ignorant of the expression of bewilderment on her face, he made himself comfortable.

"Yeah, I can see the screen quite clearly from here. I am short sighted you know."

The humour, the way he curved his lips was so familiar that she nearly screamed.

"You know," he paused, his attention still focussed on the screen on which a movie was about to begin.

"The way you looked at me back there, I could have... Well, maybe I look like somebody you know because since I booked my ticket, I have pressed the search button in the small computer I call my brain and can swear I have never set my eyes on you. My memory is one thing I can count on, if nothing else. But the way you stared," he concluded lifting his shoulders and allowing it to fall in a helpless gesture.

"Who is your father?" she asked, before she realized she had been too forward. "I 'm sorry," she apologized when his head turned sharply to look at her. "I mean," she tried to explain, averting her eyes. "Err..."

"Dr Frederick Peters," he answered, more out of curiosity. "Or, do you know him?" he asked, narrowing his eyes.

"No." She replied, looking out of the window. "Just wanted to know,"

"Don't tell me you are one American looking for her roots, or precisely her lost brother and father."

"Of course not," Glamour replied. "My parent stay in Atlanta, Georgia. You look like..." she paused, but continued after letting out a sigh.

"...You look like someone I once had a crush on..."

"Ooh... my," the stranger exclaimed, "I am flattered. Hope that crush extends to me, his look alike. M - e - n, I don't know you but if an angel like you ever gets to have a crush on me, I'd rather turn my back to the world than let her down."

Ignoring his compliment, she looked out of the window, staring at the crowded New York airport.

"I would understand if you want to be left alone," he said when he noticed she did not respond in the least to any of his compliments. "You don't seem to feel too well, maybe I should just allow you rest. In case you feel like talking, I'll be at the back," he concluded making to get up.

"Please don't go," she said suddenly reaching out to touch his arm but quickly withdrew it when she realized he was embarrassed.

"I'm sorry," she apologized, looking away. "I mean," she paused not knowing what to say. "I mean," she repeated. "Its okay if you sit down. I guess I just can't wait to get back to France and put some memories behind for good."

"Mmh," the stranger started, leaning back into his chair. "Bad memories," he continued, "let me see," he paused. "Okay, you went to see your fiancé and you caught him in bed with your best friend."

Surprised at his outspokenness, she turned to look at him and they both laughed.

A month later, Glamour called her dad to break the news of her engagement to Johnny.

"G - a - w - d," Rex groaned. "Are you sure you are doing the right thing?"

"Papa." Glamour called. "Don't take it that way, I have never been so sure in my life. After my exams this summer, we will come over to The States and then, to Nigeria for our wedding."

"Why Nigeria?" Rex asked, getting a wrong notion.

"He wants the wedding done in his home town papa, he…"

"Is he a Nigerian?" Rex asked surprised.

"Yes papa, he is very nice, humorous and intelligent. If after you meet him, you still don't approve of the marriage then papa, I swear that I will break the engagement."

Thinking of what Glamour just said, he thought it was worth giving them a chance.

"Alright," he said. "When are you coming over?"

"Six months..." she paused, "...maybe less."

"That soon?" Rex said surprised. "Or... have you… err… I mean are you…"

"Papa," she said gently cutting her fathers' sentence. "I'm still very much a virgin if that is what you mean, I haven't slept with him yet…"

"Glamour!" Rex exclaimed, surprised at his daughter outspokenness.

"I… err, well… I didn't mean it that anyway. I know you wouldn't do a thing like that, so…err," he continued, "I guess we'll look forward to your coming home."

"Alright Papa, I love you."

# Chapter 11

*"B*ig daddy," Ayo exclaimed recognizing Rex's voice on the phone. "Where are you calling from," he continued removing his glasses.

"My house, in Ikoyi."

"What…" Ayo exclaimed. "When did you come in?"

"Just last night… you know Glamour's wedding is in a week time, and we have to get some things in place before then. You will come won't you," he paused

"Of course… I will." Ayo answered. "Glamour has never given me a chance to give an excuse. For the past eight months, she has been calling me, reminding me to keep that day free of any business appointment."

"That reminds me," Rex started. "How about coming over this evening, with your wife. I want you to meet the young man. He is really an idol."

"Really?" Ayo asked, surprised at Rexs' seriousness. "Why not," he continued. "I'll come," he paused then said slowly. "My wife, she is not feeling too fine. After she put to bed you know she needs to rest."

"Okay," Rex said, aware of the fact that Ayo always found one excuse for Cynthia's absence at any public function. "I think it would be better if we come over. Four of us… err let's see, Okay," he concluded. "Lets say seven o'clock this evening. That should be okay with you, or should we…"

"Thanks Rex, you've always been an understanding friend. I will expect you."

"C'mon Ayo," Rex drawled. "I think I want to see that little girl of yours. Whom did you say she looks like?" he asked.

"Like Cynthia's mother," Ayo replied. "It was like reuniting her and her mother again. Since she put to bed," he continued "…she has done nothing other than hold tight to her baby."

"But…" Rex paused on second thought but spoke all the same. "Is she still planning on filling a divorce?"

"I don't know Rex. She does not come out of her room and of course you know I don't go there, except when Sca' is around.

He seems to be the only one that can talk to her."

"Alright," Rex sighed. "I'll see you later today," he continued, not wanting to engage any further in the conversation because once they started talking on Ayo's private life, it usually lasts for hours.

"Okay Rex," he replied. "Thanks once again," he said before dropping the receiver. He stared at the intercom for a while before finally picking the handset.

The phone rang on and on till the line went dead. He punched three numbers again and waited till the line went dead before he quietly dropped the piece back on its cradle. Ayo stared into the mirror on the wall for some minutes before he turned as if on reflex and left the study.

Slowly, he turned the handle when no answer came from within after a tap on her bedroom door, but paused when he saw she was asleep. She was sleeping with the baby lying on her bosom, her hand around her possessively. He watched her for some minutes, adoring the scenery they gave, mother and child. As he turned to leave, gently pulling the door behind him, she spoke making him stop in his tracks.

"Do you have to be a peeping Tom to see your daughter," she said opening her eyes.

"Not really," he replied stepping back into the room before he shut the door. "Just did not want to wake either of you," he added now by the bed.

"The buzz of the intercom is enough to wake us, so why think we should still be asleep. Why not just come if you want to say anything, instead of using an intercom."

"Thought you wanted your privacy," Ayo Protested.

"Not when I now have a girl, my baby, our child. You can come and see her. I mean, you don't have to wait for Sca' before you see your girl do you."

"Yeah," Ayo replied, taking his seat on a single chair close to the window. "So I presume you now see me as less dangerous," he continued, "to grant me free access to your room or..." he paused.

"Of course I know you will be harmless now," she said a smile crossing her lips before she continued. "You can't rape me with Yetunde around, can you?" She concluded giggling.

"It's a free world," Ayo shrugged. "Say whatever you want," he continued. "You own your mouth." He concluded, not paying attention to her sensitive jokes.

"So what brings you or what was so urgent that after you called and I refused to answer, you summoned enough courage to look me up."

"Rex called," Ayo explained sitting on the edge of the seat on impulse. "He said he would be coming over later this evening with Wendy and the young couple; Glamour and her fiancé," he added allowing the message sink. When she did not speak, he continued.

"He had wanted us to come over but I explained that you were not strong enough to leave the house yet, so he decided to come over since that will provide him an opportunity to see Yetunde, and you to see the couple. He…"

"Cut the long story short," Cynthia Said at last, when she realized Ayo was beating around the bush. "You want me," she continued "…to come down for dinner isn't it?" she asked.

"Err… actually," Ayo started, taken off guard. "Not if you are still weak you know, but really, I think…"

"Who told you I was weak?" Cynthia asked Ayo, enjoying his confused state.

"Well…" Ayo said making gestures with his hands. "I thought after… err… actually," he paused not knowing how to explain himself.

"You'll be down-stairs wouldn't you?" he simply asked.

"That was what you should have done since, ordered me to come down for dinner."

"I'm not…" Ayo paused about to protest but she did not give him a chance, she continued.

"You are the husband, aren't you? You are supposed to be the boss, or…" she stopped when Ayo called out her name.

"C - y - nth - ia," Ayo drawled. When will you stop all this, when will you start looking at things from a different angle.

"Ahh…" she answered, "so I have been abnormal since…"

"Please Cynthia," Ayo called.

"What?" she replied.

"Are you coming?" Ayo asked.

"I don't…" she stopped as Ayo's plead interrupted her statement.

"P - l - e - a - s - e," he drawled, staring at the floor. "Honestly, I did not bargain for all this, I just…"

"Okay I'll come," she said as her baby stirred.

"Thanks," was all Ayo could say before he got up and walked towards the door. "7 p.m." He added before opening the door, not attempting to look back before he shut the door behind him.

"Big daddy," Ayo exclaimed, hugging Rex at his doorstep. Pulling back, Rex exclaimed

"Boy - o - boy! You look good my friend," he continued sizing him up. "Cynthia is sure taking good care of you," he concluded looking towards Cynthia before leaving Ayo and taking Cynthia into his arms.

Realizing Rex was just trying to play his way into Cynthia's heart, he ignored the compliment and simply gave Wendy a slight peck on both cheeks before looking up to see the young would be couples who had stood all the while watching the scene created by the reunion of two old couples.

Glamour's full-blown figure took him by surprise because he hadn't seen her in some years, but the young man beside her knocked the breath out of him for what seemed like hours. Ayo could not believe what he was seeing because, to him, it was like staring at himself in a mirror some twenty-five year's back.

"Won't you hug me too?" Glamour asked when she saw Ayo got the surprise she really wanted him to get.

Like a dummy Ayo's hands went out and she went into his embrace squeezing herself deep against his chest before pulling back.

"Uncle," she started, "...meet John Peters." She continued, turning to face Johnny who stood there embarrassed at the way their host stared at him.

"Darling, meet Ayo Arigbabuwo, my adopted uncle."

"It's a pleasure sir," the young man said, taking a slight bow.

"Come in," Ayo said, jerking out of his reverie.

## *Chapter 12*

*A*s they ate in the dining room, Ayo wondered who the young man was and how it was they had such striking resemblance. He was not the only one stricken by the strange resemblance because Cynthia kept wondering if the two men could pass for twins especially, when age difference was written off.
Suddenly, an idea occurred to her. There was only one way to satisfy her curiosity, she had to ask some questions.

"What do you do?" she asked Johnny, surprising Ayo and Rex.

"He is a..."

"Glamour," Rex called, "Johnny can speak for himself can't he?"

"P - a  - p - a!" Glamour exclaimed, embarrassed and shocked at the fact that her father did not think it wrong correcting her in public.

"Its okay love," Johnny said reaching out to touch her hand before squeezing it in consolement. "I'm a medical doctor," he continued. "My father has always wanted me to become one, so that I can manage his chains of hospitals.

"You mean your father is a doctor?" Ayo asked surprised, making every head at the table turn towards his direction.

"Yes sir, he owns St. Nicholas hospital, Dr Fr..."

"Frederick Peters," Ayo concluded making the young man look on in surprise.

"You know him?" Rex asked. Getting interested in the discussion.

"Yes," Ayo answered focusing his attention on his food. "We go a long way," he paused. "A long way," he repeated, before picking his glass of wine.

There was silence at the table for some minutes as nobody wanted to ask any question that might reveal what most of them are afraid might be true - a link, relationship, blood relationship, between Ayo and Johnny.

Rex broke the silence clearing his throat before turning to

Cynthia.

"How is the baby?" he asked.

"Fine thank you," Cynthia replied. "She should be down in ten minutes," she continued but paused when Rex spoke.

"Don't tell me she has started walking already."

"Don't be funny," Wendy defended. "She probably meant the maid or her nanny would bring her down stairs."

"Oh…" Rex said, trying to cut a piece of the chicken thigh in his plate. "Hope… ohpps," he gasped, dropping his fork and moving back simultaneously as pepper splashed from his plate onto his *babariga*.

Immediately, Glamour who was closest picked a serviette and tried wiping off the stain from her fathers white expensive *Guinea brocade*.

"Ah… ah…" Wendy laughed. "Reminds me," she continued "…of the first night Rex visited my house, at my parents request of course," she added. "He was becoming elusive. Rex splashed pepper on his three-piece suite because he was nervous and my mother had to have him pay for her wasted stew. She never allowed anybody waste her food."

"Impossible papa!" Glamour exclaimed, "…did you pay?"

"Err… well," Rex stammered.

"Of course he did," Wendy interrupted him. "Or else, I wouldn't be sitting here."

"Really?" Cynthia asked, giggling. "I guess that is a big warning to Johnny," she continued, "…yours might be too big a price to pay."

"Try him." Glamour said defensively.

"Okay," Cynthia replied, thinking. "How about your left ear."

"What?" Glamour said surprised.

"I thought you said he'll pay anything. So…" Cynthia continued, "…would you give your left ear?" she asked.

"I guess we all have to wait till I spill my soup, before deliberating on that."

"That's my boy," Rex laughed "…and definitely, I know you'll rather not touch any tough piece of meat than loose your left ear."

"Positive sir," Johnny replied, smiling.

They all finished their dessert and left for the living room, the ladies with the baby while Rex, Ayo and Johnny discussed the crises in the Middle East.

"I think we should leave." Rex told Ayo, at a quarter to ten. "Tomorrow and, as a matter of fact the next six days would be hectic. So, the earlier we get to bed the better... well..." he paused, looking at Johnny for support.

"Maybe that applies only to me anyway, or..."

"Of course I have to be in bed too sir, I have some arrangements to make tomorrow and a meeting for two p.m., tomorrow afternoon."

"You talk like one hard working chap?" Ayo asked on their way out.

"With a father like the one I have, one can't help but work hard sir. I guess it's an inherited gene or something I've been used to."

"Talking about your father," Ayo interrupted him. "Tell him to give me a call, its been quite some time, I'm sure he would be surprised I'm still alive."

"All right sir," the young chap replied before receiving Ayo's hand in a strong handshake.

"Bye baby," Wendy cooed reaching out to hug Ayo. "Take good care of your baby, and your wife especially. I trust you anyway," she pulled back patting his cheek.

"What should I get you for your wedding present," Ayo asked Glamour who was about getting in beside Johnny.

"A Yatch on the Mediterranean for our honeymoon."

"Wow," Ayo's eyes brightened. "You two are one couple I would like to watch," he said shutting the door after her.

"I'll see what I can do," he concluded waving them off.

"Any message for me?" Ayo asked his butler, dropping his coat on the sofa.

"No sir... but... well," he paused as if to think. "Someone came, but madam spoke with him so I did not bother requesting he leave a message."

"Madam?" Ayo asked surprised.

"Yes, madam." The butler said, afraid he had said something he was not supposed to say.

"Where is she now?" Ayo asked bending down to pick his

coat but sprang up without picking it when the butler spoke.

"In the kitchen sir."

"In the what?" Ayo asked shocked. Slowly, he turned and walked towards the kitchen. He pushed open the double swing doors and halted at the door- step, holding both wings with both hands. She was setting the table, dressed in a pair of blue Jean trousers, a sleeveless sky-blue silk blouse and an apron tied around her waist. He entered the kitchen, allowing the doors swing past each other.

"You're back?" She said, ignoring the surprise look on his face. "Why don't you get out of those shoes," she continued staring at his pair of shoes. "Or preferably, take a shower before coming down to eat." She paused, turned and walked towards the shelf to pick a hand napkin in a bid to elude his penetrating eyes.
Afraid to say anything stupid and spoil the night, Ayo only turned and left like a programmed robot.

After a cold bath, he slid into a pair of trousers and a long cream coloured sleeveless *Jalabia* before leaving his room to join her downstairs. His mind was running riots, different ideas coming into his head.

What in the heavens came over her still remained a mystery to him as he entered the dining room and nearly screamed from anxiety when he saw she had been upstairs herself to change. Now, she wore a red shiny short-sleeved long body hug, fish tailed end evening gown. He wanted to fall on his knees if that was the only way he could beg her to let the cat out of the bag, but on a second thought, he told himself it would be best not to push her. Who knows, he told himself pulling out a chair. This might as well be, a farewell dinner. Maybe her divorce was through as their agreement had long been overdue.

Her voice jerked him out of his reverie and he shook his head to clear off all the strange thoughts that clouded his skull.

"I am famished dear," she continued. "Are you going to sit there or pray, so that dinner can commence?"

"We commit this food we are about to take into thy hands, Oh Lord."

"Amen," they both chorused before she set out to serve the food.

"How was work today?" She started, as she dished his food

before slightly turning the table, which was fixed, into a hollow rod making it revolve horizontally. After the table swirled round, bringing the other empty plate to her, she continued.

"I hope you will like the stew, it was my mothers favourite." She concluded, picking her cutlery.

Anybody that walked in, Ayo thought would think them the best couple on earth but would not realize they were bound together by a bond, a bond from a business agreement and not of love.

Suddenly an idea occurred to him, the visitor. Who was the visitor? Does he have anything to do with this he asked himself? There is only one way to know he decided.

"Cliff said someone called earlier," he started not raising his head. "Someone I know?" he asked, still not raising his head.

"Ah yes," she answered, "Dr. Frederick Peters."

At the mention of the name, Ayo nearly choked, dropping his fork and knife simultaneously before raising his head to look at Cynthia.

"Ahn... ahn... ahn," she shook her head, "...nothing comes from my mouth until you eat your food."

# Chapter 13

"Can I speak with his wife?" Frederick said to the butler, settling himself into the sofa, a little tired.

Just then, Cynthia appeared at the top of the stairs.

"Afternoon Sir," she greeted the strange looking man before she started descending the flight of stairs.

"Afternoon madam," Fred replied, rising to his feet before taking a slight bow.

"Forgive me for intruding into your lovely afternoon, but I thought it was better I see Ayo before tomorrow," he paused and watched her take her seat in a single chair opposite the sofa in which he lowered himself after she was seated.

"I presume you are one of his very close friends?" Cynthia asked, not too surprised the way the visitor addressed Ayo by his first name. Only Rex, she thought and probably Sca' another voice told her had she seen call him by his first name.

"Yes." Fred answered, "…we go a long way. A long way," he repeated, his face broadening into a smile.

Suddenly, she narrowed her eyes, remembering the way Ayo answered Rex. *I thought it was better to see Ayo before tomorrow*, he had said. What was tomorrow, she thought. Glamours engagement ceremony.

"Are…" she started, stopped but continued on second thought.

"Are you Dr. Frederick Peters."

"Yes, how did you know?" he asked, surprised at the way she figured out who he was.

"I can see Johnny's eyes in yours and his nose too." She lied, trying to keep a smile on her face.

"Really." He said, narrowing his eyes.

"Yes." She answered quickly, lowering her gaze, afraid he might see through her eyes.

Observing the fact that she averted her eyes, he realized Cynthia too must have seen the resemblance. It was too striking, father and son, a mirror image of their time.

"You are as smart and intelligent as you are beautiful," Fred said when she finally raised her head.

"Thank you sir," she replied. "It was nice of you to observe," she added feigning a smile.

"Ayo is a rare breed," he paused but continued almost immediately. "And... I hope you realize you are lucky to have him.

After his wife died, I looked forward to hearing that he has remarried but for twenty - five years, I did not hear anything. Then I heard about the wedding of the decade. That was quite a wedding you guys had," he paused laughed then continued.

"I wondered how it got that much publicity, but... well, for a mogul like Ayo, one could not have expected anything less."

"Would you mind a drink?" she asked getting uncomfortable with the way the stranger talked. She wondered, why all these or... no, Ayo hadn't seen him in some years so he couldn't have sent him.

"No, I don't mind. Scotch preferably," Fred answered.
She got up and slowly walked to the bar.

"Add a little lemon if you have any," Fred called out as she poured the drink. "You're very homely," he continued when she lowered the drink and some ice cubes on to a glass stool by his chair.

"I hope this is how homely you are, when Ayo is around."
Surprised, she straightened up, narrowed her eyes before returning to her seat.

"What makes you feel I'm not?" she asked after taking her seat.

"I never said you weren't, all I meant was that Ayo deserves to be happy. He deserves to have a loving and caring woman in his life, he..."

"Why are you telling me all this?" she asked trying to keep a smile on her face.

"Mmh," he sighed, dropping his glass on the stool before he leaned back in his chair. "Before his wife died, she gave birth to a baby boy. After a series of unsuccessful attempts to have a child, she finally got one. But at what expense," he paused. "At the expense of her life," he continued shaking his head.

"What baffled me most was that Ayo, unlike most men did

223

not marry another wife or have a mistress bear him children outside matrimony. Instead, he suggested they adopt a child, but Yinka would not hear of raising another mans child." Fred paused, but continued after some minutes.

"If only she knew that someone else would raise her own child, but...you see," he paused again, looked up and realized she was sitting on the edge of her chair, obviously interested in his story. He took a sip from his drink, then continued but stopped almost immediately when she asked, "Do you want a refill?"

"No. Not at all," he replied. "I don't drink too much these days, age is telling on me you know. That is why I prefer my scotch with lemon, it helps sooth the nerves.
So mnh... mnh," he cleared his throat. "Back to my story. You see, Ayo took the news of her death with great shock. If only he saw the smile on her face before she died. The smile that came with tears of joy, joy from the fact that at last, she gave him a child, a son, an extension of his lineage."

Fred paused, brought out a small *Sony* Walkman, stared at it before looking up at Cynthia.

"In this tape," he continued shaking the Walkman, "are her last words. Her apologies to Ayo, and advise to him.

I wanted to play it for him but he went berserk when he heard she had gone. He... well," he shrugged. "I think I should play the tape, so that you can listen or get a feel of the scene on this day," he concluded, pressing the play button.

"Tell him," a female voice, choked with tears started on the tape. "That the happiness we both shared, the happiness I always wanted him to have, he will get front this boy. Tell him," the voice paused, followed by a series of sniffs before it continued.

"So far apart I'll be in death, but still close my heart, with him will rest.

Tell him to put any grief aside and get a wife that would take care of our son, but of all, tell him... tell him I love him. I always have and even in death... oh..." she paused.

"How I wish I could stay, only for a few months with you before I go, but we now have a son. Take care of him. Ayo, please, take care of him."

Then, Fred stopped the tape, leaned back before he continued, not looking straight at her.

"The boy, I could not release to Ayo. Not in that state, a psychologist even advised me not to, because he might treat the poor boy with scorn, blaming him for his wife's death. As things were, Ayo buried himself in his work and with time..." he paused. "As he, I mean, the boy." He added, "...grew up, it became difficult to tell him I did not sow his seed. The boy that called me father. How would I tell him? Will Ayo accept him? These questions have bothered me all these years. Now come to think of it," he raised his head to look at her.

"Who is a father?" He paused, then answered the question himself. "One that cares for and loves a child, bringing him up with good morals.

I gave him everything; even my hospitals now are in his name... who else would be the heir when it is apparent I can never make a child.

But, he would never forgive me if after I die, he realizes who his true father is. Moreover, destiny has brought them back together and who am I to say no to their fate."

"Soo... o." Cynthia drawled, wanting to get straight to the point. "Johnny is Ayo's..." she paused, not wanting to believe how fate was working.

"Yes," Fred nodded. "Johnny is Ayo's blood, you knew from the very first time you saw him. I could tell you suspected when I came in earlier, but you're too smart not to want to raise a feud or misunderstanding between two old friends."

"Mmh..." Cynthia sighed, leaning back into her chair. All along, she had sat on the edge, paying attention to the shocking revelations.

"But why now?" Cynthia started shaking her head, "why a day before his wedding?"

"He is now a man," Fred continued. "A man I built out of him. He likes Ayo already and I guess in no time, even if I don't tell him, he will know.

Moreover," he continued, "...what other opportunity than now. I mean... it is the best wedding gift I can ever give to him but you will promise me one thing?" he asked looking straight at her before he continued when all she did was shrug.

"Promise me, that you will take good care of my friend. Make him happy at least, that was what Yinka died for; to make him happy. That, you will take Johnny as a son. Though he is now a big boy,  ...man rather," he corrected "...but all Yinka made me promise to do was to make sure Ayo marries another wife. One that would give father and son, the love they deserve.

Promise me now that when I leave the country, soon after Johnny's wedding that I might feel fulfilled. That..." suddenly, he stopped, his jaw dropped in surprise when she broke down in tears.

"Madam," Frederick exclaimed. "All I asked for was a promise, is that too much a thing to ask."

"No… not that," she started wiping her eyes with the tip of her fingers. "I have been so unfair and ungrateful to Ayo." She continued, telling Fred about her childhood, her father, her mother and her proposal to Ayo. The conditions, how Ayo broke one, and it resulting to a baby girl.

"Mmh," Frederick sighed, when she finished. "You only have to thank God that you have not and will never file a divorce. Not after tonight."

"I don't know," Cynthia said slowly. "You see, even when I treated him with scorn, he was ever so understanding, so nice, too soft, always caring that I wonder which specie of men my father came from."

"That is why I told you that he deserves to be happy, he is a rare breed. I guess your mother did not want a reoccurrence of what happened to her to repeat itself with you that was why she specifically selected Ayo for you. You believe in life after death, don't you? Do you believe that even in death, she still watches over you. If you do, then don't let Ayo slip from your grip," he concluded getting up. "Work your way back into his heart.

You never can tell maybe it is in the world to come that you'll get to meet again, someone, a gem like him."

Fred turned and walked towards the door as Cynthia got up, too weak to think. At the door, Fred turned to face her.

"I don't think I should play that tape for him again," he said. "Probably it was meant for your hearing. That was probably why I never got to play it for him to hear. The past is now gone and the future is at stake. But today is the key to the future, so make sure you do not break the key."

"Thank you," was the only thing she could say, staring at the floor.

When Fred stretched out his hand for a handshake, she simply raised her tear filled eyes, looked at him before she threw her arms around his neck.

"Thank you so much Fred," she said. "How I wish I had a father like you, I probably would have been a different person entirely."

"No," he answered pulling her back at arm length. "God knows best," he continued looking into her eyes. "Things might have been worse than it is today, and you probably would have made the mistake of marrying the wrong person.
Every thing that happened was probably meant to bring you two together. Make you value each other. It could be said to be the designs of destiny.

Now, with Ayo by your side, I bet a queen above all, you will be.

All the same," he added on second thought. "I can adopt you don't you think, I can adopt you as my daughter. Whether Ayo wants it or not, Johnny will still know me as his father. I guess two Fathers are better than one," he added laughing. "I can as well have a daughter too you know, making a father with two children instead of one."

"Ah... ah... ah," she laughed in between sobs. "From today henceforth, I shall call and know you as father." She replied, going back into his warm embrace.

"Get prepared, the earlier the better. Off you go, straight to the kitchen to cook your way back into his heart." He concluded before taking his leave, leaving Cynthia staring at the closed door for so long that when the clock chimed and she realized it was less than an hour before Ayo returns, she hurried on, with a new zeal.

"Please I am dying of anxiety," Ayo said after some minutes, unable to eat his food. "What have I done to deserve all these, what..."

"Hey," she drawled, "...can't a wife treat her husband to a surprise meal without any good reason."

"Not after a whole year in marriage my dear. That reminds me, you said Fred called."

"Yeah," she answered not raising her head. "He said..." she paused to think. This is not the right place to break the news she thought, maybe...

"Yes, I am listening." Ayo said, breaking into her thoughts.

"He only said he came to catch up on old times," she lied. "He also said he will check on you, tomorrow evening"

"Tomorrow what?" Ayo asked surprised. "But, tomorrow is supposed to be the traditional marriage ceremony, isn't he..."

"Please Ayo, we are on the dining table." She said gently, making all his anxiety melt into vapour, disappearing into the coolness of the evening.

"Moreover," she continued, stretching her hand to pick the dessert bowl. "He knows best," she concluded dishing out some fruit salad into a small glass dish.

"Want to try some of this," she said turning the table to shift the bowl to him.

Ayo stared into the bowl, wondering how delicious the nice looking fruit salad would taste.

"Come on," she urged. "Taste it."

"Did you make this yourself?" he asked picking a dessertspoon.

"Why do you ask?" she replied. "Are you afraid I might have garnished it with enough love portion?" she asked.

"As long as it is love portion and not food poison, I wouldn't mind," he paused, took a spoonful, looked up at her and said, "I think its working already, or..."

"Can you do me a favour?" she asked cutting him short.

"I'll be your genie, if you allow me." He replied, dropping his spoon to pay attention.

"Sleep in my room tonight," she said, wanting to burst out laughing at the surprised gaze that followed; Ayo stared at her in bewilderment.

"Come on, say something," she urged when he did not reply.

Slowly, he picked up his spoon, stirred his dessert absent-mindedly before he spoke. "And you are not afraid I will rape you, if we are alone, even with Yetunde around"

"I thought you volunteered to be my genie," she said tilting her head seductively.

"Yes my queen, I did."

"So, will you be my guest tonight and always?" she asked.

"With all pleasure... of course, with all pleasure," he

228

repeated, sitting back in his chair, confused at what her game was.

"So…" she shrugged.

"So," he repeated after her, looking into her eyes, watching the wicked smile play around her lips.

"Shall we?" She said, dropping her spoon.

Ayo slowly pushed back his chair, helped her out of hers and with the power of a stallion, he lifted her into his arms, carrying her like a baby, close to his heart as they made their way upstairs, to the beginning of a new life.

✧

# EPILOGUE

What else could life offer, after so many ups and downs. Once beaten twice shy, you would say, but when twice beaten, could a third try be worth the while? Could it bring love, happiness, peace and joy?

"Daddy... daddy," Yetunde called as she ran into the garden, waking Ayo from his trance.

"Baby," he replied swinging his legs off the garden stool. He crouched, arms outspread and she ran into his arms.

"Mmmnnhhh," he groaned, hugging her close to his chest.

"How about me, big daddy?" Ayo junior said, making him look behind Yetunde.

Ayo junior stood there, his ball in one arm and the other outstretched.

"Come on Junior," I didn't know you were there, he continued taking him into his other arm.

"Mummy said that I should tell you that the photographer is here," Yetunde continued pointing towards the platform that overlooked the garden.

Ayo looked up and smiled at Cynthia who shrugged and smiled back.

Slowly he picked both of them, one in each arm before strolling towards the house.

From the entrance to the house, he saw Johnny coming down the flight of stairs and almost immediately, Ayo junior started shouting.

"Daddy... daddy," while Yetunde shouted;

"Uncle... uncle..."

Ayo then gently lowered them both, allowing them run into Johnny's waiting arms.

Glamour who was at the top of the stairs and Cynthia who was still by the door leading to the platform laughed at the way both kids left father for son.

Ayo admired his son, an enigma of strength, just like he was at his age.

How beautiful it would have been, to watch him grow. But,

what could he do? Fate, wanted it a different way. The imaginary line beyond mans control, strong whirlwinds that sometimes bring sorrow, barricade between today and tomorrow destiny is very cruel, it leaves you in limbo - the way his life was designed - a very complex network entangled in an intwined web - a network of heartbreaks and sad moments, but an end that every heart craves for. An end, he thought. Is this really the end of the mischievous planner called Destiny? Well, he shrugged. Only time would tell, he told himself walking up to take his position in the family group photograph.

"Yes," the photographer said, moving back to access the sitting position.

"That's just the way it should be," he continued moving back to his camera.

"Now," he continued viewing the arrangement through the lens.

"Perfect," he exclaimed raising his head, all smiles.

"Alright," he said, bending down, to take the shot.

"Say cheese," he grinned, and he snapped.

Printed in the United Kingdom
by Lightning Source UK Ltd.
104506UKS00001B/36